MY LIFE AS A DOG

MY LIFE
AS A DOG

REIDAR JÖNSSON

Translated by Eivor Martinus

THE NOONDAY PRESS
FARRAR·STRAUS·GIROUX
NEW YORK

Chapter 1

1959

The snowflakes had a hypnotic effect on me. I was getting more and more drowsy, but I needed to keep my eyes open. What if I missed my station and got off at the wrong one, rushed out into the white arctic tundra, totally dazed, only to be met by wolves who were ready to tear me to pieces! Now, that would be unforgivable and unworthy of a true Trapper. A Trapper must never make mistakes. One single mistake in the art of survival, like failing to light a fire or looking after one's dogs properly, and you pay with your life.

It was getting dark and the large fluffy snowflakes rushed towards the misted windows of my compartment. The lights from the train scooped a tunnel out of the passing landscape and white drifts of snow exploded again and again into billions of little pieces as the train chugged along and I became more and more exhausted.

Unfortunately my own wolf-dog, Sickan, had been pensioned off. I expect she was lying in front of someone's open fireplace somewhere, fat and sloppy, dreaming about past adventures while I had to manage as best I could on this narrow-gauge railway in the depths of Småland.

But luckily there were no wolves in Småland in the winter of 1959. I just pretended there were. I often pretend. You feel as if you've got company when you pretend you're someone out of a Jack London novel. Sometimes I even get the feeling that I am just an amalgamation of various characters out of fiction. It's a bit like being a hotel where people check in with all their belongings, but where they don't have to pay the bill as long as they keep me company. It gets a little complicated at times, though. But then I've always been warned by grown-ups that it is not good to sit in a corner reading books. All that stuff you read about might seep into your brain and clog up your childish mind in the end.

They weren't to know that I was looking for something special when I was reading books. But I'll talk about that another time.

At last the train pulled in at the station. My uncle stood on the platform waving just as he had promised, and I wriggled out of the train, quite proud of the fact that I had managed to change trains all by myself and that I hadn't lost anything on the way.

My uncle didn't say anything. His eyes were running and so was his nose. He was a walking disaster: he stammered out a few sentences but I didn't understand what he said. I thought it was kind of exciting with just the two of us on the deserted, snow-covered platform, with the departing train puffing and hooting. It was Russian in a way.

He took my bags and we started to walk alongside the sombre station building, then up the hill past the church which lay dark and silent, surrounded by its tombstones like an Alpine landscape in miniature. I sidled up to my uncle. When we were struggling up the hill, he told me that we were on the way to Lundkvist's Taxi. If we were lucky we might get a lift with someone else who was going in our direction.

Did I mind waiting for a while?

I realized that it must be cheaper that way and I was obviously costing money. Now money is something I do understand. For ages I've been a financial burden to other people. Actually, it was partly for financial reasons that I went to stay with my uncle. Other people's greed had brought me down and that's why I didn't want to stay on any longer with the Manufacturer. But I'd rather not think about that. I'd rather think about my uncle who smokes a pipe with the bowl upside down and whose sad expression has lightened a bit now.

The snow was still falling in large fluffy flakes past the streetlights when he stopped and made a joke about skiing the rest of the way. He put my cases down and pretended to ski downhill, but he skidded into a snow drift and disappeared out of sight. I tried to laugh. He meant well. My uncle is a light-hearted, irresponsible sort of person. At least, that's what my grandmother tells me. She's told me ever so many stories about him. Most of them are about the time he decided to become a sailor and how he got lots of new clothes before he left, but came back without a stitch on. In every story my grandmother tells about him he always ends up without a stitch on. And then she always says how irresponsible he is too. She's told me one story about a

2

canary and another one about a coconut and a third about an old wind-up gramophone and then a terribly long one about the tattoos my uncle's got all over his body. I think that's what really shattered her. She tried to frighten me with stories about him, but she didn't realize that it had quite the opposite effect on me. I too wanted to be irresponsible and come home without a stitch on. I too wanted to wiggle my ears and cover myself all over with tattoos. I wanted to get out into the world, drink and fight but still remain a child at heart. My uncle's adventures gave me some hope that all wasn't lost yet.

At Lundkvist's house we waited in the kitchen and I was sweating in my blue duffle-coat. Why did I have to get a blue duffel-coat when everyone else wore a black one? A black mourning ribbon stands out like a luminous band on a blue duffle-coat, but if I'd had a black one, it wouldn't have shown at all. But I'd soon grow out of it anyway. The large warm kitchen with its whistling Aga stove was very far from my memories and very far from home. I fell asleep against my uncle's soft over-coat, and he moved a little to make room for my head on his lap.

Wrapped in his coat, I inhaled the strong smell of Hamilton's tobacco as I was carried off towards the big black taxi. We drove in silence, the smoke from my uncle's pipe hanging like a cold veil in the car. The smells from my uncle's overcoat took me back so far in time that I was sure I'd be born again when we arrived at his home. Nothing at all had taken place and everything would start right from the beginning again. Only this time we would all know how to live.

But I didn't feel especially reborn when we got there. I shut my eyes and pretended to be asleep while people were whispering about me. My aunt thought I had grown, but my aunt's mother thought I was painfully small. I couldn't help them, I'm afraid. I'd love to be small and thirteen but who'd want me if I acted my age? After all, the only one I could trust was myself. My uncle was a most irresponsible person, my aunt was just a housewife and my auntie's mum, whom I called Auntie Auntie, was neither one thing nor another if I'm going to be really honest with you. And I'd better be honest and sober in case my uncle should happen to break his neck for instance. It wouldn't surprise me if he did just that. That's how irresponsible he is, you see. Once he bought a coconut which was hollowed out like a real Red Indian's head and he pulled my gran's leg and said that it was a real skull which had been shrunk by a real head hunter. After great pangs of anguish and a private chat with God, my gran decided that the Indian must be buried in her garden. Actually, she came to an agreement with God that she would hand over the poor shrunken head to the parish priest, but she didn't dare when it came to it. But the secret burial preyed so much on her mind that, in the end, she decided to unearth the head and carry it to the priest after all. It is a terrible thing to do to a person who has never seen a coconut before. It is irresponsible. That's what my gran said, because she didn't want to tell us about the priest's reaction. But I agreed with her. Choosing my uncle as a guardian was my life's greatest gamble.

The voices around me continued to disagree about my size. According to one person I was quite big for my age and according to another I was pitifully small. I decided to take it in my stride, fell asleep and let the matter rest.

I have an incredible knack of doing the wrong thing all the time although I am always trying hard to do the right thing. That thought struck me the following morning when I woke up and switched on the light. I was undressed and tucked up on my auntie's and uncle's convertible sofa in their living room. And from where I lay I could see tiny black indelible bloodstains on the ceiling. Ingemar Johansson has been here before, I thought. Ingemar Johansson, that's me. I might as well own up to it right from the start. And those dots which stared at me from the ceiling were my doing. I switched the light off in order not to see them. But then it was as if they were transformed into all those little mosquitoes which had been buzzing around before I killed them with a rolled-up newspaper against the whitewashed ceiling.

The sofa was an old acquaintance of mine. And the train had chugged along with me to Småland once before. Last time it had been early summer and I remember the heat was oppressive.

4

Chapter 2

1958

In the spring of 1958 I married Little Frog. We made our tepee out of grass as there was a shortage of buffaloes that year and consequently it was hard to get hold of buffalo hides. By the entrance to our home we buried two toffees and asked the great Manito for prosperity and happiness.

Our wedding was simple but dignified. I made an incision in my thumb and let my blood drip on to Little Frog's tongue. She grimaced but mixed the blood with her saliva. We put our mouths together and mixed it all up. And that was it. We were happily reunited again. I had just come back from the children's home on the other side of town. The stay at the home was a kind of exile. It was a disgrace for an independent individual like me. That's why I hadn't dared meet Little Frog to start with. I'd rather have dropped down dead than show her the state I was in. My brother and sister and I had all been moved from the Great Wall of China to the children's home because our mother was ill for the umpteenth time. But one day in May, after a year which had dragged on like a whole century, rumour had it that she'd be coming back and we packed our bags and ourselves on our bikes and pedalled away from the children's home–which we hated more than anything in the world.

Our mother was our only passport to Happy Heights. That was the name of the area we lived in. And our house was called the Great Wall of China because it was very long.

We stood there with our bikes and our bags and looked at her through the window. My school cap was pulled down over my forehead so I could hardly see her, but I sort of sensed that she was happy and I was suddenly aware of my incredible ability to do everything wrong. The idea was that she'd be able to rest properly without us around. We weren't welcome, in other words. I decided to move out at once to lighten the burden for her but also because I didn't like hearing her sighs. I sniffed

5

around in the usual places, wondering where to settle down. In the attic it was horribly dark; in the cellar, someone had put a padlock on 'my' air-raid shelter. Who had squealed about my alternative living accommodation? Had Little Frog been sitting there all through the winter, crying and yearning for me, until someone discovered her and our home which was made of cardboard boxes and some rag rugs?

Little Frog and I were used to makeshift living accommodations. We were like nomadic Red Indians. Sometimes we lived on the balcony where the mums used to beat the carpets; there we had a tarpaulin sheet for cover. And sometimes we lived in the cellar and at other times in the attic. Once we even dug a tunnel underneath the railway embankment. We dug a deep hole and sat there feeling the earthen walls vibrating when the trains roared past. We sat there staring into the darkness without saying what we were thinking. Was it really a good idea to sit there like two stupid rabbits and be buried alive just for the pleasure of living together?

Normally, Little Frog lived on the third floor a bit further down the Great Wall of China. Her father was a jailer. Sometimes on Sundays he'd let us come with him to the prison where we could have a peep at the prisoners through a little hatch in the door. It wasn't much fun, but that was the whole point of the exercise. Her father is not just a jailer: he is also a youth leader in the Good Templars' Association. It was good for us to know where we might end up if we strayed from the teetotaller's path.

Anyway, Little Frog and I were reunited. We built our tepee, got married and moved in. And in the beginning our marriage was quite untroubled. At night we lay there in the dark hugging each other and during the day we cleaned, hunted and looked after our children. 'Our children' was me. One moment I was out there warring or hunting buffaloes and the next moment I was crawling around on all fours crying: 'da, da, da'. There were times at school when I wasn't sure whether to say 'da, da' or 'ugh' to my teacher. We alternated so that one night I was a baby and one night I was grown-up. There wasn't much difference between the two nights, mind you. But I preferred being a baby because then I could relax more. I was a bit stiff as a grown-up. We lay there, side by side, like two lifeless logs breathing on each other. Sometimes I'd touch Little Frog a little

6

here and there, but to be honest with you, there wasn't much to be touched. Besides, I knew exactly how it all worked: right down there they have a hole like on a bottle. And that bottle is hanging there inside them and at the bottom of that bottle there is a kind of cake which little children hang on to and eat from until they are ready to come out.

Somebody showed me in the cellar once. He put his dick in a bottle to demonstrate, but then he turned terribly red in the face and started to sweat because he couldn't get it out again. It didn't look much fun, him standing there with the lemonade bottle between his legs hissing at us every time we tried to help him pull it off. Somebody had the bright idea that a vacuum may have developed inside the bottle and that's why it had got stuck there. We started to hit the bottle to help him. It didn't even sound like glass. But in the end the blinking bottle broke after all. But then it looked even worse, because the bottle neck was still hanging on like a torn collar. The bloke started to cry and scream and said that we had knocked his prick off. Some mums who were in the wash-house heard him screaming and rushed in like sweaty angels in their flower-patterned pinafores. They carried our unhappy bottle-screwer into the wash-house and laid him down on a bench in there. Then they rubbed some jelly-like soap onto his sore dick and plop - he was free again. We thought that was great fun. But then one of the women shouted that that sort of thing could happen for real if little children tried to do what grown-ups do. Small children don't have the right kind of bodies for it, they explained. We have to wait until we're old enough to have soap between our legs.

No wonder I was scared.

What if I got stuck in Little Frog's bottle and someone had to smash her to pieces in order to get some soap between her legs so that I could get out again . . .

No, I preferred to wait until she could produce that soap herself.

But that was just an excuse, of course. Something I made up so that I wouldn't have to do it. I was afraid of getting stuck in more ways than one. If you screw somebody your souls get fused and then you're stuck and can't live without each other. Not even with the help of soap. That must be awful.

Apart from a certain lack of intimacy, our marriage was quite happy and practical. My mother was able to rest while I was

7

keeping out of the way. And if she were to fall ill again, I always had my own family. Everything in the garden was lovely, in other words, except for Little Frog's sister. Although we invited her to our wedding she still grassed on us after a couple of weeks. Suddenly, when we had decided to have a 'grown-up' night, Little Frog's dad came snooping round and saw what we were up to at once, even though he couldn't really see because it was pitch dark in our tepee. He went right through our grass ceiling as he stood up and he shouted and waved his hands about like an angry bear and said he wanted to have a word with me! I knew at once what he meant by that so I ran off as far as I could – all the way to the rubbish dump which is a very good place for defending yourself. You have a clear view right down to Happy Heights and you can spot anyone who wants to attack you. The dump itself is surrounded by bare trees with dry twigs, and beyond the trees there are fields on one side and the canal on the other. Every autumn when the fruit trees are full of tempting fruit we always try to venture past those fields, but never manage to. It was always too dark before we got there and then it was time to go home again. Someone got frightened or someone's wellies leaked. We got tummy-ache from all the plums and apples we'd pinch from the small farms along the dirt roads. Old men who couldn't stand straight any more sounded like crows with angry cracked voices, harmless and feeble, but we had strength in numbers. We were like the locusts in the Bible who descended on their gardens, we were their recurring disaster.

When I was on my own I felt a bit scared in those open fields. But I didn't mind wading across the canal, maybe fifty metres upstream so no one could trace me – as long as the grass snakes weren't hungry.

Once we killed a snake which had half a rat in its mouth. It was just about to swallow the reluctant water rat and seemed capable of devouring almost anything. Even a child. The only protection against snakes is rubber boots. We had them on so we killed the snake. I think it was rather impolite of the snake to have its dinner just where we always waded across pretending there were huge boa constrictors lurking in the reeds.

I worked myself up while I sat there watching the smouldering rubbish dump. What would happen to me? I invented another story worse than the one before. I do that sometimes because then reality never seems quite so bad.

Sometimes I work myself into a frenzy for no real reason at all. The inside of my head is all white. When my mother was in bed as usual, coughing worse than a souped-up engine, she once tried to tell a neighbour how nice it was to be on her own. I got all worked up because of that. Strange, isn't it? I heard every word although I kept on chatting all the time. She was so tired, our mother, and there were so many of us and we were such a nuisance. And how could she ever get any rest with a son who was more like an orang-utan, hanging from the curtain, crawling under the bed and saying nonsensical things which no one wanted to hear?

I ran around with this question like a motor in my head, until the neighbour forced me to stand still for a moment. She pressed me against her disgusting fleshy body, smelling of fried bacon, and screamed that I ought to know better and did I mean to kill my mum?

I had done it again. I had killed her a little again. It was like lightning flashing through my brain and I heard someone say that he was probably more difficult than usual because he was reaching the menopause. And 'he' was me, of course.

In the end, the disgusting creature let go of me and called me the little professor. I collected myself enough to flee, but no further than the hall where I crouched under our big aquarium. I could pretend at least that it was dangerous to hide there. Two hundred litres of water right above my head, a quiet slurping, rippling noise going on while the angelfish systematically bit each other to death and the swordfish squirted four inches of black thread and the voices from the grown-ups droned on in their feverish wishful thinking about freedom. But mother's plans of escape ground to a halt for the simple reason that she couldn't get very far with that cough. It was worse than thunder. She wouldn't even be able to hide in heaven.

This wasn't the first time I had been called the professor. Actually, it is my most common name after Ingemar Johansson. It was really because of my glasses. And I suppose I'm not that easy to get on with because I've got this hotel full of guests that I mentioned earlier. Jack London's and Selma Lagerlöf's characters have got fifteen double rooms at least. Rudyard Kipling is on his own with his elephants and mongooses – and I have let some biblical characters into the attic because that way they haven't got far to go to heaven. I'm quite well versed when it comes to the Bible.

It all began a long time ago when two angels came to see me. Two young men, looking exactly alike, with well-pressed dark suits, well-fitting black overcoats and narrow ties of an undecided watery colour and pure white shirts with button-down collars. They wore sturdy shoes and thick white socks. According to Raymond Chandler, there is only one kind of person who wears shoes and socks like that. That's right! American cops. And these two guys were some kind of spiritual policemen. They told me in funny but perfectly correct Swedish that as children of God they would like to spread the Word. I have never seen my mother so excited before. It was she who called them God's little angels and invited them into the living room where the afternoon passed like a knife-throwing act at the circus. But it was worse in a way because we couldn't see the knives. You just saw the effect of the carving. The two angels were stripped like two pale onions without a centre. And my mother laughed all the time – when she wasn't coughing or talking, that is. I had never seen her like that before.

She knew everything. The angels flicked through the flimsy pages in the Bible as if they were cigarette papers and all the time they tried to prove that they were right, but my mum was always ready with her Bible quotations, which just about finished them. I think they even started to wet their fingers like you do when you're about to count paper money. But in the end they gave up. My mum won on a technical knock-out. Without a doubt. It was fun but at the same time a bit dangerous and quite incomprehensible.

And sure enough, they got at me when they were tying their cops' shoelaces in the hall ready to cover some new ground, this time with their wings clipped.

They weren't just spiritual policemen. They were also angels of Death. It was they who told me that my mother was going to die. You could tell that a mile off, they said. She was on the bottom step on the way to Hades. And she could only be saved by a very clever boy: if I read their magazine I would find out how. Then they disappeared and I started to cry. How was I going to lift her off that bottom step? That's when I started my great search and I learned whole chunks of the Bible by heart. Then I discovered with horror that the world is full of books which tell you quite contradictory things. There were even things written on the back of cornflakes packets. And that's how Jack London and all the rest got into the picture.

But that was a little while ago. Now I believe that the only time we really meet on this earth is when we are buried in it.

But to return to the rubbish dump.

I got all worked up. I imagined that all the jailers would get together and put an iron ring round the dump and then slowly, slowly they'd close in on me.

I had really cooked my goose this time.

I hadn't even touched Little Frog – maybe just a tiny bit – maybe just inside her knickers – but her dad would probably kill me or ban me from the Youth Club at least, which amounted to the same thing in the end. The punishment was postponed like a time-bomb inside me. And one day it would have ticked its last. 'Tick, tick', then 'Bang, you're an alcoholic! Go to prison without passing Go!' And all because Little Frog and I had got married. There was no talk of having children even; nor making any. I was both father and child at the same time. Why hadn't I been crawling around in the grass outside the tepee crying: 'da, da,' instead when the jailer turned up?

I started to cry. A cheeky rat stared intently at me and I tried in vain to kill it. It just backed away lazily as if it knew that I didn't have a mongoose on me. That's what I needed all right: a tame mongoose to bring me some food. Or a real wolf-hound. Sickan just ran away as soon as you let her off her lead.

Light wisps of yellowish smoke enveloped me. The acrid stench was coming from a fire on the dump. There was always a fire on that dump. I sighed and decided to go home and take my punishment like a true Red Indian. I wouldn't move a muscle when they started to cut me to pieces in the cruel light of the full moon.

But as usual, I had only managed to get myself into even more of a muddle. My trousers were torn and my glasses were gone, although I could have sworn they had been on the tip of my nose all the time.

Going home without my glasses was like volunteering for San Quentin's gas chamber. I would suffocate from all the nagging I would get. Nobody would ever believe me. It was obvious that I had *thrown* them away in order to ruin my mum.

I rummaged around the rubbish and rags, turning over some

11

boxes of indescribable contents while the rats were squeaking angrily. So was I for that matter. And I was stronger and bigger than they were, so they ran out of the way during my furious search which actually got more fun the deeper into the rubbish heap I delved. It's fun digging in old junk. It must have been one of the first things I did in life because it comes so naturally to me. I was quite beside myself the first time I saw this rubbish dump. Just think, we'd moved to a place which was next to a dump! It was as if a kind uncle had offered me a first-class ticket straight into the Arabian Nights. Somewhere in the middle of all that rubbish we were bound to find the solution to our family's problem! Perhaps in the lining of an old handbag or in a secret drawer of a discarded old bureau, well hidden from the rest of the world until I and no one but I found the precious stones, the gold nuggets or the valuable old stamps!

The first thing I'd do is send my mother to Switzerland because everyone gets well there. The air is good but expensive. It is so expensive that they put you in the papers if you just go there to breathe it.

I can just see the headlines:

Young Hero Sends His Sick Mother to Exclusive Resort in Switzerland

The hero of the day is our young Ingemar Johansson who miraculously found one million gold ducats on the council dump last week. Here he is waving goodbye to his mother who is on her way to the most expensive resort in the world. Her high expectations are already adding a touch of colour to her pale but otherwise beautiful face which, incidentally, bears a striking resemblance to Greta Garbo's.

I would point out that last bit discreetly to the reporter. But he wouldn't find it difficult at all to write that because my mother actually did look like Greta Garbo.

I once asked my grandmother and she told me that mum was as beautiful as Greta Garbo in *Camille*. But then she didn't want to talk about it any more – and I understood why because my mother didn't carry on like the Lady of the Camellias. My mother was an honourable woman who was going to be rescued! And I was a young man with a whole dump at my disposal!

But not all to myself, of course. All of us from the Great Wall of China used to muck about in it. At least everyone under fourteen. And the reason was very simple. You have to go where Fate wants you to go – there is some terrible boot-licking going on round that Fate. Up to now, I've only known two people who haven't grovelled to Fate, Fortune, Happiness or whatever they call it. One was my grandfather and the other was my mother. But they were quite convinced, of course, that they had already met their Fate. I would love to say a few words about my grandfather, but I'm a bit cross with him and can't quite figure him out so I don't know what to say. He gets angry because things aren't straight and simple in life. No, he is not a surveyor. He is an honest Swedish worker and he says that that is his Fate. I even think he goes around fretting because he hasn't had his balls surveyed. He believes in Swedish quality and muscles of steel. Everyone else pooh-poohs daft opinions like that and would rather believe in Lady Luck as it is obvious that you can't get rich by honest work. But you never know for sure, of course, so there is no harm in a bit of healthy scepticism. For years now I've been standing underneath the benches in the circus just in case some careless person drops some paper money through the wooden slats. I've dreamed endless dreams about money notes fluttering down like cheap confetti from skyscrapers to welcome some local hero. I've never been small enough to squeeze underneath the boards in a telephone booth outside the People's Park, but if I had been, I know I'd have stayed there for good. As it was, I had to make do with getting up early every Sunday morning, then running along with trepidation to lift up the slats and check if some drunken fool had dropped his money through them on Saturday night. I know you have to work for Fate. Especially if by Fate you mean Fortune. You can't just sit there like grown-ups and chew your pencils while you fill in the lottery coupons. No, you have to keep at it. You have to be around.

Normally there would be quite a few fortune-seekers on the dump, but this was a Sunday and the cinemas were already showing their matinee performances. I was alone and I had the whole dump to myself. At last, the sole proprietor of a field of treasures!

It was sweaty work, searching for treasure. The closer to the fire you got, the greater the chance of finding something. That's obvious.

You can't just walk up to a dump and pick up millions as if it were a simple mushroom-picking expedition. So I struggled and searched among the burning boxes, torn mattresses, rags, broken pieces of furniture, rotting food. I forgot all about my glasses. The smoke enveloped me like damp fog. Thick and yellowish, it stuck to my clothes, worked itself into my nostrils and eyes, and opened up all the tear ducts. I could have drowned in my own tears if I hadn't given up.

I am sure all that stuff about expectations and innocence is a good thing, but I lost them both when I got my very first pair of swimming trunks.

I had to nag for at least five years before I got a pair. Before then I was never told why grown-ups wore swimming costumes. You don't need any, I was told. Why? Was it because small children should be toughened up? Why should I sit with a bare bum in the water when all the others were properly dressed? The only explanation I could think of was that at a certain age you become a little less hardy and the swimming trunks serve as a kind of protection. I can't describe my happiness when I ran out into the water wearing my first-ever pair of swimming trunks – and my horror when I discovered that they weren't waterproof.

For years and years I had believed that swimming costumes were waterproof. And there I was with the same shrivelled-up prick as usual.

The chance of finding a fortune in that dump must have gone up in flames by now. And I had lost my glasses, torn my trousers and my clothes reeked of that stinking smoke. The whole of me was smeared with horrible greasy soot. But worst of all – I had lost my wife, Little Frog. Our home was in ruins and a description of me had been issued in Happy Heights because I was accused of indecent assault on a minor. In the distance you could hear dogs barking. I was defeated and too tired to run. I just sat down on a heap of old rags and tried to become part of the landscape. An old newspaper lay in front of me. It looked interesting. I read that two professors, Martin Olsson and Carl-Herman Hjortsjö, had opened Erik XIV's grave and found that the old king was full of arsenic and that it was possible to prove that the poison had been in his body before he died. Fat chance for future poisoners!

I read and read for all I was worth, hoping that no one would discover me because even I had forgotten that I was there. But a dog ran up to me and took a bite at my trainers.

The dog was Sickan.

Good old Sickan. My very own wolf-dog who did everything wrong just like me. She couldn't understand why we wanted her to retrieve the things we'd thrown away. And we thought that was a sign of her superior dog's intelligence, because you must be a bit dog-stupid to run after the same things again and again when people have clearly shown that they don't want them any more. At least we consoled ourselves that that was the case.

The fact that it was Sickan who bit my shoe made me wonder whether it was all predetermined by fate – as if it was my heart and not my shoe she was chewing. She'd been recruited for this particular task and she had betrayed me. My best friend acting as a retriever for the enemy camp! In a way it made me happy. Show me a dog that wouldn't enjoy chasing an under-age, oversexed Red Indian? I quite understand her. The fact that it was her somehow made it more important. The only thing missing was my brother acting as superintendent. That would have completed the picture. Him running up to me shouting that I had been arrested by the best police dog in town.

But he didn't shout anything when he finally did turn up. He just prodded me with his air gun and wondered why I was not wrapped up in a parcel like the rest of the rubbish.

One day I'll be the Cain of this century. I am afraid I might kill him, even if he is twice as big as me – it wouldn't be easy. I'll never manage to reach up and hit him. Once I crushed his knee, but it healed up again, luckily. Another time I hit him so his eyebrows burst open against the table-top. That was the only time he was bent double in fact. I helped him by pressing down extra hard. There was a WHAM and thick blood kept squirting out into the room. He cried like mad because he thought he'd go blind. But then he was stitched up and I was given a good tanning with the carpet beater by our mother. She came into the room like a fury and hit everything in sight and then it was my turn to scream worse than my brother. It nearly always ends like that. But it always starts with him being twice as big as me. My only chance is to lie down and kick, or he'll beat me up at once. He is very crafty. You can hardly ever tell by looking at me that he's beaten me up. It's only when I hit back that somebody notices. He twists my arms, bends my fingers, pulls my ears and gives me 'the death blow' under the bridge of my nose. I promise. Millions of drunken canaries dance round in my head calling for revenge!

'The death blow' is something he practises a little now and again without any effort at all. I can't do much about it. I have to wait until I can feel my arms again. They go all numb and prickly and I can't lift them – as if you've been sleeping on them all night. They are just like old logs, useless and hollow. I've heard people say that you can have lead in your veins, and that's just how it feels.

And it's not much fun being called Ingemar Johansson then. Because of the name I'll get a few extra blows and the general paralysis becomes an icy starting point for the soul to fly off like some home-made sputnik.

(I am not saying that God is wrong but I have strong doubts about the soul leaving the body when we die. I personally believe that childhood is the true soul and it runs away with the first morning sputnik to God as soon as the torture starts.)

It's not until my soul has gone that my arms wake up from their deep sleep and revenge takes on a furious new form. I'll use anything to hit back with; there are no rules any more because those in power have perfected the rules for their own purposes. I am out to kill.

Besides, Sickan belongs to him.

At least that's what he claims. It was he who paid twenty-five öre for her, not me, although the idea was that she was going to belong to both of us. Later, I gave him twelve öre, so he retained superiority by just one öre.

We bought her from a farmer. Sickan's father must have been an Alsatian. The mother is a mixture of spitz, cocker spaniel and collie. Roughly speaking, Sickan looks like an Alsatian, but she is a bit smaller, maybe only half as big. She's got black, curly, silky fur, drooping ears and some white marking on her front. Even our mother fell for her. She laughed when we came home with Sickan in a margarine box. Then Sickan got leased out like the rest of us, but she too came back. That was absolutely vital because if you can't be faithful to your own dog, you might as well put spruce twigs on your front doorstep like they do at funerals. You can't mix blood and saliva with dogs or kiss them like I did Little Frog, but you don't have to do either of course. Everyone knows that dogs were sent here by God to try us: if you bite your dog then all hell breaks loose!

(Fortunately, Sickan is at a dogs' kennel at the moment.)

But to go back to my brother and the rubbish dump where all the other dogs had now stopped barking and no new arrivals seemed to be in sight. In fact, my brother appeared to be the sole member of the search party. He waved his horrible air gun about while Sickan was busy chewing my trainer.

To break the silence, I started to tell him how you could discover traces of arsenic poisoning in a body several hundred years after it had been poisoned. But he just said: 'What's the point of that? By then, everyone would be dead anyway.'

He is exactly like grandfather.

If things aren't naturally straight then they must be made straight!

He just can't identify with the problems of childhood when people like Olsson, Hjortsjö & Co. run around accusing their previously respectable forefathers of arsenic poisoning. What's dead and buried should remain so – it is worrying enough with people who keep wondering about the cause of death. Everyone should find their own answer to that one.

I told him I was looking for a treasure.

He thought I ought to look for my glasses. He was off to chase rabbits. He looked disgustingly clean and proper with his horrible air gun. He'd hidden it because he didn't want me to find it. But it was easily accessible, so sometimes he even brought it home with him.

Once I woke up to something cold and hard brushing against my forehead. That was the first time I saw his air gun. My brother grinned and waited for a tenth of a second behind the bath to give me the idea that I was a living target – and then he pressed the trigger – Poof! It was just air, but I got so scared that I wet my pants, something I hadn't done for years. But then he also got scared so he helped me take off the sheets and my messy pyjamas. He tiptoed out of the room and threw it all down the rubbish chute, then he made me promise not to squeal about the gun. In return, he promised that I could borrow it sometimes.

We have our secrets, he and I. He is terribly clever.

It was the same thing at the dump.

17

He just prodded me with the air gun, got a little bored, loaded it, aimed and asked how my rat chase was getting on. And by the way, he told me, everyone at Happy Heights knew by now that I had screwed Little Frog.

'You might as well give yourself up,' he said. 'You'll have to leave school, go to work and support her if she's pregnant. You may end up in the papers. As teenage parents.'

He turned round and shot at an imaginary rat and asked if it was really true that I had screwed Little Frog.

'Of course,' I said.

He was always boasting about having screwed someone, even though he hadn't. It was about time he realized that he had a little brother who had actually done it.

He was under the illusion that you screw someone just for fun, just anyone at random. To him it's just like screwing with a bottle. But all the same, he gets quite weird when he talks about it. His eyes become all shiny and his mouth as large and open as Boot-Carlsson's, a loony who always wanted to see our rubber boots. He used to walk around the streets with a hand-cart, collecting junk, and as soon as he saw a pair of boots he started drooling at the mouth. We thought it was so funny that we kept showing them to him. But if you got too close to him you'd had it. He'd go mad, shout and scream, pull off your boots and do all sorts of things to them which made you look away, and then you had to get rid of them. You never wanted to put your bare foot in that boot again. Believe me. But Boot-Carlsson is not alive any more. He was dispatched during the great reconstruction period when they built all the new housing estates.

My brother got his funny eyes when he enrolled in the voluntary Army Corps. They meet in each other's homes and sit down in a circle on the floor comparing pricks, showing how stiff they are, like real soldiers. Then they masturbate for king and country. That's the sort of story my brother tells me. He likes whispering in my ear about stiff pricks and stained uniforms with patches that look as if they've been dipped in sugar, and he especially likes to torment me while I'm doing my mathematics homework.

Mathematics is the worst subject I know. The figures just jump about like poor little frogs on my squared paper. It feels as if I've got sand in my eyes, the kind that flies around when dry April winds blow. It's on occasions like that that my brother has a go. During the spring we were living in the children's home he kept telling me disgusting stories like that.

As far as the Little Frog-Jumping Panther (that was my Red Indian name) affair was concerned I had definitely made him a little insecure. He must be bluffing. The search party for me was just a figment of my imagination. I grinned, certain that he had turned up because he was intrigued by my affair with Little Frog. I was sure I could think of something juicy to tell him if he helped me look for my glasses. We could let Sickan have a sniff at my nose and then ask her to track down my glasses.

But he wasn't joking. He really was the search party sent out to look for me. The idea was not to frighten me with Little Frog. He was asked to get me home as soon as possible because my teacher was waiting for me by our mother's bedside.

In the children's home I had let my brother say all those slimy four-letter words so I could write them down. It was quite fun really. He said them all in the dark and I sat there with my torch and wrote and wrote – but in my maths book, I'm afraid. I played with the words, swapped them around, piled them one on top of the other until in the end I was as skilled with all those filthy words as a girl juggling with five balls at the same time and swapping them behind her back as well. It became a habit – a way of making the unknown less dangerous. And that's why my maths book ended up full of my brother's jelly-like fantasies. When my teacher snatched the book from me, the story about the bottle inside girls' tummies was kids' stuff compared to some other things in that book.

Now, my teacher was an ambitious person. I understood what I had coming to me and felt quite lost when my brother walked off shouting that I shouldn't forget my glasses like that. He disappeared across the field with his gun slung over his shoulder and Sickan happily following. She was tied to a clothesline which gave me some comfort as it meant that he didn't believe Sickan would go with him voluntarily but would prefer to stay with me if she had a choice.

Why should an age difference of two years be so important that one person can wander off like a free man while the other is trapped and frightened on a council rubbish dump? Why wasn't I him and he I? Why weren't we born the other way round? Or why wasn't I born an American instead?

That's not a joke. If my grandfather had stayed in America

and sent for our grandmother and mother instead of coming back here then I would have been an American. That is a fact. I was born at the wrong time and in the wrong place. I can just picture myself wandering off across the field, away from civilization, into the American wilderness, the afternoon sun warming the hair at the nape of my neck like a friendly fatherly hand; a light southwesterly breeze tickling my nose, entering my nostrils and all the blood vessels in my head bubbling like happy exclamation marks. My knapsack is light. I eat the fruits of nature and drink from rippling streams and springs and rivers. And my constant companion walks beside me like a watchful shadow with the very essence of wilderness in her every fibre: part wolf, part dog and part something super-human as she seems to understand what we mean long before we are conscious of our own intentions. Side by side, we delve further and further into the wilderness where we put our lives at stake. We are not wholly dog nor human being. We are the best of both – one for all and all for one.

Oh, Sickan! Why didn't you bite off the clothesline? How could you know the difference between twelve and thirteen öre? There I was in the wilderness, sitting on the dump looking at the smouldering rubbish and the thick black columns of smoke that rose from them – meanwhile you were having a good time chasing rabbits with my brother.

What is a rabbit chase compared to the joy of looking for my glasses?

I sat there for a while replaying my adventures in my mind before I thought of trying to send some smoke signals to Little Frog. Who knows, she might be sitting on the carpet-beating contraption spying on me?

Among some fabric I found an old blanket and threw it over a smouldering pile of steel springs and old rubber tyres. I pulled and tore at the blanket but it got stuck in the twisted springs and got really messy from the burning rubber. In a few seconds, smoke appeared and then fire. I tried to sort out one tyre as a sort of signal but it was impossible. The frizzling black chunks of rubber stuck to my trousers and worked themselves through the material even though I tried desperately to remove them with a piece of wood. My legs started to smart. I ran as fast as I could towards the canal, taking a short cut across a mountain of rubbish, but skidded and fell, blinded by smoke and tears. I fell right down the steep slope. Half-rotten cardboard boxes, news-papers, tins, broken chairs without any seats, an old pram, wet mouldy mattresses, half eaten by rats which used them for their big communes – everything just poured over me like a sharp stinking blanket with wet awkward edges. I crawled around screaming not only with pain but also with fear. Suddenly I stopped. The scream travelled towards my mouth but once there, it hit a lid of surprise – a stunned surprise mixed with fear which was greater than the pain: right in front of me I saw a small child's hand waving . . . slowly, slowly, like a sad farewell before it moved on and dived into the last spasms of the rubbish heap and silence returned to the place.

It must be the result of those Voluntary Army Corps exercises. They have all started screwing now and they throw little child-ren on the dump so they don't have to go out to work to support them. When mankind has sunk so low it must end by people murdering their own innocent dogs too!

The words rushed around in my head like meaningless sharp crystals, with no other purpose than to dislodge the lid that covered my mouth. But I couldn't produce a sound. Not a sound. Everything turned black and I disappeared.

High up in a block of flats, a little girl was wondering what would happen if she threw herself on the black newly tarmac-adamed parking lot which looked quite deserted in the early morning light. She had woken with a start and a black hole inside her. And inside that black hole, she both existed and plunged at the same time. She had already forgotten how it had come about in the first place. The pain was so great that the black hole seemed to have drilled a tunnel right through her. And now it was a reality, just like the rubbish chute in the quiet block of flats. And it was her parents' fault entirely. It was they who had inflicted that pain on her. But she was going to take her revenge. For the rest of their lonely life they would walk remorse-fully back and forth to her beautiful grave where she'd be resting with an eternal smile on her lips. The simple but pointed inscrip-tion 'Serves you right' would be a wonderful revenge!

But would she hurt herself in the fall? Maybe her body would turn into a mushy mess? Her beautiful slim body would just be a memory before the coffin lid was finally nailed on. Maybe they'd have to sweep up the remains and put her in mum's

Tupperware boxes, but that would look rather horrible with all the various parts visible through the transparent plastic. At least she would last forever in a Tupperware box, but maybe her parents would prefer to get rid of that mushy mess as soon as possible?

The little girl tiptoed across to her bed and looked at Sara-Lisa who lay there, her innocent eyes closed and her long black eyelashes flickering in the light breeze. She would have to sacrifice Sara-Lisa. Without thinking too much about it, afraid of changing her mind, she yanked a surprised Sara-Lisa from her bed.

And she waved her arms about and cried for her mother as she came floating down towards the hard concrete.

It was terrible. The little girl heaved herself over the windowsill as far as she could, but it was difficult to see what had happened to Sara-Lisa. She had to creep down the stairs carefully.

The tarmac was already warm, the sun shone mercilessly on Sara-Lisa's head. Her arms and legs were several metres away from the trunk, which was completely flattened. A slight wind made her eyelids move and the little girl shuddered when, for a moment, she thought Sara-Lisa was still alive. She hitched up her nightie and quickly collected the various pieces. Then she ran upstairs and stole into her bedroom, where she stayed, filled with remorse. It didn't seem such a good idea, throwing yourself out of the window. She found a shoebox for Sara-Lisa, had a little think, then went to the kitchen for a bottle of tomato ketchup.

There! Now, Sara-Lisa looked really dead.

The little girl tied a string round the shoebox and went to the rubbish chute where Sara-Lisa fell – straight down a horrid black hole. At the top of the building a hatch closed. The little girl rushed back to her bed and thought it was good that there were dolls to play with and decided that all black holes had gone.

Encouraged by my own story of the little girl with the black holes, I carefully dug my way forward, afraid to bump into the gory hand and afraid to ruin my own brilliant explanation. Millimetre by millimetre, I pulled myself up from the rubbish so as not to touch the burns on my legs.

I crawled out of the dump and limped across to our lianas. My glasses ought to be there somewhere. I recalled losing them there before I started to look for treasure. But now they were gone of course. I climbed into one of the cement pipes and stared straight up at the trees, at all the bicycle tyres swinging there. With or without my glasses I was a loser, unless I did something really fantastic which would be the talking point of the whole Great Wall of China for weeks! With the help of the bicycle tyres suspended across the canal I could try and swing myself over to the other side. The Tarzan of the rubbish dump. The king of the rats. No one had done anything like that before. I'd be famous all over Happy Heights!

But how would I be able to prove that I had swung myself across the canal?

Never mind.

I'd probably end up head first in the mud where I'd remain as a warning to other children in years to come, a terrible deterrent with my trainers barely visible in the low tide. That's what happens if you don't do your sums properly!

I was thinking about this and that in my cement pipe. It was leaning a bit to one side. Sometimes we used to cover the entrance with boards and cardboard to keep the rain out, but even so the cement pipes didn't make very exciting huts with their ready-made walls. Besides, they were too close to the lianas. People wouldn't leave you in peace there. But a little further away there was another cement pipe. Perhaps I could make a new hut for Little Frog and me? A concrete shelter that would keep all jailers out!

I climbed up the pipe and limped through the dry sprawling brambles which were underneath the alderberry trees. Somewhere in the middle of those brambles there had to be another cement pipe. I had seen it once before but I hadn't thought about it at the time. That was several years ago, just after we'd moved in to Happy Heights. Mother and I went there to pick blackberries. She was happy doing that, I remember. Every time I dropped a blackberry into her basket, she praised me. We were united in a holy rite. The prickly thorns were there to test my endurance. The twigs and branches got twisted round our legs. I penetrated further and further into the undergrowth, drunk with happiness. I ran back and forth to fill her bowl and to feel her hand on my head like a quick blessing. And then I rushed on, healed and protected. No sharp thorns could prick the two of us. At last something I could do, at last something we did together.

We were alone. We'd come from grandmother and grandfather where she always fell ill and spent the hot summer days on the living-room sofa. My brother and I brought her two bottles of sea water every afternoon and she locked herself in grandmother's larder with it every time. That larder is so big that four people can stand upright in it. Grandmother's incredible collection of preserves reaches right up to the ceiling. At waist level there is a wide shelf covered with wax cloth. She's also got a spirit stove in there, hissing away every day because the big cooker in the kitchen is not on during the summer months. But the door to the larder is almost always locked and the key is in my grandmother's apron pocket most of the time. Your stomach almost sticks out of your ears as you stand there listening. The narrow window with its crocheted half curtain lets through a filtered light. If you shut the door and hide under the shelves and lie absolutely still you may be lucky enough to get locked in. Then all the secret smells come out and dance around in the meshed light. They are so strong they are almost tangible.

That's where I went to try and find out what she was using the sea water for. At first mother lit both burners on the spirit stove. I heard the quick pumping noises and then the hissing sound after she'd struck the match. She hummed to herself, alone and locked in the larder. She never used to hum like that with us around. I heard the rustling sound when she stepped out of her nightie – a zinc bucket scraped against the stone floor. She laughed and giggled. Then a quiet splash as her song rose and subsided with her breath – like a secret message in the form of a whisper which could only be produced in that dark warm larder at my grandmother's. With bated breath I slowly stuck my head out between the jars, closed my eyes and tried to make up my mind whether I wanted to see her naked or not. No, I'd rather not see her naked. I don't think I ever had before either, but the desire to watch her using that sea water became stronger and stronger and in the end I opened my eyes wide. She was covered in all the colours of the rainbow, as the light was reflected from the window and from the blue flames of the spirit stove; her eyes were closed and she held one arm above her head. She covered the top of the bottle with her thumb to make the water squirt better as it sprayed down on her naked body, which was thin and firm with small flat breasts and none of grandmother's enormous hips. I'd seen grandmother in the nude many times, when she was washing herself in the sink or when we all bathed together in the steaming bath-house. But this was the first time I saw my mum like that, reflected in jam jars and bottles. She shifted from warm to cold colours, the shadows suddenly split and were elongated into dancing figures on the ceiling while her song rose from her half-open mouth and her absent minded face showed a wild and strange expression which I had no part in. She was enjoying herself, playing with the water. She was rid of us, rid of me!

It is amazing what a simple bottle of sea water can do; the effect on our mother was such that I or my brother and sister and the whole world for that matter was obliterated by the sheer enjoyment of it all.

I suddenly felt an irrational hatred . . . I was confused by the black wave which took hold of me. I was ashamed and closed my eyes hard while she scooped up some ordinary water to rinse off her body and then dried herself. I hated the whole rite. But luckily it was all coming to an end because a week later we were going back home again. My brother and sister – I haven't said anything about her but maybe I will one day – were allowed to stay on a couple of extra weeks, but I refused, so after a long struggle I was allowed to go with our mother, although she really would have preferred to be on her own. That's when our blackberry-picking days began. But no sooner was she running around in the brambles, strong and healthy, than she had a relapse. She closed her bedroom door and laid down her rules: twice a day I was allowed to knock on her door to ask her how to prepare the food. It always ended with her screaming that it wasn't her fault that I couldn't cope with the cooking – she hadn't asked me to come with her. And the bucket full of blackberries started to go mouldy and rot. Long entangled green and yellowish webs covered the berries. Every time I opened the door to the larder the horrid stench hit me in the face until I started to cry one day in front of her closed door.

I didn't dare open it any more.

But now, once again, I was on the blackberry path. I strolled along and didn't mind the prickly bushes.

In there somewhere, completely covered by the dry scrubs

and straggly alderberry trees, lay Little Frog's and my future home, in perfect seclusion.

A house of stone at last! Here we would rear a new tribe. And I was the king of the rubbish dump.

Unfortunately, there were a few obstacles in the way which had to be overcome. First, I had to get a radio so I could follow the World Cup. The teams had already arrived and I didn't want to miss a single match. Secondly, there was an alderberry tree growing in the middle of the cement pipe just as if it were saying 'up yours' to me. And all round the pipe new shoots were sprouting hopefully, so it looked more like a huge flower pot than anything else. How was I to cut down that mini jungle without as much as a scout knife on me? There was only one thing to do: set fire to it and remove the ashes with an old tin box when the trees were burnt down. There was no shortage of fire and every true hero knows how to use it for his own benefit. It didn't take me long to make a torch just like the one they use to light the Olympic flame, then I ran around on padded feet to light the Olympic fire . . .

Hooray, hooray!

I stared at the bonfire and saw how our future tribe would arrange an Olympic rubbish game with a gigantic fire in a cement pipe. The flames flared up and soon had caught hold of the tree. But all too soon, I'm afraid. My great Olympic fire was like a furious prisoner, it wanted to break loose. The sizzling tongues greedily attacked the other trees and a shower of sparks started to fall on top of me while I stood there transfixed, trying to pretend that it was raining. In the end I snapped out of it and ran down to the canal, snatching a rusty old tin on the way. I returned with water splashing in every direction but hardly any left in the tin. Never mind. I threw what was left into the hungry fiery sea. With the help of my clever minions we would organize a human chain right down to the canal. So let's get going!

Back to the canal, race around a bit, pick up the tin, run for it again, take the tin and pass it on to the next man.

This is going fine!

I ran up and down along the bank of the canal, pretending that I was putting out the fire, but I didn't dare turn round.

There was a terrible din: it sounded like a gun going off. What was the point? The whole copse would burn down, it would end up looking like a charred field, stripped of its protective layer.

And everyone in Happy Heights would look at that naked shameless picture postcard from their windows and it would serve as proof of what they had all said in the council estate: Sven Hansson won't give up until he has developed all the land right up to the dump!

The sparks started to fall on my back. I squatted and stared into the muddy waters of the canal where the tall flames danced gracelessly. There was a squeaking and rustling sound going on around me and when I looked down I could see the mice and the rats pushing and shoving – as if they knew that all the water snakes in the canal were waiting for the banquet of the year on the other side of the water. The snakes were probably lying there with their mouths wide open like garage doors ready to swallow everything whole. It was just a question of walking straight in and parking permanently. I stood to attention for the rats and told them to go first as I was the captain and I wanted to be the last man to abandon ship. But they were not that easily duped. They just multiplied around me, and even though we were in the same predicament it was still a bit of a problem. When the sparks started to singe my head I didn't have much choice left. The two alternatives open to me were cremation – in the company of scores of paralysed rats – or human sacrifice by way of offering myself as a tasty dish to the water snakes. I chose the latter because there was no sign of them yet. But I screamed as loudly as I could when I threw myself into the muddy slimy arms of the currents where slippery vegetation effectively concealed everything that might prey on me. My scream was meant as a 'get out of the way'. But I hadn't reckoned with the rats.

The first thing I saw was a man scratching his crotch apparently without any embarrassment. And he didn't stop when I looked at him disapprovingly. In the end he pretended he was looking for his handkerchief, and got it out to wipe the sweat off his brow.

'Hi there,' he said.

He was a cop.

I sighed and tried to turn around. Strangely enough, something seemed to cling to my legs. I looked down and to my great surprise saw heavy bandages which ended in loops – which in their turn were tied to the end of the bed. I supposed someone had put me in a straitjacket but the wrong way up. I was stuck. There was no doubt about that. I squinted and tried to think of an escape route, but the only thing I could see was a screen which surrounded most of the bed. And the only opening in that screen was where the cop was sitting.

'Hi there,' he said again. No doubt about it. A real intelligent conversation was about to take place.

I sighed again and tried to shut my eyes. But the crotch-scratching man didn't give up that easily.

'My God, it's hot.'

He must have spent several hours trying to think of something we might have in common when I woke up. It really was warm. I wasn't even sure that I had any legs left inside that parcel. You never know, it could have been some filthy old canal water splashing about in there.

Bang! There it was. I remembered the dump. Somehow it must have got stuck inside me and I didn't even need to decide to throw up – it just came shooting out of its own accord. The man flew to his feet and scratched his head for a change. There was probably nothing in his book of instructions about how to interrogate vomiting children. In the end, he collected himself enough to call for a nurse and she took care of me and told me that I wasn't allowed to speak.

She was an angel. Obviously I couldn't speak. Every time I woke up that bloke sat there scratching himself and it got warmer and warmer and my legs melted in the heat and I threw up now and again just to keep up appearances.

One day he must have got fed up with me because suddenly he wasn't there any more. And that was a pity because I learnt through Sister that Sven Hansson just wanted to thank me. To him I was a real hero, a real settler who helped to clear the disused land so that he could build more blocks of flats for more large families, although the council had refused him building permission. He disappeared when the other fellows in the ward started to joke and say that maybe he had encouraged me to burn down the trees round the dump. Anyway, he had won a years-old battle thanks to me and now he would flatten the dump and extend Happy Heights right across it. To him, my misfortune was a great fortune. Who knows, he may even advocate a statue of a little boy coming out of a cement pipe.

I lay there making up stories like that until my brother came to see me. He told me that the whole Great Wall of China was in uproar. In one great big fire I had destroyed a whole paradise for treasure seekers, so I couldn't hope for a very popular return. My brother tiptoed into the corridor, looked around and returned with a smouldering cotton reel in his hand which grandmother had sent with him to make me well again. I have witnessed her magic powers on several occasions in my life. No kidding. She can conjure and look into the future. She always tries to prevent minor accidents, but it's impossible because no one takes any notice of what she says: if she says I shouldn't go down to the big coal harbour because if I do I'll fall into the water and drown, well then I'll just go straight ahead and do it. And when I get back home in dripping wet clothes she says: didn't I tell you so? But accidents like that may not be quite so difficult to foretell. She is not the only one going on about drowning. But grandmother has always got the edge on the others. She has an uncanny way of passing on her predictions to grown-ups. And they'll always come true. Grown-ups could avoid all sorts of accidents if only they listened to my grandmother, but nobody cares. They are just like children. I go mad when I think about it. Anyway, when my brother turned up with that smouldering cotton reel and told me that it was from grandmother I didn't suspect anything at first. It was just like her, doing something like that.

He said I was to suck it to get well again.

And I sucked and sucked that dreadful smoke into my lungs. It felt like swallowing barbed wire.

'Keep it in. Keep it in,' whispered my brother while holding his hand over my nose and mouth.

My head was reeling. I felt like throwing up again before he let go and I could breathe out.

'Now you've smoked a proper cigarette.' He grinned.

No sooner had I got out of one tight corner than I landed head first in another one.

This was an obvious case of blackmail. He had me completely in his power. If I told anyone that I'd seen him at the dump, then he'd tell that I had been smoking. That's as far as I got in my thinking. After that other problems turned up which worried me more. I couldn't get rid of the smoke when I exhaled. My stomach was rumbling, my intestines were swishing about like loose shoelaces. I felt sick and needed to go to the toilet. But my legs were still tied to the bed. Normally Sister would help me and I'd pretend that I was in another room. But this time I simply crapped in my pants. It just gushed out and I wanted my father to come and rescue me and make up for earlier disappointments.

Everything repeats itself. It's as if I had a pre-ordained course to follow, and every time I run around it the end gets worse and worse. I run round in circles like a sweaty circus horse ruled by the rein and the whip. But at least the horse knows who's in charge. I don't.

This is how it all started:

I was born with chronic bronchitis. It is an important fact. It was fun being born with chronic bronchitis, at least that's what I've gathered from all the stories I have heard about myself ever since I was old enough to understand things. But then there is one more important fact.

I was a very beautiful little boy. I was both beautiful and thoughtful. Most of the time I crept into some corner and fell asleep and just wanted to be left alone. But my chronic bronchitis and my peaceful disposition made me the centre of attention right from the beginning. (I wonder what my brother thought about that at the time?) First, I wasn't allowed to come home like other new-born babies. Then I went in and out of hospital like a precious piece of luggage. I flashed my eyes and coughed discreetly while the staff kept brushing my thick flaxen hair which fell in seductive curls. And then my grandmother turned up and tried to change my insides into stewed fruit to counteract the bronchitis. But one day it all suddenly collapsed.

I was like one of those pampered royal princesses at Haga Palace who, after several years of lying on soft down mattresses, suddenly wakes up with a start and is transformed into a nasty frog.

My mother disappeared, all those lovely angelic nurses disappeared too and I was just a nasty frog whom a farmer took pity on. There is not much to say about that period in my life. You just have to grin and bear it sometimes, don't you? Living in the countryside was good for me. Even my chronic bronchitis disappeared when I inhaled that dung-filled air.

But I was terribly homesick. I desperately wanted to get away from there. I wanted to go home and find my mother.

Summer came and with it the highlight of the farming community – the annual market day at Kivik. We all went and I wandered off on my own as soon as I could, to spend my wages. The whole farm with all its possible dangers had been under my vigilant eye because I was looking after the three-year-old daughter of the house as she toddled about. I followed her around like a kind old dog, lifting her out of danger whenever necessary. It was worse than being chained down. A very painful occupation. But I was paid at least, cash in hand at that; enormously heavy coins to carry around. So I handed them over to the first stallholder I happened to come across in return for a pair of binoculars. They looked interesting, like those used by spies, and I thought perhaps they might make it easier for me to look after the little terror.

But some stupid person must have put a lot of naked ladies in the binoculars. I was just going to look at the pictures before returning them with a complaint, when suddenly a giant's hand snatched them from me. It was the farmer. He was furious when he looked at those pictures. His face turned quite white with anger.

How could I explain to him that it was all a mistake – with his hand ready to strike?

I decided to go on the defensive and suddenly turned lame.

At first I feigned surprise as I tried to get out of the kitchen sofa where I was sleeping, but then I rather enjoyed it when the whole family gathered around me and carefully squeezed my legs in various places. I was going to give that bloody farmer a lesson. He must have hit me so hard that my brain got dislodged. He hadn't reckoned on that. His face looked like a cold steamed-up bottle of milk. Sweat poured off him until he reluctantly agreed to send for my father. Usually, father would come out for weekends and work for the farmer. That way it didn't cost so much to have me staying there. This time he came rushing out to fetch me.

But when we were back in town I still couldn't move. I didn't realize that my imagination could be so powerful. We had to go to hospital. And when I arrived there I thought for a moment that I was better even than grandmother at conjuring, because the whole waiting-room was brimming with paralysed kids of my own age. The word that explained it all bounced off the tiled walls: PARATYPHOID. A terrible word. On with the nightshirt and then sign in. It was worse than the war. And I who had planned on going back home. Instead I was dragged up some stairs, screaming and shouting. In the end I didn't know why I cried: whether it was because my father had rapped me over the knuckles or because I hadn't had a chance to revenge myself on the farmer.

I certainly knew how to put a foot wrong, even in those days.

Not even my paratyphoid was like other children's. Just to be on the safe side, they gave me an injection in both thighs. I wriggled and screamed so much that they needed three people to hold me down and a fourth to put the needle in.

I am sure that that sort of thing ends up in your medical record. Why else would they tie my legs now at the hospital? And turn me into a little paralysed parcel which had to stew in its own shit? It gets worse every time. If you aren't paralysed to start with, they soon make you, that's for sure. All you can do is laugh at it. It was so sad, it was almost funny. My brother sniffed around in a troubled sort of way and lit a match to get rid of the gases. But then Sister came and my brother was taken out and they changed my clothes.

I wonder what Sister wrote on my chart at the end of the bed. Never mind. Things couldn't get much worse, I thought, and made up my mind to become a model prisoner with my legs in a parcel.

In a way, it wasn't too bad, I suppose. I didn't have to go to school after all. I didn't have to face that filthy maths book and soon they were going to abolish corporal punishment. That is what my mate, an old man in the bed next to me, told me anyway. Life was great. The World Cup kicked off to a good start. We weren't having such a bad time in the ward. The grown-ups pitied me in a respectful sort of way. They took it in turns to entertain me with stories of their various complaints and they told me what I ought to say to Sven Hansson when he came back again. Sometimes they went too far. The old man talked about how they were going to vote in the local election and if only they got a chance they'd show that Sven Hansson a thing or two. It got a bit boring, in the end, listening to them. But they calmed down when they were allowed to shuffle out into the corridor and put their vote in the urn. The result was a draw. I preferred the subject of football. I lapped up their stories and speculations about each and every goal in all the football grounds in the country.

But even I recovered in the end and the Manufacturer himself turned up to take me home. There is a lot I could say about him, but that'll have to wait for another time. Anyway, he called my mother a nightingale. That's how they knew each other. That is when her lungs were still in their full splendour. She had been singing in a choir and he was still crowing in it. That's what I gathered anyway, but I am not absolutely sure. There's definitely something fishy about it, because they keep everything very secret.

The Manufacturer was grim and said that everything was in a bad way and I struggled to keep pace with him as best I could. He is so tall and thin that it felt like running after a couple of unfriendly knee caps.

When we got home, the flat seemed very empty because my brother and sister weren't there, and I had no idea how my mother was looking because I kept staring at the floor while the Manufacturer told me that they had had a discussion about my future. I was to go to my uncle's in Småland and stay there for the summer. My mother couldn't look after us any more. My brother had gone to grandmother's of course and my sister, ah well, she had plenty of takers, lucky sod.

He went on and on about things I didn't really want to hear. I just waited for that other voice to utter one little word.

But I have never experienced a silence like that before.

The Manufacturer was as unaccustomed to packing a suitcase as I was. He dashed around and asked my mother through the bedroom door what I needed to take with me. She didn't mind talking about this, that and the other to him. I wasn't entirely unused to packing, actually. In fact, I had moved about so much in my short life that I probably could have managed it myself. But I made myself awkward just to be difficult. That's what my mother told the Manufacturer anyway.

In the end we had packed everything and I was ready to leave. But then I had to unpack it all again. The Manufacturer had had a brilliant idea for my future safety:

'You must always keep a list of personal belongings taped to the inside of your suitcase. Then you'll be quite safe.'

And the train chugged along towards Småland which I didn't know anything about. I chewed up the ticket just before we changed trains in Alvesta. But it didn't matter because I had a piece of paper tied around my neck which said where I was going. Somebody lifted me onto the next train and said that I should seize the opportunity to enjoy the narrow-gauge railway. Soon it would just be a thing of the past.

I really hoped they were right about that. I couldn't sit down. The train shook and rattled and the hard benches grated against the burns on my legs. I got up and pretended that my clothes were a tent whose walls I wasn't allowed to touch. I went out on the platform of the last carriage and saw the railway tracks disappear in the distance. I got the feeling that I was disappearing too. My skin was coming off. They hadn't done their job properly at the hospital. What had they used to stick it on with? Liquid was seeping out. I was shrinking inside my clothes. Maybe there'd be just a bundle of clothes left on arrival. That would make them take note, all right!

They'd stand there with egg on their faces and they'd have to return the empty bundle that was me to my real home – but too late, alas! I would have dissolved into a puddle by then and become part of the ground water in Småland. And in my new capacity I would turn up as a welcome guest in many a thirsty mouth. Especially those I liked the least. And with them I'd get really awkward, so awkward that they'd choke on me and their last word would be 'yuk' before they had to spit me out.

Yes, I always chose to be really awkward whenever it suited me in life.

Chapter 3

1959

There wasn't time to say good-bye to Little Frog in a stylish manner before I left. The deportation to Småland happened with the speed of lightning and I ended up on my uncle's and auntie's convertible sofa before I could say Jack Robinson. I lay into the small hours listening to the chat about the World Cup on the radio while fighting those mosquitoes with a rolled-up newspaper. Smack! It was great fun. When I saw all the bloodstains on the ceiling it was too late to do anything about it. I felt so embarrassed that I decided to ignore my birthday the next day.

But that was then. The second time I set foot on Småland's soil everything that should never have happened had already taken place. My brother and sister were wandering about somewhere else in our tragedy. My only consolation was that Sickan was all right. She was probably having rabbit steak for Sunday lunch. And she wouldn't need to have more than two baths a year. As long as she didn't get completely paralysed with homesickness she'd probably manage until we got back.

But to tell you the truth, I wasn't thinking of Sickan when I stood there looking at the village school down by the church. No, I was thinking of a bull I'd seen at that farmer's place where I'd stayed once. I don't really like barking up the wrong tree because I was cured of my chronic bronchitis after all, but surely he ought to have understood that I was far too small to hold a big angry bull at bay? As soon as that bull set off across the meadow we ploughed hell for leather through the fresh manure. Many years later I was looking at the village school in a winter dream. The lit-up windows seemed friendly and welcoming, but all I could think of was that bull that had dragged me around in the cow dung.

Strange, isn't it?

That bitterly cold day I had a sudden urge to howl, but I

35

decided to keep quiet after all. It was the first time I had had that urge and it frightened me and surprised me at the same time. I felt more desolate than the winter landscape. The taxi driver had left. He'd been talking all the time in the car and he'd said that next time he wasn't going to wait for me at the crossroads. I had to be there on time.

He couldn't drive the same route twice just for my sake. But it was nice of him, anyway. When he found me wandering about in the middle of nowhere, he didn't know that I had no intention of going to school. He drove me to a picture postcard landscape with heavenly music and harmony.

The heavenly music streamed out of the classroom. It was pure and clear and it seemed to go on forever. I went in and faced the music: that is twenty-five masters of the recorder, all playing 'All things bright and beautiful' with glowing cheeks and star-spangled eyes. What about that? All for my sake! I was both moved and impressed. I, who couldn't even play a tune on a comb. All the same, I always appreciate the effort of an expert when I come across one.

Once I asked mother if I could possibly have saxophone lessons, at least for one term, but as expected she said no, of course. Everything that cost money was scrapped from our family budget. Yes, we actually had a family budget. I don't know where the accounts book is now, but I can easily remember that beautiful slanting handwriting of hers which drew up the two columns of debit and credit and which finally produced a crushing 'no' whenever we asked for anything. My grandmother told me that in her childhood there was something called 'the English disease', a deficiency disease which luckily they managed to avoid, she always added.

She knew nothing about our family's deficiency disease of course. She thought everything would be all right as long as you had stewed fruit with your porridge. She had no idea how it felt to drive a pretend car in the sandpit when you wanted a real racing-car like a Fangio's – just to give you one example from 1951 when Fangio won the World Championship with his Maserati. I suppose it was a little unreasonable to ask for a Maserati, so let's take a reasonable example instead: new skis or skates, a new pair of trousers or a bike. No chance. And if ever we got anything then there had to be a lot of fiddling with the budget and things. Now I think that kind of deficiency disease is worse than the one grandmother was talking about. Mine has become bigger than the Bermuda Triangle even. It is like a bottomless pit.

I will always think of accounts books with neat slanting handwriting where the figures never add up. Sorry mate! Not enough.

When the last notes died away, the recordists stared intently at me and I realized that they were wondering what I could do in return now that they had played so beautifully for me. None of us needed to wait very long for my response. I managed to achieve more in one day in Algutsboda village school than they had ever dreamed possible.

Someone coughed behind the organ and a white head of hair appeared and after much hullabaloo the first male teacher in my life revealed himself!

Nothing but a dithering old man, but a man all the same!

He patted my head and hoped that one day I would belong to the musical circle too and he asked if my name was really Ingemar Johansson. I didn't deny it. The giggles made me embarrassed as I walked up to the teacher's desk to hand over my report book, but in the end I was shown to a place right at the back of the classroom. It was a fine corner.

The musical score on the blackboard looked like blurred spiders. My spectacles were now a thing of the past and 'All things bright and beautiful' wasn't my kind of tune anyway. I was never going to play anything so stupid on the recorder. In my corner of the classroom I could spend the winter in greater comfort than under a draughty fir-tree as I had first planned. I thought it would take a bit long to build a proper house with a palisade, you see. I curled up and pretended I wasn't there, although everyone kept staring at me. My teacher turned the pages of my report book slowly and glanced at me now and again. He was beginning to realize that I was the false note in his heavenly harmony. When he started to speak I almost thought he was Moses himself:

'In this class we like playing the recorder!'

It sounded like something which he, inadvertently, had forgotten to include in the ten commandments.

Apart from his teaching job he worked as a church organist and he would be very upset if I didn't play the recorder like all the others. He was also a little surprised at the question marks beside my As for Behaviour and General Conduct. And I don't blame him, because so was I. For years now I had heard of Bs and Cs which would fall like broad-axes from the sky and make short shrift of my future if I stuck my head out too much. My A? was like a royal pardon to a man who is condemned to die. There was nothing else I could say about it. I took it like a man. As long as you've nothing to hide, you're all right. And with a B in Home Economics I think I could say I was OK. I had B in Art too. As long as they'd leave me alone in my little corner, I'd be all right.

The B in Home Economics was a mistake and I was very embarrassed about it, because only girls get As and Bs in Home Economics. But my teacher was convinced that my interest in cookery came from the heart. She was incredibly flattered when I remained still while all the other boys put dishcloths in the potato mash or mixed chalk into it – or covered the girls' crocheted oven cloths with egg and flour, then fried them until they turned a nice golden colour. But my little secret was that I felt sick all the time. What to her appeared as a firm steady look when we were making the sauce was just my seasick eyes about to pop out of their sockets. I think it was the sparkling orderliness that made me seasick. The cookery teacher wasn't to know that I and my brother and sister lived in the hysterical hope that one day in the lunch break we would be able to invent the perfect quick dish, provided the kitchen was silent and the door to the bedroom remained shut. Most of the time the afternoons were veiled in screams and smells of burnt leftovers, and suddenly a voice would be heard from the bedroom: 'I'll die if you as much as talk about food!'

That's why I was sick with happiness when the cookery teacher took my wrist and guided it carefully while we were making that sauce together. I melted like butter in her warm hand. She was better than mother and her big warm breasts almost wrapped themselves round my ears like soft cushions whenever she stood behind me. Fancy, we were actually making a sauce!

But at the same time I wanted to throw up. I felt sick and ashamed. And it didn't help that she gave me B in Home Economics. I realized I was worse than all the other guys put together. They could at least fry an oven cloth! What could I do? My cookery classes were like a rising dough in my head!

The A? in General Conduct made me more interesting in the other pupils' eyes and so did my Fail in Swedish language. The squinting old man actually read out loud from my report book. Maybe he was just absent-minded or maybe he was using me as a warning to the others. Anyway, I was the monster of the year in Småland – A? in General Conduct and Behaviour and Fail in Swedish – that's worse than a calf with two heads. We were a charming little bunch, full of contempt for each other. They weren't to know that I had been wondering for years whether to improve my handwriting or conceal the fact that I believed in alternative ways of spelling a word.

Mercifully, there was a knock at the door and two men who introduced themselves as policemen came to my rescue. Of course, I thought. It sounded so funny when they asked after Ingemar Johansson that I had to laugh.

A small, blond, broad-nosed scoundrel with enormous jaws put his hand up and said that Ingemar Johansson was in New York and was just negotiating with Cus D'Amato about a match with Floyd. You bet we laughed! Even the cops laughed. But I laughed more than anyone else until I discovered that I was the broad-nosed scoundrel.

Things like that happen quite often to me. It's nothing to worry about. My life doesn't always belong to me exclusively. I really do try to hang on to myself, but it's not always possible. But it must be worse for the real Ingemar Johansson. I had shamed him. At the same time as I heard about our national hero from Gothenburg I wanted to change my name for his sake, but how could I when my second name is a girl's name – I am named after a lady who forced an English king to abdicate and who dishonoured his royal family. She even changed the pages of history. What could my mother have been thinking of when she decided to give me a name as terrible as Wallis? Did she think that I'd have the same Wallis charisma and that I too would be able to attract blue-blooded customers as if they were just iron filings? Or was I the sticky fly paper that my mother stuck to when she was aspiring to her crown? What did she have to give up for her Wallis?

So you see now why I have to call myself Ingemar. And in front of those two country cops I promised never to drag the real Ingemar Johannson's name in the dirt again, because our whole nation's hopes were pinned to his fist.

When I walked off into the corridor with the two policemen I vowed that this was the last time I'd make a fool of myself. One of them offered me a tablet, such a cheap trick that I tried to run through the door and into the vast empty snowscape outside. I suppose it was the strain of it all. I'd come to Småland to start a new life and once there I found myself under police guard, encircled and caught by two tablet-pushing wrestlers with some terrible tactics in cross-examination:

'Now what about telling us something about those street-lamps a week ago?'

Streetlamps?

It sounded as if I must have been in Småland longer than I realized myself. But I didn't know anything about streetlamps. There are times when I wish I were somewhere else, but that is a different matter, isn't it? This time it seemed as if I'd been to a glass-smashing party without having any recollection of it at all. Some bits of life are as blank and black as the inside of a sack of coal – was it really possible that I had roamed about like a demon smashing all their streetlamps?

I suppose it could be.

I started to scream: 'Yes, yes, chain me down to the wall, fetch the police car!'

What am I saying?

We city-folk have a tough skin. The cops didn't get a word out of me. They wandered off into the glistening snow in the school playground with disappointment written all over them. 'We'll be back. Don't worry.'

But they never returned. My musical organist teacher persuaded them that it is very hard for little boys to be in two places at the same time even if they boast an A? in General Conduct and Behaviour.

Whose idea was it in the first place to put the blame on me without knowing when I was going to arrive? Great, wasn't it? What was I going to tell my uncle? Maybe he knew already that he had a juvenile delinquent staying with him?

Anyway, in one great swoop I had surpassed everyone's expectations. I who didn't think I could do anything for them! The whole classroom turned round when I came in and sat down at the back. I might have been the teacher, the way they looked at me. And the organist was reduced to the sort of person who spends most of the time spitting in church – he was tolerated but that was all.

To keep the interest alive I went into the playground during break and threw an icy snowball straight through one of the windows. No, I'm only joking. It was a mistake, actually, organized by all the other guys. They really were clever. They lined up with their backs against the wall with windows and threw snowballs at me. The girls were standing outside the shooting range, giggling. One moment they chewed their mittens and the next they didn't dare look at me any more. I was like a criminal, hunted by the police – so terrible and so cruel and dangerous that they wanted to touch me to see how wild I was.

What could I do with all these snowballs coming at me? Refrain from returning them? Never. I could have thrown tons of snow at them because they were so blind that they didn't realize how I longed to be their friend!

So I squeezed my snowball until it turned to ice.

Crash!

Even on my first day at that school I was put in the front row so the organist could keep an eye on me. He looked as if the air had gone out of him. Another one who's going to have a nervous breakdown for my sake, I thought. Apart from my mother there was my first teacher. But she'd been my brother's teacher before she was mine. So I can only take the blame for one and a half nervous breakdowns. She got so nervous looking at me that she lost her capped teeth. I suppose there might have been a few other factors involved. Whenever she told me off she always shouted and told me to look at her, but when I did she didn't know what to do. She got so nervous that she started to cry. Her teeth just popped out of her mouth like a bunch of cherry stones when she tried to say that I didn't have a soul. It sounded like one of my spelling mistakes, completely incomprehensible. But it was always fun watching her crawl around on all fours, looking for her teeth.

My recorder-playing teacher was a kind man with nerves of steel, even though he was on that precipice they call retirement. Year after year they took kids away from him, reduced his grant, removed the little he had. The remaining pupils were borderline cases. The village school with its single class left was doomed, but we weren't.

By mistake they had given him an enormous mobile box on wheels with several doors on it. In that box there was a science laboratory for experiments in Physics and Chemistry. That box was his favourite toy. He always started off by sticking to the subject, but when the different phials were brimming over the top, he was moved to tears by the mystery of life.

It was impossible to put a stop to his discussions. Before we knew why, we were looking up passages in the Bible to compare chemistry and religion. And we believed him. He loved us borderline cases, as long as we learned to play the recorder.

So what was more natural than that he should love me too?

But unfortunately, someone had crossed over my recorder in the accounts book. However much the organist teacher tried to persuade the council, they still wouldn't give him any money for more recorders. I had to take over a broken old recorder which was repaired with some insulating tape, then I practised during breaks and after school while I was waiting for my school taxi to arrive. I had a bit of catching up to do, but if I pulled myself together he promised that I could play in church at the end of term and at the confirmation service.

And did I pull myself together?

I tried to produce some sounds through the broken piece of wood with the strange holes in it while the organist was beating time with his baton and pointing to a lot of flags and dots, which seemed to jump about like drunken sparrows on telephone wires on the blackboard. And it wasn't I who cried at the result. The organist and my recorder howled worse than starving wolves in the winter.

Once back in my uncle's and aunt's kitchen I was exhausted from all the puffing and blowing. Something was cooling on top of the stove while wonderful sounds were coming from the first floor. My uncle was sitting by the stove farting little blue flames. I laughed every time he set light to them, one after the other. But auntie put her foot down and slammed her fist on the table: 'That is enough of that!' The only trouble was that on that same table was Auntie Auntie's half-stuffed sausage skins and now they were suddenly flattened and a grainy substance came spurting out all over her dress. Uncle laughed so much that he fell down from the stove and broke his pipe. Auntie ran into the bedroom and pulled her dress off. How do people look without their clothes on? There are all sorts of shapes and sizes. My aunt is the thin sort. She is the 'thin and interesting sort', at least according to my uncle. He is quite crazy about her. As soon as he saw her without her dress on he crawled after her on all fours, growling like a dog. He jumped up and pulled her down on the bed, he snorted and sniffed around her and asked if he could bite her ankle. Are people allowed to behave in any way they like? Yes, it seems like it. I thought it was fun, though, so I growled and followed after on all fours too to the bedroom, where I expected my fair share of female flesh, to be honest. Into bed and munch away!

That's what I thought. For a tenth of a second I stared at the yellow flowers on the linoleum and when I looked up again the door was closed.

Anything can happen in life. You think you're hatching the golden egg and it turns out to be hollow, after all. That's why you should never let go of your target. Look at me. I've lost sight of my target somewhere along the way.

I am not saying that I've been running away to my beloved Marian like a happy-go-lucky Robin Hood, but I must have done something wrong. And just like Robin, I've been punished for it. He lost his Goddethorn because that bastard Guy of Gisborn perjured himself and murdered Robin's best friend Trusty. How can anyone be so mean as to kill a dog?

It was because of Trusty that Robin was made an outlaw: *And his wrath quivered in him like the arrow just before it leaves the bow.* After Trusty's death there was only hatred and revenge left in him.

But how could Robin be so stupid? Messing about with that Marian instead of being with his dog? I am all for Jack London's Weedon Scott. He took his wolf-dog and best friend with him into the big wide world. That's what you should do.

I scratched on the door of my aunt's and uncle's bedroom, but to no avail. And Auntie Auntie was knitting away by the kitchen table as if nothing had happened. I crept back across the desolate tundra in order to examine the flattened sausage-skin and for no apparent reason I asked about Mr Arvidsson. I thought it was a bit funny Auntie Auntie sitting there knitting away while Mr Arvidsson was all by himself down in the basement.

She just purled two and plained two while saying a few words about Arvidsson's death. He had died just after Christmas.

43

Why hadn't my uncle told me anything? Why did people never tell me anything until it was too late? What was going on around me? My Auntie Auntie was a widow. She didn't have anyone any longer. And there she was, knitting away as if nothing had happened.

'Auntie, Auntie,' I called.

It sounded good. Maybe she'd be a little happier if I made her into my kinswoman. The best phrase I know when I am on my own and the authorities want to 'take action against me' is next of kin. If you don't have any next of kin you're in bad trouble, because then the authorities can take any action they like. I said 'Auntie, Auntie' a few more times. It felt good. But she didn't comment about it. As a matter of fact, I think she is the quietest person I know. If she ever cries I think she must have some secret outlet. She is always the same dry old stick. And she is scrawny too. I am sure Mr Arvidsson thought she was thin and interesting once when she was young. Somewhere deep inside her I can see a likeness between her and my aunt: a young and happy woman who could bang her fist on the stuffed sausages and who didn't mind having her ankles bitten. I know a woman's legs are for biting. Not hard – just so. Maybe if I nibbled a little at Auntie Auntie's leg she'd feel the wings of love brushing against her?

I crept along and looked at the thick blue veins twisted all over her thin legs, and I came to the conclusion that it might not be such a good idea after all.

'But my dear Ingemar, don't cry! Arvidsson and I will soon meet again.'

That's exactly what she said. Maybe she was just knitting a winter sweater for Mr Arvidsson – one with holes in it so he could stick his angel's wings through them. Why do people never give up? Why did she go on knitting and why did I carry on at school as if nothing had happened? Angels scatter their ashes closer and closer to our hair. As soon as I started to grow up I seemed to be forever sad. First I thought it was enough to lose one human being, but I realize now that I have to get out of here and fight again and again.

I am growing strong and lonely. And maybe I'll end my days by knitting a sweater for the frosty climate in heaven, that is if I decided to stay around that long.

Is that sort of talk called sensible talk?

While I am on the subject of sensible things, I think my uncle married my aunt because she looked like his big sister. You see, my mother used to look after him. She was the sensible one, after all, as my grandmother used to say. Little Frog is also the sensible one of us two. When I was buying a leather jacket she came with me to give some sensible advice. I had earned some money digging up potatoes during the summer holidays and I was looking forward to a smashing leather jacket with a fur collar and big pockets with zips all over, but I only had enough money for a horrible green shiny plastic jacket. It was an imitation job, completely useless. I decided on delayed gratification and was ready to postpone my purchase until the next potato-picking season, but Little Frog said that the plastic jacket was much more sensible anyway. She meant well of course – like all big sisters, mothers and grandmothers – when she betrayed me in front of that sales assistant: 'And you can always wipe off the dirt with a wet sponge. And the reflective bands are as good as a real life insurance, because life insurances are only valid after the event but reflective bands work before.' And what would I rather have? Before or after? Alive or dead in other words?

Her sensible nature won the day. I opted for life and bought the plastic jacket, even though I had never seen anything so horrible in my life. We trotted off home to my mother who was ill in bed at the time and she inspected the jacket while I wriggled about in it like a worm in a tin box and Little Frog went on about her 'before' and 'after'. According to her description of my jacket, it was more like an armoured tank. Nothing could hurt me while I was wearing it. And with reflective bands like them I was perfectly safe.

In a way, she was right. As soon as the temperature dropped below zero my jacket got stiff and cold. It was worse than being inside a freezer. But I was practically unbeatable in every fight that winter of course. I didn't bat an eyelid when my opponents sprained their wrists and fingers on my armoured jacket.

Maybe I am exaggerating a bit now. But you have to when you talk about life, don't you? There are no sensible truths. Your prick is just as cold whether you are wearing a pair of swimming trunks or not. But that is not entirely true, actually. Anyway, you get the feeling that nothing is waterproof.

So it doesn't matter if you're covered all over with reflective bands if you decide to step outside yourself and say good-bye to everything. Life is deadly serious and something we've just got on loan. Isn't that funny? The best thing I've got in life is just a loan?

The only way of avoiding the inevitable is not to be around when it is time to give it back. I just parked and left, put my gloves on the shelf and said: 'Thank you very much, I am not interested.' Many people don't understand what I am talking about. I mean, many people are even surprised if they catch mumps. Why me? they ask, instead of Why not? But they haven't seen a thing; they haven't realized that reflective bands simply don't help.

In the end my uncle came out and said that aunt had taken all the spunk out of him, but he didn't seem to mind. Aunt sneaked into the bathroom and when she reappeared her dress was as red as her cheeks. Never mind. I thought it was nice that they were so madly in love with each other – as long as they didn't slam the door in my face like that again!

Fresh sausages were sizzling on the stove, fuelled and supported by crackling birchwood logs, and the supper almost jumped into my mouth of its own accord. It was delicious. Auntie Auntie never seemed to eat anything. I suppose putting all that lovely food on the table was enough for her. People in Småland eat differently from us. You might sit there with a potato dumpling in one hand and a cream cake in the other. Did I say *sausages*? They have invented their own kind of sausages in Småland. Uncle says it is a mixture of elk and badger: they put the two animals in a tent and there they have to fight each other to death. After that, they leave the tent standing in the sun over the summer. Now and then they spray it with water to make it shrink – just like the Red Indians used to do when they put their prisoners on cowhide to dry in the sun. After that you hang up what's left of the elk and the badger inside a chimney and the smoke will do the rest of the job during the course of the winter. That is how you make those special sausages. I like them. But my uncle doesn't want to go near them. He's been a sailor, so he only eats bacon and eggs. As Jack London said about his dog, you become what you are if you are where you are. And if you move to a new place you become someone else. Since my relations were evidently never going to move, I was looking forward to a life on sausages.

Outside our kitchen window the winter evening stretched like a big black hole, but in every house around the glass factory workers were eating their sausages. Everything was peaceful and quiet as far as my eyes could see. Our kitchen was just like a fart in the universe, but I had found a way home. No navigation problems here. I had greater precision than LUNIK 1. By altering its course by a tenth of a degree it had already missed the moon by 3,500 kilometres and it was now rushing into space at 11,000 kilometres an hour. On the radio it sounded as if LUNIK 1 would have to circle round the sun's gravitational field forever and I, for my part, was immensely grateful that I had completed my new orbit. I didn't want any more adventures. I just wanted to live a peaceful life in the country. And if I got bored I always had my uncle and he'd had enough adventures for both of us.

I looked at him. He wasn't like any of us. Maybe my mother's father. He had the same thick curly hair, the same big nose. His mouth was as big and wide as mine of course. You just can't miss it.

He probably wasn't as irresponsible as my grandmother used to say. Her stories were typical mother's stories and I know from experience that mothers are always disappointed in their sons. Just ask me. I have been both child and husband to the same woman and I've been her little brother too.

From now on I intend to back up my uncle. He always comes out with funny expressions like: 'We'll see how it all unfolds' or 'Don't worry – I am not fussy.'

I especially liked the last expression because he always farted as he said it.

After dinner my uncle and I struggled into the living room. The strain that we'd subjected our digestive systems to was clearly reflected in our absentminded smiles. I collapsed into the nearest chair and stared out through the window across to Mr Fransson's roof. But Mr Fransson wasn't there. He usually sat there hammering away on his roof, summer and winter, day and night. Mr Fransson was a phenomenon when it came to harmony. A long time ago I used to think that people like him were mad. But now I know better.

I am sure Mr Fransson is going to celebrate his hundredth birthday on top of his roof – that is if he doesn't end up in the mill pond. Repairing the roof and bathing in the pond in the middle of winter were his favourite pastimes. When he couldn't make it to the roof any more, it was time to pack up and park. That's why his roof was the best-repaired roof in Småland. It took him a whole day to put down one single roof shingle. A few years ago he'd started working nights as well. He hung there on his roof-rick in the wintry night like a sloth. He got smaller and smaller. One day he'd probably end up like a dried-up roof shingle himself and swirl away in the breeze – that is if he didn't drown in the current before then. If he wasn't on the roof, you were sure to find him in the water. It didn't make any difference to him whether it was summer or winter, day or night. He'd come stumbling past with a shabby old towel slung across his shoulder when you least expected it. During the winter he used a kick-sled, but he had his own method of getting about. If the piste was good he'd carry the kick-sled and if he saw a bare patch on the ground he'd put the sled down and struggle past it. The sled squeaked and shrieked as he pushed it along, insisting that it too was put on this earth to work. And when he got down to the water, he'd undress and climb into a hole in the ice. The freezing cold water would rush at his tall twisted body as it was lowered down with the help of a rope. Kind people had hacked a hole in the ice for him. But on one occasion the village children tried to charge a fee from the spectators. They put up a notice by the roadside demanding twenty-five öre for the pleasure of watching the oldest winter bather in the area. It turned into a real performance. Fransson refused to get out of the water, but he got stuck to the frozen rope. People had to saw the rope off to get him free before carrying him into the glass factory to thaw him out in front of one of the furnaces. But he got so angry that he ran straight home and climbed up on his roof.

I have heard this story from others and I don't care whether it is true or not. It must have looked fun anyway with Fransson stuck in that block of ice in front of the furnace like some kind of prehistoric animal. I could just picture Fransson coming back to life under protest with the block of ice slowly melting around him. Here was his chance in a million to live on another couple of hundred years if only they'd put him in a freezer!

Auntie Auntie's husband, Mr Arvidsson, had been so jealous of Fransson the summer before that he used to spit like a cat every time he heard Fransson hammering away. Behind his drawn sun-bleached blinds Mr Arvidsson would lie in his bed listening to the dull beats which were like an ominous reminder of the passing of time.

Mr Arvidsson regarded that noise as an insult since he had put his own tools away, even though he was just a baby, according to Mr Fransson.

Suddenly to use one of my grandfather's expressions, a vertical line appeared. And if I followed this vertical line from the very beginning of my life – from the second I came out of my mother's womb – I could see lots of old 'phenomena' strung together like wild strawberries on a blade of grass. Neither Boot-Carlsson nor Fransson were exactly your typical 'wild strawberry', but they turned up at regular intervals with all their extraordinary secrets, one after the other, and they made me wonder about the meaning of the word 'madness'. Boot-Carlsson went a bit too far with his constant masturbation, but as long as he didn't do it in my boots you could almost put him in the category of 'wild strawberries' on my vertical line. Not at the top of the line, mind you. I could make a long list of those happy madmen I've come across in my life, ending with myself. Fransson was one of those people that I took a great liking to right from the start. Both he and I were fighting against time. But he had the edge on me with his ninety-eight years, of course. I wasn't even fourteen yet. But what really surprised me and gave me hope was that he wanted to live to be a hundred and twenty at least. Now, if a geezer of ninety-eight manages to ignore all the distractions around him and just gets on with repairing his roof and has the odd dip in an ice-cold stream, then surely I'd be able to find something to make my life worthwhile too?

I really felt happy as a dog when I lay there in my armchair philosophizing with my bloated stomach. Again and again I registered the details in the room: the furniture, the carpet, the pictures, my uncle's lazy look – everything in the room. I didn't want to forget a single thing. I was swimming in a big wide river. Everything flowed so quietly. There were no strong currents, no sudden precipices. Mr Arvidsson's death didn't mean anything. Auntie Auntie was making a noise over in her corner with her knitting needles. Forever and ever. Amen.

But in the middle of this peaceful setting my uncle suddenly exclaimed: 'Caramba!'

He speaks fluent Spanish sometimes. He told me once about

his adventures in Buenos Aires. This time he was worried because their son had left their double bed for the first time. He spoke to me as man to man. Surely I had noticed that he and auntie were enjoying a second honeymoon?

Funnily enough, I had forgotten all about their little Erik. He used to hang around me like a leech the first time I was in Småland. Every time I stopped he had his nose right up my backside. That's how close he was to me. He was always a pain in the arse. He was the little brother I had been when I used to follow my brother around. But you don't tell someone off who isn't even your own brother, especially when you're only on probation yourself. There was always the risk that I might be sent back home again. I learned to disregard him and obviously I'd succeeded so well that I didn't even know he was there in the end.

Poor uncle. His talk couldn't keep pace with my thinking.

It was embarrassing. He revealed that I had saved their love life when I had vacated the convertible sofa for their little Erik. They had only let me stay there the first night as a kind gesture. After several years' struggle, my uncle had finally managed to get Erik out of their bedroom. The sofa was now occupied. I got the general idea, but I still didn't quite understand. In other words, there was no room for me in their two rooms and a kitchen. Talk of precision landing. Talk of making fun of the Russians when they miscalculated with their LUNIK 1! I couldn't even find the right sofa.

'It doesn't matter. I've got Auntie Auntie and she says I can always stay with her,' I said, and he beamed like the sun.

I always do things like that. I wouldn't have survived one day among cannibals, that's for sure. They'd only need to hold out their knives and I would cut myself up into several delicious little pieces for them. Luckily, I had just made Auntie Auntie into a kind of relative. Anyway, there was only a double floor between me and my real uncle. I ought to be able to keep track of him as we were living in the same house after all. Their second honeymoon was going to reverberate from the walls.

That's what I thought anyway.

But it wasn't going to be like that. Auntie Auntie had been dispatched. The house wasn't theirs and the glass factory needed it for a bigger family, a family who'd come from Hungary and who had a lot of x's and y's in their names. Auntie

Auntie had been moved to a flat on the other side of the road. She was lonely and wanted some company, someone to talk to. And that someone was to be me.

They might as well have given her a hedgehog to cuddle.

My uncle really was a most irresponsible sort of person. He had tricked me into coming to Småland without really wanting me there. For days now I had looked forward to it and I had forgotten to be on my guard. I had laughed and learned to love them and I'd almost peed in a corner to stake out my territory, then what does he do? He tells me that I don't belong there after all. '*Andale Burro*,' as he used to say.

'No, wait,' he said, as I tumbled down the stairs and ran into the black hole of night without my jacket on.

The road stretched ahead, straight and narrow as a ditch, into the arms of the snow. I sank deep into the soft snow but I wasn't going to give up that easily. I ran until I found a hard crusty surface. I shall vanish into the night, disappear for good and live on the produce of nature, without asking anyone's advice.

No one ever puts up a sign saying 'Drive carefully' for my sake. Things happen and I lose all the nuts and bolts at once. I don't know how many times I've run away, but it's so many that I strongly suspect that people must have picked up someone else occasionally when they thought they'd found me. Every time I've run off, I've left a part of myself somewhere, and I keep coming back defeated.

My brother and I have run away many times. Every summer when we used to go to one of those camps run by the council, we ran away. We thought it was enormous fun. It was fantastic to be so important that all the staff organized a search party for us. Once I happened to throw a javelin right into a fellow's leg. That time my brother and I shot straight into the forest. It was I who wanted to run away then, but usually it was him. The staff ran after us in the rain. We darted off into the forest with some large rhubarb leaves as protection against the rain. It was ridiculous. I gave up at five o'clock and my brother gave up at six, because that was suppertime. We were defeated by our own hunger, beaten by insufficient protection against the rain. Rhubarb leaves, I ask you! You couldn't even stuff them down your trousers when matron gave us a good thrashing after-wards. I got five strokes and my brother got seven. He'd been gone one hour longer than me, after all.

But why try and run away from my uncle?

I was a loser the moment I opened that front door. Where would I go?

To the right was the glass factory. That was bound to be as warm as usual and I was sure to find somewhere to hide in there. There was only Stuff-the-hole Hardy who walked his eternal round to feed the two insatiable furnaces with logs. Maybe I could become Sweden's youngest vagrant and live a Stuff-the-hole Hardy life in the local glass factory?

Hardy had told me himself that he missed the old time vagr-ants. The welfare state had taken care of them and put them into homes as antiseptic as operating theatres. And the tramps them-selves were so clean that they'd die on the spot if they as much as looked into that starving hole. Stuff-the-hole Hardy always complained that the welfare state had boiled up all the old tramps. But I was starting out as a young tramp so maybe I wouldn't die if they caught me?

Cheered by this thought I ran straight into the furnace room and straight into Saga's arms. She was standing just inside the door, peering at a lot of people who were mucking about with something in front of the furnaces.

Stuff-the-hole Hardy and 'Jesus' were standing there glaring into the dark. Jesus looked more peculiar than usual. He had big white bandages wrapped around his hands and he held them straight up in the air. And in front of one of the furnaces, the resident artist was talking to Saga's father who was the sales director of the factory. The managing director and a lot of other unfamiliar faces were also there and all the ovens were open. The fires were roaring away, making all the faces red and warm. One photographer seemed to be in command of things. He ran around placing the artist's things here and there, moving tools around and tugging at reluctant glass blowers who didn't want to be photographed. He chased after them, his camera clicking away.

'Shhh,' said Saga, even though I hadn't said a word. She pulled at my sweater. 'They are photographing the American collection.'

She was just her usual self. She didn't even say Hi!

And I suppose I looked my usual question mark because she whispered to me that the artist's birds were to fly across the Atlantic to America and her father was going there to sell them. It was the greatest thing that had happened in the history of the glass factory. The artist had made it at last.

'Come,' she said, and disappeared through the door. Saga was always fantastic at taking the lead. I trudged after her into the same wintry night again. She walked fast, a few steps ahead of me, and she didn't turn round until we came to their big white house.

'Keep quiet now and we'll sneak up to the attic.'

I nodded.

Saga's attic was better than nothing. We tiptoed up the stairs. I could hear voices and laughter coming from the TV somewhere in the house. It must have been the TV. Saga's parents were the only people in the village who had a TV set. Everyone else said that it was boring with TV. I don't know. On the two occasions I've watched, it snowed so much on the screen that we had to guess what was happening – and that was quite fun too. But most people, including my uncle for instance, say that the best programme they have watched on TV is a series in twelve parts about the art of building a kayak. Nils Erik Baehrendtz was hosting the programme but that's only because he didn't want to show the other Ingemar Johansson on the box.

The door to the attic creaked ever so slightly. The moon cast a shaft of light across the empty wide floorboards. It was an enormous attic, at least three times the size of my uncle's and aunt's flat. We stood there holding our breath in silence. And I wondered what she wanted from me.

'There,' she said, and walked over to the window.

She sounded pleased with herself. Her black hair disappeared, her pale face with its determined mouth looked bluish-white and I took a few cautious steps forward.

'What do you mean "there"?' I asked stupidly.

'Here you are. Now IT has happened.'

She knew. It wasn't a question. The whole village knew about it. I was somebody who had arrived because IT had happened. Everyone talked about it.

I sidestepped the issue by asking why Jesus had bandages round his hands.

'He's dipped them in an acid bath on purpose, because he

doesn't want to work. That's what daddy says anyway. Now he can preach as much as he likes.'

Saga was as strange as Jesus and Stuff-the-hole Hardy put together. She had changed. She wasn't older than me, but she looked as if she were going through some sort of an acid bath herself, actually. What had happened to her? She stood there by the window as stiff as a steel pen. Their house was situated on top of a hill in the middle of the village. If I looked beyond the trees past the big road I could see the narrow path meandering across to uncle's house. During the winter that path was never touched by the snow-plough. There was no need, because nobody owned a car over there anyway. As far as you could see there were other red houses nestling in a semicircle round the village like small random dots in the heavy snow. The smoke from the chimneys rose like stiff white pillars straight into the sparkling winter night. She took my hand and pulled me closer. It felt strange. Saga wasn't the type to pull anyone close to her. I would have preferred to turn the light on. I think she sensed my surprise, but she thought I was frightened so she asked me what I was scared of. That must mean that there was something to be scared of. There was something going on right in front of my very eyes and I didn't understand what it was or why I was frightened of it!

'You're not like the others. You're not from around here. We are growing up. Have you thought of that?'

What a question! I didn't know what to answer. I wished I was still a baby with lovely curly hair and lots of sweet nurses fussing over me. Much better than spinning round like a cat in a tumbler drier. Nothing but the laws of gravity kept me on the surface of the earth when I was spinning round like that, being nostalgic about my childhood. And she was asking me if I realized that we were growing up!

I released my hand and stood there on the other side of the window pointing to all the stars, just to change the subject.

'The first one crashed in outer Mongolia, the second one near the Virgin Islands. Why shouldn't the third one crash here? Wouldn't that be fantastic? It might turn up with a long tail of fire behind it.'

'You and your sputniks.'

'Imagine yourself circling round the globe, just waiting to be burnt up. And you're just an innocent Eskimo dog.'

'Poor Laika.'

It was obvious that she couldn't identify with a dog, even though she had one herself. Her family had a boxer called Oscar which they boasted about all the time. Saga thought Oscar was intelligent. But if he was so intelligent, why didn't he put some kind of clothes on? I thought he looked naked in a funny sort of way. Dogs without long-haired fur don't look quite dressed. They look as if they've lost their overcoats. There is a difference between dogs and dogs of course.

But Laika we must all feel sorry for, because she symbolizes human progress. She circled around in space without knowing why, stuffed with pipes and tubes in every muscle, and with threads through her heart and silver anodes screwed into her brain so she could transmit signals home. I am sure she would have begged to be taken down – if she could.

I always get upset about dogs.

Saga slid across to me. There was a breath of wind turning into a waltz around the sliver of the new moon. Saga breathed her faint sweet smell close to my mouth and at the same time she told me that she had been waiting for me.

That was a lie. She would never wait for me. She was not the type to wait for anyone. That's what I thought anyway.

I couldn't get away from her. I stood there pressed against the windowsill wondering what she wanted. Why did she say things like 'we are almost adult now'? In what way was I different from the others around the village?

'I am starting to grow breasts. Isn't that awful?'

Poor Saga. Now I understand. That really is something to worry about. For her, of course, it was a catastrophe. How was she going to play in our football team in the spring? I was more or less assured a place. But what was going to happen to our best inside left? It was terrible. We couldn't have anyone with breasts in our team. The previous summer we had managed to get to the top of the local league table without letting on to the other clubs that we had engaged in some irregular practices like including a girl in our team. It was cruel that she of all people should have breasts. She was the toughest of us all. I almost wished it was I who had them instead. I was not half as good as her anyway. I thought a long time about the possibility of taking them over in some incredible way but then I got another idea:

'Can't you strap them in?'

'Maybe. I hadn't thought of that.'

She quickly pulled her jacket and shirt off. Her breasts were not very large.

'How quickly do breasts grow?' I asked.

'I don't know.'

We took her scarf and wrapped it round them. I pulled a bit and tied a knot behind her back. She looked as flat as usual. What a relief!

'If we get hold of an elastic bandage, we can pull even harder,' I suggested. 'And then no one will notice anything.'

She turned round and I untied her scarf. Her short hair fell forward and left the nape of her neck bare. In the moonlight she didn't look so tough and strong at all. Usually, you had to watch out with her. She lashed out without thinking. Fast and straight. Bang! And there you were on the ground. She was totally unpredictable. She could hit you for the slightest reason. Some people tried to tame her with arguments like 'You ought to know better, being the sales director's daughter and all.' But that only made matters worse. Saga was no ordinary girl. But her breasts put her in her place. She couldn't ignore those two growing buds. I am sure she wondered what use they'd be to her. So did I.

Suddenly she turned round and laughed, still with nothing on top. The only difference between her and me was those two buns she had growing on her thin muscular body.

'I am so happy that you came. This will be our secret. Will you promise?'

'I promise,' I said.

But I didn't know how we could keep a secret like that. I thought it was common knowledge that girls grow breasts. It would be quite a feat eradicating such knowledge. And one more thing: at the glass factory everyone knew everything about each other. If Saga hadn't grown any breasts they would have known about that too. It would have been written in the smoke from the chimneys, it would have been spelt out in capital letters, grey and white against the black sky. It would have been visible at the bottom of every coffee cup, it would have been cut up into little pieces like the cake with the coffee. You just couldn't get away from things like that. Especially as Saga was an extraordinary 'package', as my aunt used to say.

But now we were discussing the future of our junior football team. That's why I was prepared to tell a few fibs until we were satisfied. Elastic bandages and some clever procedure in the changing room would be the salvation both for her and the team as a whole. It was just a question of keeping a straight face in front of the other teams. We didn't mind her being one of us because she was the best player we had, but a year ago we had promised not to say a word about her true sex. We called her Pelle after Pelé from Brazil. That's how good she was. But we couldn't turn up with a Pelle who had suddenly turned into a girl. They'd laugh at us. I just had to help her strap those bumps in. Saga was absolutely vital to us. It wouldn't be difficult to persuade the others in the team of that fact.

But I wished Saga would put her shirt back on again. It wasn't good for any of us that she ignored her breasts like that, unless she wanted me, as her first strapper, to get used to them. It wasn't an easy job to do without the support of the rest of the team. It felt so private. Every time I glanced at her breasts they seemed to grow. And time almost stopped: it lay there on its back like a dead fish that's floated up to the surface. Saga came closer again and the moon retired coyly behind a cloud, and I wished I could do the same. The sweet smell from her breath transported me into a strange hypnotic expectation. I closed my eyes and suddenly I wanted to do a lot of things with those breasts apart from strapping them in, but I knew that it was wrong to feel like that because technically I was still married to Little Frog.

I opened my eyes and looked into Saga's. A thousand years passed and then she asked the question I wanted her to ask:

'Do you want to touch them?'

What a question!

Of course I didn't.

All of a sudden I didn't want to touch the breasts of our inside left. Looking at them was one thing, but only from a strictly professional point of view, mind you. Touching them was just like breaking up a chain. I played outside left myself. Now how do you think it would affect the game if the outside left and the inside left started snogging? Maybe it was all right. But I didn't dare take the risk. It just wasn't worth it. Besides, how was I to know – she might decide to change her mind a second later and land me one instead. Why do something that I might live to regret?

57

But how could I tell Saga all this?

Maybe she didn't want to carry on with the football? Maybe she preferred someone to touch her breasts so she could change from being a tough inside left to being an ordinary giggly girl in skirts and hairband? Maybe just one quick touch and she'd change into another person: an enemy who'd be strutting about on her way to the bus stop the following day, quite aware that she was the only one from the village who went to the grammar school in town. Our ball-games might be reduced to mere memories.

We were still standing close together. It is true that I may not be like other people. My brother would say that it is not normal to worry about whether you should touch a girl's breasts or not. He believes in grabbing what you can. But I need time to think things over. And she gave me time all right. She seemed to be nailed to the floor beside me, immobile and stubborn. The moon got tired of being excluded and wrapped Saga in a silvery light while I was getting goose pimples under my sweater – my way of sympathizing with her. But I still didn't know what to do.

The best thing was probably to run away. I pushed past her, but I only managed to take a few steps before she knocked me to the ground with a terrible jab from behind. We rolled around on the floor in silence. Then she sat astride me and I could hear from her voice that she was crying.

'Tell me that you've grown too.'

She was crazy.

Of course I had grown too, but that didn't mean to say that I needed an elastic bandage. Our problems were not congruous. (Fun word. The only word I'd picked up from the thorny world of mathematics.)

I relaxed. There was no point in fighting her. She was both angrier and stronger than me and I suppose I had to put up with her until her anger subsided.

But she squeezed me with her legs and – oh boy, what slim football muscles were working away there against my sides!

If the owner of those legs had been allowed to grow in peace without any interruptions in the form of breasts for instance, then Småland would have made history in the football world. That's a fact. But it didn't turn out like that. I lay flat on my back and let her decide. Hopefully, she'd give up in the end. Her sales director father and his wife and their dog Oscar were

58

probably waiting for her downstairs. If Saga was gone for too long maybe Oscar would come up looking for her, being an intelligent dog and all that, I mean.

I could just picture Oscar: his wet sloppy face with that floppy creased mouth of his. He'd probably be very surprised to find his mistress half naked in the attic. The poor thing couldn't wag his tail, because he didn't have one, but with his talent he'd probably conclude that Saga was half naked just because he was.

I thought this idea was so amusing that I started to laugh.

Saga got so surprised that she rolled off me. She fell down on her knees and looked at me in wonder as I curled up in hysterical laughing fits. When I finally stopped she had a thoughtful finger in her mouth. She really looked worried.

'You're a bit bonkers, aren't you?'

'Yeah,' I said, 'get dressed now.'

'Aren't you going to show me how you've grown then?'

What could she mean? Did she want to start some kind of bartering? If I showed her mine I could touch hers. The same old thing we used to do in the Great Wall of China. I shook my head even though I was afraid that she might start another fight. But instead she withdrew into the darkness and her thin voice suddenly echoed across the attic like a sharp saw-blade at full speed towards me:

'I suppose you don't dare because you've wet your pants.'

I knew what she meant all right. I slowly responded to her cutting phrase which she repeated again and again.

It was lucky that it was dark in there. I exploded into a billion pieces and flew off like a burst balloon. What you tell someone in strictest confidence can always be used as a weapon against you at a later stage. I had opened one tiny little door to the past and told her about my time at the children's home, but she had promised not to say anything about it. Now she might even tell all the others. She hadn't forgotten and nor had I. My memories flared up in front of me: a room of white tiles, the stench from twenty kids lining up for the bathtub suddenly entered my nostrils and I felt those hard hands pulling us down one after the other, to be scalded in the same bath water. A small, misshapen boy with webbed feet stood in front of me and I struggled and screamed because I didn't want to be dipped in the same water as him. Maybe he was contagious? What if he were?

Saga's blackmailing scheme was as clear and hard as a steel

blade and couldn't be evaded. If there was one thing I didn't want the others to know about it was certainly the time I'd spent at the children's home. I screamed that she could have anything she wanted.

'Shh. Not so loud.'

She came up to me in the dark, smiling – pleased now with her cunning. I was surprised at myself – that I didn't put up any more resistance. Maybe I wanted to play the same game too?

She took my hand and led me to the moonlit area.

'This is a good place. Now I want to see if you've grown too.'

That was below the belt! What could I offer her? I was the one who would end up feeling embarrassed, not her. She had something new on her body, but I didn't. At that moment I wished I was an ass in more ways than one. Then I could have scared the wits out of her with my size at least.

I froze in my position and my hands travelled down to unbutton my trousers.

If only a sputnik had crashed on top of us at that moment – then nothing else would have happened!

My uncle was excessively worried when he finally found me at the crossroads, still deeply hurt by his deception, but more confused about Saga's strange new hobby. Even if I was defeated by the world around me, at least I didn't show it. But he said he was sorry and worse than that: obviously I was to be tossed from one kind of blackmail to another because he asked me if I really wanted to disappoint Auntie Auntie. She was so lonely and had looked forward so much to my company. And I who had been on such good terms with her and everything.

I could have asked him if my own disappointment didn't matter at all, but I didn't bother. If you're always swimming against the tide you're bound to get strong muscles in the end, but even the strongest people are known to have drowned when they haven't taken a rest. I just couldn't fight against the tide any longer and I needed somewhere to be. Never mind where, as long as the currents weren't too strong.

He pointed to the road which disappeared into the darkness. Someone had broken the streetlamps. Then he told me where Auntie Auntie lived and asked if I could go there by myself. Of course. I stepped straight into the coal sack, while whistling to myself because I was scared. Then I sang Paul Anka's 'Diana' and when I got tired of that I cheered myself up by singing Little Gerhard's 'Buena sera senorita! Buena sera! It is time to say good-bye to Napoli!' It was not that I was afraid of the dark, but it stopped me from thinking of things I didn't really like thinking about.

I survived anyway and got to my Auntie Auntie's and she was knitting away as usual. I was so preoccupied with my solitary rock concert that I asked her who she liked best: Tommy Steele, Elvis, Little Gerhard or Paul Anka. But she answered Pat Boone, someone outside the competition, a real drip. It was typical that she knew about him and his endless Christmas song. Pat Boone was the parents' own manufactured sleeping pill, created to stop us from being swept away by the gigantic wave of rebellion that belonged to the real music world. That's what I told her. She ought to know the facts, I thought. One day that huge revolutionary wave will splash across the threshold of the music school where I had just started and the recorders would bow with modesty and the organist would cough with fear as we started up with 'Jailhouse Rock' instead of 'Twinkle, twinkle little star' on speech day. Auntie Auntie thought that sounded great fun and asked me to play one of those tunes on my recorder. But I had to tell her the truth. You're not always as good as you think you are. I hadn't quite lived up to my own musical expectations.

She suggested I take lessons from old Mr Holdst who lived in the flat next to us. He could play all kinds of instruments which often made the whole house shake. She said she'd asked him if I wanted her to.

I hesitated. The organist seemed more than enough.

We sat in the kitchen talking, and I thought it was rather nice of her not to mention that I had run away. She had never doubted that I would come to stay with her, so she had taken my satchel with her. In the end, I began to wonder how the rest of the flat looked and finally she suggested that we should make our beds. She disappeared through a door which obviously led to my room, or so I thought. It sounded as if she was in need of some help so I went after her – and bounced back at once, because there was no other room. In one corner of the room the tiled stove was hissing away. Just in front of the stove there was a clear space, but apart from that the room looked like a warehouse. The furniture was stacked on top of each other. She hadn't had the heart to get rid of anything from the past. We pulled the dining-table to one side, as far as it went, and in the end we managed to make the convertible sofa into a bed. When she started to pull out the under bed I realized that we were going to sleep in the same bed, practically. She got my pair of pyjamas out and suggested that I undress.

What can you reply to that when it comes from an old lady you hardly know?

I slipped into the kitchen and put on my pyjamas quickly then tiptoed back into the room. Creeping into bed with a bang, I pulled the cover over my ears before she could say Jack Robinson. How old could she be? About the same age as my grandmother perhaps?

Don't think that I am always making comparisons with the children's home. Once my brother and I stayed with an old lady who had a house like a manor. We used to count the rooms. There were thirty-eight spread over four floors. My brother was living on the second floor and I was on the first. In the evenings, I would open my door and my brother would slide down the banisters, straight into my room. That was during the summer. We used to creep out on the verandah and listen to the old lady when she was entertaining guests on the lawn. They took their evening tea there, as she called it. She used to talk a great deal about us to her friends. She felt sorry for us. So did we, but we didn't like rubbing it in. Anyway, it all came to a sad end when I said that I hadn't had my pocket money although she claimed that I had. She called me obstinate. (I have acquired quite a language through mixing with old ladies!) That same evening my father came to fetch me home again. He left me in the power station among the turbo-motors and covered me with his overcoat after he'd given me a good hiding. He worked night shift and said he didn't know what to do with me. The best I could do was disappear for good. So I ran away – as usual. I walked to the end of the town, but a heavy mist hung across the fields. It may have been the first time I ran away. Anyway, I don't remember what state I was in on my return.

I was woken from my daydreaming by a rustling sound outside the bedcovers. There was a sudden thud as Auntie Auntie threw a log on the fire, shut the damper and closed the doors to the stove. Her bare feet made a funny noise against the linoleum when she walked back towards the bed. Oh my God, maybe she was just as embarrassed as me – she even got sweaty feet at the prospect of having a stranger in bed beside her. Mr Arvidsson must have been lying in my bed with his white hands fumbling on top of the covers. Maybe this bed was the last thing he'd tried to hang on to in life?

I could feel the bed bouncing. She sighed a little and made herself comfortable. Then it got dark and quiet and I could pull the cover back from my head again.

When I peeped down towards the foot of the bed I could see a glowing square which seemed to be suspended in mid-air. It was the fire behind the tiled stove doors. The fire sparked off reflections in the crystal bowls and vases on a sideboard which was standing at an angle beside the stove. Mr Arvidsson had been one of the best crystal glass polishers at the factory. Small samples of his art were now visible in the otherwise dark room. They danced and glimmered in the crackling light from the fire and I realized why she had found it so difficult to get rid of the big heavy furniture she had. It was the only place left for displaying Mr Arvidsson's crystal glass in a decent way.

I turned my head slowly in her direction and pretended that I was asleep. But there she lay – her hands carefully clasped across the bedclothes and her eyes fixed on something in the ceiling. I assumed the same position and looked up. A dancing reflection from the fire was moving along up there, a bit faint but fully visible and as lovely as a dawn at the Antarctic. Suddenly she sighed and said:

'Well, well, life is a difficult thing sometimes.'

'It is worse than worst,' I said.

And after that, words of wisdom poured out of both of us.

Auntie Auntie wasn't that bad after all. Over the years, I have got used to adapting myself. I was already wondering whether Auntie Auntie may be my Weedon Scott perhaps. We had quite a good time together, she and I. The stove was crackling away, it was nice and warm in the room and we understood each other well.

I thought of the summer before and of all the people I had got to know in the village. Oddly enough, no one was at the same school as me. But I hadn't been included in their calculations so I couldn't make any great demands. Our football team would reappear in the end. Saga's problem was best avoided, I thought. All snow melts in the end, after all. And you'd be hard put to find a grown-up who won't say that time heals all wounds. I had to be my own pressure bandage until such time.

I probably couldn't get much closer to the border of nothingness. Auntie Auntie had no one to keep her company. That was for certain. We could lie there together like two experienced old oracles talking about life.

I dozed off and felt how our age joined the dancing figure on the ceiling. It is true that I wasn't fourteen yet, but I am sure there was an older person already inside me. I was aware of the various parts of my body and without understanding why I suddenly panicked. I had thin ribs, scrawny arms and my legs were like sticks which were separated from the rest of my body. And through all that was me, old age broke out – an old person struggling to deliver himself. There was no way I could stop it. I would have to fight against this growth all my life, carry burdens I didn't want to carry, run away from feelings I didn't want to have. Oh, how I wished I could get rid of that worm-eaten creature inside me and shed my skin: like being underwater in a dark lake when you suddenly feel a great need for oxygen and you fight your way to the surface with all your might to draw one enormous wonderful breath again, and all sounds and colours return to you with double force.

Here I am! Here I am!

And that's all there is to it.

Time stands still. I float around in circles, unperturbed about which direction I am taking. On the horizon there are waterfalls. But they are so far away that they don't really exist. They are in another world and in another time.

Auntie Auntie may be swimming out there heading towards the currents.

She may not be so afraid of that aged guest inside her body because that aged guest has already forced itself upon her.

That's how my thoughts strayed when I, without any previous warning, suddenly saw something I didn't want to see. I saw unfinished beings struggle against the terrible pull of the currents, I saw how they waved their hands about, imploring and screaming in despair because they hadn't finished growing up yet. In the distance there was a roar from the waterfalls. I recognized a hand, a face and a floating head of hair and the voice that cried: 'No!' And I was quite sure that she wasn't finished, so I cried 'No' too. But who could hear us amidst that groaning and moaning?

64

'What are you doing?'

Auntie Auntie grabbed my shoulder and shook me a little. I stared at her in surprise and wondered what she meant. But she looked so strange that I didn't dare ask. I had been unconscious for a while. I never want to think about it. I never want to go there again. The ribs in my chest felt like the large heavy wings of a gigantic bird which had just landed. They pumped and pumped until I crept towards Auntie Auntie whose two questioning eyes were wide open with fear.

'Did you sing?' she asked.

How should I know? If I'd been able to speak or sing where I had just been then it must be buried like a secret loop inside me and it would never be unearthed again.

I laughed a little and sang in a low voice so as to stop her from asking any more questions:

'Buena sera, senorita! Buena sera! It is time to say good-bye to Napoli!'

But I realized that my mother's death had made its presence felt in my bed and I wanted to have the last summer back again, because that was before anything had happened. I wanted to hang on to it, like a dog to his favourite bone. And my memory blossomed and the voices became more and more clear.

Chapter 4

1958

It was a wonderful summer. I had promised myself not to make a big thing about my birthday, but no one else knew about my resolution so I took back my promise when people started crowding round my bed ready to congratulate me. My uncle, my aunt and their little son Erik sang for me, but they slowed down a bit when they saw all the red marks from the squashed mosquitoes on the ceiling. However, they soon recovered with a 'Hip, hip, hurrah!'

It was the Sunday of my life. Uncle was wearing a track suit and a peak cap, just like Kalle Svensson, and carried a football under his arm. He tossed a parcel to me and told me to come downstairs in five snappy minutes. I opened the parcel and pulled out a pair of shorts, a real football shirt and a pair of fantastic football socks. The shorts were white, the shirt was white with blue cuffs and a blue collar. On the back were the letters BIK. The knee socks were also white and blue. They were the nicest presents I had had in my whole life. If the shirt had been green and yellow, the colours of the Brazilian flag, I suppose it would have been even better, but why aim at the stars when you spend most of the time on the ground anyway?

'Ball, ball,' said little Erik.

'Ball, ball,' I repeated.

What else could I say? We were in the middle of the thing called life. All of us, old and young alike, were in a feverish mood since the Swedish team was heading for the very top. There were even moments when we thought that the Brazilians might bite the dust. I had slowly realized the psychology behind what seemed just like a dance to the Brazilian players. You have to keep the ball *inside* your head. Then you don't need to run after it. You only need to place yourself where you know it is going to land. You've got to let that leather ball conquer your whole inside – and at the same time you've got to pass on your

66

soul to the ball. And you've got to learn to dance the samba. That gives you the right rhythm and bounce. Preferably you should be born with the samba in your blood. It won't do with the 'hambo' or the 'polka', which is just two-step. Since I'd learned how to do the jitterbug with Little Frog at the Teetotallers' Sunday dances I suppose there was no risk of me being too stiff. But I had to find someone else who could do the samba so I could keep it up.

I slipped into my shorts which felt cool and comfortable against my sore thighs. I could only pull up my socks halfway because my legs were still painful after my adventure on the rubbish dump.

But it worked.

The shirt fitted perfectly and my old trainers were also a perfect fit, almost too small as I clambered down the stairs with little Erik's 'Ball, ball,' behind me.

My uncle and I jogged towards the football ground while he gave me a short run-down of the local club's football history. As a goalkeeper, he relied on inspiration. He spoke Spanish and said 'Caramba'. He'd brought back both inspiration and the samba from his travels on the seven seas.

And I was a godsend, provided I wanted to play outside left in the junior team.

Of course I did.

My poor uncle had no idea that he was running alongside a person who had been bespectacled until quite recently, someone who'd always been the last to be picked for the school team. But in my own mind I was in harmony with that ball – that is how exciting and wonderful it felt to be jogging beside my uncle.

All the people who worked in the glass factory were already there. And all the mosquitoes in Småland had also turned up for a feast. We ran out onto the field. My uncle introduced me to several of the players, but I was so busy trying to tense my calf muscles that I hardly managed to memorize all their names. He ran into the goal and shouted to us that we should warm up with a few balls before the match started. Great! I ran forward and was just about to parry a great shot at the right-hand gate-post when I suddenly felt a compact body coming in with a hard tackle. It seemed impossible, but a boy who was smaller than me and who had dark straight hair had actually pinched the ball from me.

The tackling finished with a perfect ball that singed the grass, then nestled into the net close to one of the posts. The aim was so cleverly disguised that my uncle threw himself to the wrong side and all the spectators around the field applauded.

I tried to brush off the grass stains, hobbled away and decided to get really tough next time the ball rolled in my direction.

But at that point the referee ran out onto the field and blew his whistle. One of the players pulled me behind the goal and said we could be ball boys.

'What are you staring at?' he asked.

'Nothing,' I said.

I couldn't very well tell him that I had never seen anyone with green hair before. That is, his hair was both green and sun-bleached, almost white in places.

'You're staring at my hair, eh?'

'Yes,' I replied.

It was nice that he had guessed and I was also relieved that I hadn't been hit over the head during the tackling. Everything was just as it should be. In Småland there were obviously people with green hair around. And why not?

We were kept on our toes for the rest of the match. After a while I realized that my uncle's inspiration might not be as good as it was cracked up to be. He struggled well, threw himself recklessly, but there was a definite sign of nervousness in his saves. More than once, he was close to bungling it. But miraculously, he seemed to be able to catch the ball in the end somehow.

My green-haired friend told me his name was Manne and I told him the truth – that my name was Ingemar. He wondered whether I was interested in going to Vackamo some time to fly saucers, maybe the same day even?

When I took a closer look at him I saw that he had slightly protruding eyes. He was of a small and slender build and somehow it looked as if he couldn't be living under the right atmospheric pressure. But there was nothing odd about that. The little Martians had to live somewhere after all while we were travelling through space. I had to wait and see. As long as no one else seemed to react I could not regard his presence as anything extra-terrestrial. In order to change the subject I pointed to the other players and asked him to tell me something about each one. In that way, I could also find out how well informed he was about life in Småland generally.

'The one on the left is Saga. She was the one who tackled you.

68

She is the best player we have, without doubt.'

As far as I knew, Saga was a girl's name. It was beyond the realm of possibility that a girl, smaller than me, could tackle like that, then fire a shot like she had done. Either the green-haired Martian didn't have a clue about boys' and girls' names, or it was someone else's fault. Maybe I had a soul-mate in that little boy? With me having a name like Wallis, why shouldn't the other poor sod be called Saga?

My attention was caught by my uncle who was struggling in his cage, not without success, but not as inspired as I had expected. He was probably nervous for my sake. I suppose he realized what a great idol he was and no one can live up to pressure like that. I always exaggerate. I think I must be suffering from mental rickets or something. I have been lacking in well-adjusted reality. Reality has become so unmanageable that I have treated it as a game all the time. Or maybe I wasn't supposed to do anything properly from the beginning. Everything had to be a game. A game is something you do instead of. Grown-ups have sharp knives, tooth-edged saws, firm keys, real tools. We had to make do with a flat wooden stick for a knife. Everyone must realize the horrendous injustice that every child suffers when it sees an adult cutting up a cod while he tries to make a hole in the armoured cod-head with the help of a wooden knife and two feeble arms. That sort of thing only leads to disaster in the end. I naturally ran off and bought a sharp knife as soon as I possibly could. Happy as a beaver I chopped off every branch I bumped into the very first day. I cut into everything I saw: I forgot time and place – and in the end I cut off my index finger too. It was possible to repair with some tissue paper which I got from the dairy. I wrapped it round the whole hand and put the wretched thing back in the torn mitten. That mitten was the only warm place in my life. It got messier and messier as the rest got cold as ice. I hobbled round the Great Wall of China twenty times without plucking up enough courage to go home. I knew only too well what would happen if I came home with a pointing finger dangling from my left hand like an extra part of my body, wrapped up like a present in tissue paper. My mother would make mince-meat out of me and I would never want to look at a knife again as long as I lived.

It snowed and it was getting dark. I stood on the other side of the canal like a lonely guard to see if my brother was going to come out. He if anyone ought to be able to save me. I stuck the messy mitten into a snow drift, thought of freezing it for the time being. On the other side of the canal, the light was shining from everybody's windows. The streetlamps were swaying slightly. They looked like drunken giraffes, but I realized that it wasn't their fault. They reminded me of someone called Edwin who's dead now. But that wasn't because of the streetlamps. The thing was, he stood down there on the pavement boasting that he could swing himself along the wire right up to the lamp if he wanted to. And he actually did. He climbed up and travelled all the way, hanging from his arms. But the trouble was he hadn't worked out how he was going to get back.

Luck wasn't on his side. It wasn't a particularly big fall, but he is no more. It wasn't fun thinking of Edwin. I pinched all his marbles that time. They ought to have been included in his estate, really. I think I've got a real beauty still which belonged to him once.

It was so horrible to think of Edwin that I decided to take my punishment and go home. The punishment for stealing from a dead child and for cutting off my index finger and for purchasing a forbidden knife. I pulled and tugged at the mitten, but could not get it out. Both the mitten and me were frozen fast in the deep snow drift. And on the same side of the canal was the Wilderness – the cruel, deep-frozen wilderness of the North.

I was aware of how serious the situation was and prepared myself for death.

I didn't actually. Heroes usually speak like that, but they don't start by stealing marbles from dead children.

I didn't want to die with those marbles on my conscience.

I don't know why I suddenly thought of Edwin as I stood there frozen stiff. I had probably a thousand other sins on my nine-year-old conscience while I was at it. Maybe it was all due to those seasick giraffes which tried to look like lampposts. I screamed and hollered, I begged and implored, but all in vain. Happy Heights had withdrawn to indoor activities. It was only me standing there with my frozen left hand. It was like drowning in eternity. Slowly and haughtily, the earth went round in its orbit and I followed after like a frozen shrivelling statue, erected as a warning to people.

I don't remember much after that, except that I was woken up by a dozen mopeds whose headlights were all directed at me.

First I really believed that I was a statue. There are a great number of old ladies around who dream that their savings should go towards illuminating some dear old church. Maybe one of them had used her money to light me up? But when I came to, I realized that the rabbit chase had been interrupted because of me. Chasing rabbits was a tremendously popular pastime among mopedists. They drove around the fields catching rabbits because the rabbits got so dazzled and paralysed by the headlights that all they had to do was knock them down.

They carried me home. First they dug out my hand and then I was a hero for two whole weeks, except at home of course. Thanks to the freezing, my index finger could actually be repaired. A surgical masterpiece. But I can't talk about the rest.

It's funny, I was going to tell you about my thirteenth birthday which was on a Sunday, but I ended up talking about a black Thursday instead. It is a fantastic exaggerated thought that the universe should turn my arm round and me as well. As if I were the centre of the universe. What does earth care about me, except to keep me down here?

Be that as it may, when the match was over my uncle had let in more goals than the opponents' goalkeeper, I'm afraid. But that didn't worry him. The samba may be a good thing, but it is not enough, as my grandfather would say.

The surprises kept coming. Ignoring birthdays isn't my invention. It is an old family tradition. There was always something in the way. But this time there was going to be a real celebration! My uncle invited the whole boys' team to cream cakes and cordial and we jogged down to the party which was taking place in the garden. We had great fun – until I stalked up to Saga and told him not to be depressed. My name was Wallis, after all. I meant it as a friendly gesture, but she hurled her cordial in my face and left, furious at my cheap joke.

It wasn't until then that I realized she was a girl. That is, she was a girl but she didn't like it.

Everyone laughed and then the party was over. Manne with his green hair reminded me that we were going to fly our saucers before he left. And I nodded to be on the safe side, because I did not want to say the wrong thing again. Meanwhile, my uncle had got a little sentimental. He drank his own cordial which he kept refilling at regular intervals. He turned up with two of his favourite possessions to help me remember my

71

childhood – or maybe it was his own? I didn't believe my eyes when I saw the old wind-up gramophone. It was quite incomprehensible that it had escaped my grandmother's attacks. But he had actually rescued it from her repeated destructive attacks which were caused by her wish to retain her sanity. I laughed until the bubble burst when he did his old trick with the only record he had. Every time grandmother asked him to throw the record away, he said it was worthless anyway, just look how buckled it is. He did something strange with it so it looked like an accordion but when you touched it, it was smooth and back to normal again.

I cranked it up and soon you could hear the notes of 'Oh, what a lovely bunch of coconuts!' all over the neighbourhood.

When we got tired of that tune we turned the record over and listened to 'I do want to be beside the seaside!'

And while that was playing, he showed me his other prized possession. That was the moment when my aunt slammed the window upstairs. I don't know whether it was because of the two brilliant tunes or because my uncle got the photo album out. At that time I was beyond all criticism as far as my uncle was concerned. I knew what was coming. The photo album was bound in leather. On the front the name VERA CRUZ was printed in a semicircle, framed by two palm trees. Underneath the palm trees were pictures of beautiful girls with colourful pieces of cloth tied round their hips. You could just glimpse their breasts here and there like warm melons under the flower garlands. 'Warm melons' was not my expression. That was my uncle's description. But those girls were nothing compared to those inside the album. And not a patch on the stories he told me about his young days as a *caballero* when all the girls were *un caballo del diablo*.

To be honest with you, my uncle seemed to exaggerate a bit because most of the girls looked confused and hungry sitting on his lap. Their mouths were too big and their shoulders too narrow with hollows around their collar-bones. They were thin all right, but I am not so sure that they were as interesting as he always claimed. And the restaurants resembled huge tiled swimming baths for orphans.

His eyes filled with tears of happiness and longing. He hugged me and said that he'd teach me a lot about life, and at the same time I managed to wipe off a little cordial against his shirt.

Then we put it all away because he wanted a nap. But auntie had locked us out. So on the spot, he promised to build a summer house where he could keep his gramophone and his photo album.

Then we could sit there and wiggle our ears whenever we liked, he said, kicking the door a little demonstratively just to show that he meant business.

It is my personal opinion that aunt locked the door because she didn't want to be one of those *caballo del diablo*.

Manne was not a Martian. His hair turned green every time he had a bath. He lived with his grandparents, but I don't know why. His grandfather was a farmer who repaired everything for the people in the village. As soon as something broke on the farms or at the glass factory, he was always called in. He had built a strange barrel of copper which was heated by the forge in the smithy. As soon as he had repaired or soldered something new he'd shout that there was hot water to be had. Manne was always clean and green-haired because of the verdigris from the copper barrel.

Anyway, he had a flying saucer.

We ran around a cow field with it. Manne's grandfather had been inspired by the race in space between the Russians and the Americans. But judging by his saucer I don't think he was the man to take the first step on the moon. The saucer itself was not too bad, but the motor was missing. The testing ground was a rusty old wire which ran from the roof ridge on top of the barn to the end of the cow field. We managed to get the saucer up there with the help of a spare part from an old well. Then he had an old hand-lever with brake linings made of iron. The iron lining was pulled towards the wooden barrel until a tail of smoke developed behind us. The motor which was never installed was used as a base for an aeroplane that Manne's grandfather was working on. He had hoisted the motor onto the same barn roof and there he was, balancing with his welding equipment, ready to measure everything up by rule of thumb, which, according to him, was the only tool needed by real professionals.

We weren't too bothered. He didn't get many opportunities to climb up to his aeroplane. Most of the time he was plagued by repairing milking machines and other useless things that farmers insist on having. Meanwhile, we flew our saucer and the sprawling iron construction that was his aeroplane looked more like a rusty version of a TV aerial than anything else.

We didn't have a dog who could come with us in the saucer. Manne wanted to experiment and measure the ionospheric pressure on the ridge of the roof. In the end, I gave in. We compromised and took a hen with us in a shoebox with holes cut out for its head and tail.

Various newspapers showed the rhesus monkey Sam's wrinkled and worried old face. He was going to be the future traveller in space in the American space programme. That explained why Manne was so eager to take a dog in the saucer. I refused to kidnap a dog, but had to give in when Manne snatched the hen instead.

Manne pinched his grandmother's thermometer as well, and I can tell you that a normal hen's temperature, twelve metres above ground in a flying saucer destined for a cow field, rises by as much as six degrees.

There might have been a slight margin of error because Manne and I cut out a little space helmet from a rubber cover of an old milking machine and pulled it over the hen's head. We just wanted to protect her from the radiation area around the earth's surface, but it probably just made the hen's head warmer and that in turn registered on the thermometer. One half degree could be deducted because of the space helmet. So far, everything was under control. And we cut out the stress factor after a few trial runs because the hen seemed to enjoy having the thermometer stuck up her backside.

That's how we carried on for several days while Manne's grandfather was either welding or measuring up or driving off in his black Ford.

In order to achieve a sense of weightlessness, on my suggestion we suspended a couple of bicycle tyres and attached the saucer to them. It was completely dark inside the saucer. Manne was wearing a kind of miner's lamp. It slipped up and down and fell about whenever we swung from the bicycle tyres. The problem with the saucer was that we couldn't see out. But that was because ordinary glass would melt on landing, according to Manne. The sheet which was stretched across the frame was painted with a non-inflammable silver-coloured paint, all according to the constructor again.

And we went faster and faster down the wire. And a terrible smoke appeared from the wooden barrel which was getting more and more charred. And the hen almost jumped into her space suit of her own accord, wanted her rubber hat on and the thermometer up her backside.

'Contact,' shouted Manne.

'Vackamo I is entering the second Van Allen belt,' I shouted. We could really feel the energy from the proton layer as we zoomed down on the cows in the field and got ready to brake.

But the smoke coming from the wooden barrel suddenly burst into flames, igniting the non-inflammable cover in turn. And one cow must have been completely stunned because it failed to move out of the way when we came crashing down like a fireball in the field. It must have been a courageous cow too. Somewhere in its cow brain it must have stored the saying 'Take the bull by its horns', because that was exactly how our flaming saucer got spiked. As for us, we were more than weightless, swinging from our rubber straps. At first we bounced forward at tremendous speed, then back again, then we shot right through the burning cloth and over the frightened cow, were pulled back again immediately and then we were stuck to the cow's back.

Actually, only I ended up there. Manne moved on and was released from the treacherous bicycle tyres. But I was stuck on the back of the cow with the tyres stretched like violin strings across the wretched beast's back. And the cow must have had a short circuit in all her nerve centres. She stood there stiff as a statue with the burning saucer spiked on her horns. Her tail was erect and from her posterior orifices something quite indescribable issued forth.

But that wasn't all. In my dazed state I could hear Manne crying desperately for his grandfather. But that's something he shouldn't have done. Manne's grandfather was a terribly clever designer. He always had lots of bold ideas and every new design could always be used in an endless number of ways. We hadn't bothered to find out, for instance, where the cable for our wooden barrel ended. All we had done was to clamber up with our saucer and then travel down again a number of times. But he had pulled the cable down over a wooden block in the barn and attached it to a chaff-cutter which turned round, cutting the straw as soon as he fed it and we set it in motion by going down with our saucer. But as he didn't have complete trust in Manne's and my enthusiasm he also attached a small motor, which ran on petrol, to the other side of the axle.

Believing all he had to do was to tear the burning saucer away from the stunned cow's head as soon as possible, he ran in to the barn and started the motor, pushed the fly wheel in and cranked it up.

He wasn't to know that I was stuck on the cow's back. Nor was he to know that the saucer was firmly lodged on the cow's horns. I don't know which of us, the cow or me, was most surprised when we suddenly shot up in the air at a majestic speed. I saw Manne's pale blank face disappear in the field before we sailed up. Then he lay down and fainted – carefully. He was completely convinced that we'd been dealt some supernatural punishment.

Luckily the cable broke before we reached the ridge of the barn roof. And on the way down the cycle tyres burst too. The cow and I came floating down separately while the saucer remained on the part of the cable that was left.

Manne's grandfather came running out to see what was left of his invention. He was rather upset at the result. But he didn't say anything, even when the hen landed in her shoebox right in front of his feet. He was mute with admiration when we explained the scientific details to him. When the poor dead hen was recovered, all its feathers came off and the thermometer had shot right up.

'Now we must devote all our attention to the flying-machine, boys,' said Manne's grandfather. 'I'll get the forge going so you can wash all that dung off. And if you keep quiet about this I won't say a word about the thermometer either.'

We promised.

But it wasn't easy for me to give my uncle an explanation when he asked why I had to bathe at Manne's place and get green hair into the bargain.

I went downstairs to Mr Arvidsson every day and gave him a resumé of events. He was always glad to see me, and kept a crystal vase full of sweets on his bedside table.

Summer rushed past outside his yellow roller blinds and we both wanted to hang on to it. I told him about our boys' club. I told him about Manne and Saga. There were so many people to tell him about that neither he nor I could keep track of them all.

He just nodded and said that's good. Then he gave me the sticky sweets and I hid some in my hand because I didn't want to show him that I never ate them. I was really more curious about him. He was sick and I didn't know him very well. It is awful but I couldn't stop looking at him. Sometimes when I ran downstairs I went past his door, determined not to go in. But then I did, after all. He was like a secret magnet.

When I'd finished my stories he always repeated the same sentence:

'You are a cherry, but cherries never change the worm. It is always the other way round.'

I thought that was well said. And there was something enlightening about it which I didn't quite understand. Then he always asked for such strange things. Once he asked me to crawl around on the floor listening for 'death messengers'.

'Put your ear to the ground and listen for knocks,' he said, and looked so worried that I couldn't do anything but crawl around listening, even though I was so frightened that I almost crawled straight through the wall.

But then he explained to me that 'death messengers' are small black beetles which feed on vegetables. During their mating season they attack wood. They can finish all the joists in a house, if you're really unlucky. Their mating song consists of the male beating his head against some wood. When the female hears this sound she just eats her way right through the wall. Mr Arvidsson thought the whole house was creaking and tapping. One of my ears was as flat and hard as a saucer before I managed to reassure him. I promised him that all I could hear was Fransson hammering now and again. He was still not convinced, though. In the end I had to look up those strange beetles in an encyclopaedia and prove to him that their mating season is not in the summer. Then he finally believed that it was Fransson hammering away on his roof.

'There are death watch beetles underneath the floorboards, believe me,' he said stubbornly.

And when I asked him who was putting vegetables under the floorboards, he just said that I was a cherry.

Mr Arvidsson was like a cold bath. Stupidly, I thought you could get used to him. But instead, I was beginning to dream that I had large ears which were pummelled against the floorboards until they looked like wrestlers' cauliflower ears. The dream always ended with a big bang inside my head, as if all the male death beetles in the world had hidden under my bed at the same time and were now knocking against the legs of my bed. It was awful. I lay on my back and tried to think of something else. I thought of my uncle who could waggle his ears and I thought I ought to be able to waggle my ears too. By using every muscle I could think of and all those I discovered on the way but hadn't thought about earlier, I learnt to waggle my ears too in the end. But then I couldn't sleep because I was afraid of losing the knack again.

But I never stayed with Mr Arvidsson for long. I ran to the glass factory almost every day. In the beginning it was just to see if my uncle was still there. But if there is something I have learned over the years it is that glass blowers are always there. Every day my uncle sat there with five or six other men in front of those big cutting machines. The water kept running over their grey-white hands. The glass rotated once and all the crossed red lines were faint incisions at first, then became clearly defined cuts.

Behind them there was a steady supply of new crates and in front of them they had a good view of the woodpile which was constantly being refilled so that Stuff-the-hole Hardy could spend his endless nightly vigils walking back and forth in front of the two large furnaces.

Mr Arvidsson was the first person to make a path from the back of the garden, straight through a birch grove up to the woodpile and from there to the door leading into the room with the cutting machines. Now, both my aunt and my uncle were using the same path. Mrs Arvidsson looked after little Erik, me and Mr Arvidsson. But I was easy to look after because I kept out of the way most of the time in order to avoid Erik. I ran to the glass factory along that same path, stayed in there for a while, looking at my uncle's tattooed Honolulu lady and 'Sailors grave' which fought a losing battle against the grey mess which dripped down his arms. Then I ran past the cutting machines which were blasting glass balls with small pointed flames, ran up the corridor along the cooling mat, which was part of a long iron tunnel, and into the room with the furnaces where they always repeated the same performance.

The glass blowers were waving their pipes about. The warm glass substance was making thousands of secret signs in the dim light, there was a whistling, sizzling, clattering sound all round as the master glass blower immersed his runny glowing red molten glass into the wooden mould. There was always someone who was sidetracked, then the glass started to go off on its own – but at the very last moment the pipe always turned round as if of its own accord. Some people hurried back and forth with their noisy clogs to take the glass to the cooling belt. Then the glass travelled all the way up the tunnel to my uncle.

At the far end of the room the master glass blower was experimenting together with the artist. The artist was always standing with his face close to the sizzling lump of glass which was spread out on a steel plate so he could make his imprints of strange birds, bulls and human faces with non-seeing eyes. When the Master was about to cut women's breasts – which were much bigger than my uncle's fantasies about warm melons, by the way – he always got angry and threw the bowls on the floor and said that he'd had enough. That always caused a big stir. The managing director came out of his office, but soon disappeared again. Master kicked the pieces of glass around and shouted that he knew where a woman's breasts should be. And that certainly wasn't on one of his bowls.

The artist never uttered a word. He just went home and wrote out a master recipe as my uncle called it, enviously. And then in the evening you could see the artist and the master glass blower swinging along, their arms linked, towards the blast furnace. Master cried and said that he loved women's breasts, the artist cried and said that he too loved women's breasts – we giggled somewhere in the dark and cried out that we too loved women's breasts. Then we ran out into the village shouting that the whole world loved women's breasts, except the ladies in the packaging department because they had to wrap them all up in tissue paper. And that's where the trouble started. Master's wife was religious and she taunted him daily, and asked him to give up that filth, as she called it.

My auntie also worked in packaging. I ran straight through the factory shouting 'hello' in all directions, and then I'd arrive at a department which was as far removed from the furnace as a young devil from mummy's little darling. In the packaging department I was a clear favourite. In there, my life was not more secret than anyone else's. And it was there that I met Berit.

She engraved names and other simple things on glass with a

little drill which looked almost like a dentist's drill. The large windows which faced south and where she sat were lapping up so much heat that she had shed most of her clothes. She walked around in a sleeveless vest and a pair of short blue gym pants and red high-heeled shoes with straps across them. I used to look in on her just before twelve when it was at its hottest. Because then you could really talk of moist, warm melons.

Every time I went, Berit asked me who I was in love with and every time I answered that I was in love with her. Then she laughed and said that she was an old woman of twenty-five who would eat me up if I came too near. She engraved her name on a ring which was almost real silver and she asked me to wear it always – if I really was serious about her, that is. And strangely enough the world didn't collapse when I said yes to the engagement, although I was faithlessly ignoring my marriage to Little Frog. I was absolutely sure that she could dance the samba so I asked her to teach me. We decided to go to the barn dance on Midsummer's Eve.

'But I can't promise you the samba,' she said, and showed me a few steps that I could practise.

And did I practise? You should have seen the effect it had on my aunt. And the grilling that my uncle subjected me to! He wanted to know everything about me and Berit, while auntie, on the other hand, said that she didn't want to hear anything at all about it. But in the end, I was allowed to go to the barn dance on Midsummer's Eve after all.

Berit and I made an appointment for six o'clock. She was going to pick me up outside my uncle's gate. At twelve I started to get dressed. It took five minutes. Then I took my best clothes off again and shaved with uncle's razor. I cut myself a little on the chin, just so that I could put some newspaper there. My uncle always claimed that all the girls fell for his curly hair so I borrowed auntie's curling tongs and sneaked out behind the garden to make up a fire. With the help of a hand-held mirror and a pair of sooty curling tongs which I'd heated on the fire, my hair soon looked really smart. But then I realized the soot would come out in the first rinse. I washed and rinsed and washed and rinsed and in the end I sported a mixture of pale green and sooty black with some strange locks which must have been twisted back to front, because they pointed straight out from my ears. The only lotion I could find in the bathroom was a jar of Vick which they used to rub into little Erik's chest when he had a cold. With the help of that I managed to subdue the curls and create a fresh aura.

Then I dressed for the fifth time, and put on my yellow shirt with a button-down collar. I picked up my tie-string with the bull's horn and pulled. And then I was ready to dance the samba with Berit.

Five minutes to six, on the dot, I got out of the bathroom. That was after almost six hours' hard preparation. But my aunt was dumbfounded by the result. And my uncle almost swallowed his pipe and Berit's red mouth was like a large letter O when she got out of the car and saw me leaning casually against the gate-post. Everyone was surprised. Me too. I thought that she and I were going to be alone, especially as we were engaged now, but she had brought a fellow with her, a fellow called Harry who worked in the factory too.

It was his car. And the car was a dark blue Dodge with an automatic gear box.

'All you need to do is put your foot down and start,' he boasted, and offered me a place in the front.

But I jumped into the back seat and decided to treat him like the driver he was. But Harry didn't have any great respect for my back-seat strategy. He adjusted the back mirror, examined my hair-do and asked if that was supposed to be fashionable.

'It certainly will become fashionable!' twittered Berit as she tickled Harry's neck. He started purring, engine and all.

Harry wasn't particularly jolly.

All the others who went to the barn dance had decorated their cars with birch twigs but not us. Harry was afraid of scratching the bodywork. The Dodge was the apple of his eye, after Berit, he said. I think he mixed Berit up with the Dodge, actually. He patted the bonnet and asked Berit to 'park' herself for a moment while he went to have a chat with the others.

Berit and I practised the foxtrot and the waltz while waiting for the samba which never came. And the evening passed with Harry turning up now and then in the barn just to see if Berit was still 'parked' there. He didn't count me in. 'Do you know what?' asked Berit. 'I fell for his car. How can one fall for a car? I didn't know that Harry couldn't dance.'

She started to cry and despite the low lighting and all the hullabaloo around us, there were quite a few people staring at us. I felt uncomfortable, as if I had caused her misery, so I suggested that I get the car keys from Harry. If only she'd wipe off that messy black stuff she had around her eyes and put some new stuff on instead, I am sure there were many people who wanted to dance with her. That is how I am. I cut myself up into little pieces and the word 'generosity' is engraved on my heart. She was engaged to me, but she was going out with Harry, and yet here I was suggesting that she find herself another Harry.

I bumped into Harry in the end. He was very drunk and was having a fight with three other equally drunk guys to see who was the best. It was difficult to make out who was hitting whom, but I didn't care one way or the other, anyway. Harry's blazer was hanging neatly on a post and I found the car keys in one of his pockets. Berit was still standing there, crying. I dragged her over to the Dodge, opened the car door and put her in the back seat. She seemed to have lost all willpower. She just bawled and cried about Harry and Thure and Gustav and a lot of others. In the end, it sounded as if she knew all the football players in Småland. I listened and tried to bring some kind of order into her confused speech, but I soon realized that all the stories were practically the same. It was only the names that differed.

'You have to stop choosing guys by their cars,' I said. I who didn't own any Dodge at all.

'You are a real little gentleman,' she said. 'How lucky I am to have you as my fiancé.'

She was wearing a black top and a wide skirt with a flowery pattern and she had a shiny patent leather belt around her waist. The car windows slowly misted up. The orchestra was playing 'Sail along, silvery moon' and Berit told me that she couldn't help loving them all. She pressed herself close to me and I tried to keep my hair away from her top. I didn't want to smear her with that Vick as well. But she started to snivel even more and said that it was such a relief to experience love without lust for a change. She pulled me up towards her breasts and asked me if I felt the same. I agreed that it made the air easier to breathe. It was wonderful. My uncle was right as usual. Everything depends on the hair. If it had just been up to me we could have remained like that forever.

But suddenly Harry pulled open the car door and dragged me out by my legs. He shouted and screamed and looked quite frightening. The part of his face which hadn't been beaten red and blue was now white. People were laughing all round us. The dance was over. Between people's legs I could see the car headlights sweep past. I was lying in the middle of a circle in full view of everyone. Berit jumped out of the car to save me. She screamed a lot of things too. But Harry didn't take any notice. He pulled me up to a standing position and threatened me with a terrible right fist which could have knocked me out in one go. Someone shouted that I was only a little boy and I tried to nod in the affirmative.

But Harry had no scruples. He lashed out in every direction – and suddenly he peeled off the little piece of newspaper from my chin.

'Look!' someone cried. 'He's cut his chin open!'

I smeared the blood from my cut a bit. Harry backed away a few steps and tried to run for it, but he didn't get very far. He was beaten up by the other guys and all the girls tried to comfort me.

'These things happen,' I said stoically, with a slight tremor in my voice.

But by then Harry had been beaten up so badly that it wasn't fun any longer. People started drifting off to their various homes. A damp cold morning mist enveloped everything in a grey-white ghostly light and the yellow eyes of the car lights rushed past. Soon everyone had gone. Harry lay on his stomach, spitting on the grass. Berit was sitting on the wide running board of the Dodge staring straight ahead without seeing anything. I wanted to go home. But we hadn't danced the samba yet. So I did a couple of steps just to show her that I really had practised. She thawed out and started to laugh. Her high-heeled shoes got stuck in the grass so she took them off and danced barefoot. Harry crawled on all fours and stared at us as if we were mad. But we weren't. We tried to bundle him up behind the wheel, but he just sank back like an empty sack. It was pointless to try and make him drive, but I reminded Berit of what Harry had said earlier:

'Just put the foot down and drive.'

'I'll never,' said Berit. Then we drove off.

But after fifty metres I discovered that Berit was rather bad at steering, so I took over the wheel. It was difficult to reach the pedals and look out at the same time, but it worked if I sat on the very edge of the seat. And slowly our bumpy ride progressed. In the back seat I heard Berit mutter something about her poor Harry and she even kissed him – I decided to break off the engagement the following day.

I wasn't too sad about Berit. My left ring finger had turned blue under the ring, but that was all. We had a lot in common, but unfortunately it wasn't enough to build a lasting relationship. I think it came to the crunch when I discovered that we didn't have the same opinion about what constituted a promise. She was no different from other adults. They think you don't need to keep promises once you've grown up. They are so adult and strong that they believe nothing can harm them any more. But when they get weak again in old age, they do a roundabout turn and start demanding promises and want others to keep promises again. But then no one cares about them. So they are back to where they started as children. It is sad, really.

But why moan about that when Sweden lost 2–5 to Brazil in the final of the World Cup. We'd all secretly wished that our Italian-trained players, Kurre Hamrin and Nacka Skoglund, would be able to withstand the samba from Brazil. But no chance. And how could I cry about a broken engagement when the whole nation was in mourning about the lost Cup?

My uncle lost his sparkle. After having been at the top of our local league for a long time we now slipped down to an enervating second place. That was close to a catastrophe. And it was my uncle who got the blame. But he didn't seem to mind one way or the other. He spent most evenings building his summer house in the garden. I thought a summer house was meant to be something fun, but he just made a boring square with one little window so high up that you couldn't see out. And it was slow work. He hammered away just as slowly and hesitantly as Fransson on the other side of the road.

Some evenings auntie called out from her window and told him how idiotic it was to build a house in a garden which didn't even belong to them. But then my uncle answered that was why it was only a summer house.

Most of the time he sat there smoking his pipe in his half-finished house, with the door open and the mosquitoes singing away. The smoke from his pipe kept them at a good distance. One Saturday night he had a terrible temper. It was partly due to his failing inspiration and partly to his relationship with auntie. He wanted to move little Erik from their double bed, but he didn't know how to. And I am afraid I couldn't help him on that score. At that time I had no wish to run away because our team was doing rather well. Saga had saved us miraculously. Even I played well. We played a soft and technical game. And if we needed to chase someone we just sent Saga along. She had a tremendous ability to make people run out of steam.

Maybe my uncle sensed that I was getting restless. He put his arm round me and told me not to be upset. We sat there in the little summer house and looked up at the window on the second floor of the main house as auntie pulled the blind down. For a short while you could see her shadow behind the blind, but it wasn't really that dark outside. The day could almost have passed straight into morning if the sun had not been otherwise engaged.

Sometimes silence can be like an exchange of confidences, so we kept silent. And our little summer house suddenly felt like our only natural home on earth. There are moments you never forget. Nothing really happens but they stick in your memory like some kind of sun spot, forever. That's how it was with my grandmother's privy. My brother and I used to run out of doors in the summer evenings in order to make them last longer. We had actually gone to bed, but we still said that we both needed to go to the toilet. There were two holes placed beside each other in a scrubbed wooden seat. The wood was unpainted and untreated except for my grandmother's thorough scrubbing job. Her scrubbing made the boards smooth and finely grained. We left the door open. The black torch used to light up the place for only a minute or so. Then it would give up, just as if grandfather had set the limit for a reasonable shitting time. But we let it go out. There were two of us after all. Outside, you could hear the odd hen clucking and there was also the rustling sound from the rabbit hutch. The flowers along the trellis shone like pink pale dots. The whitened walls gave off a faint breath of cold stone. I sat on the kids' hole with an old box in front of me in order to reach the floor. My brother had developed his own style because he suffered from a manic fear of infections. First he'd put newspaper around the edges, then he'd climb up and stand with one foot on either side of the hole, squatting. Sometimes he aimed straight, but sometimes he didn't. It was a constant worry, but grandmother must have been clever with her scrubbing brush because she never uttered a word about it. Anyway, we used to sit there like two lavatory philosophers with the summer night stretching like a great sea of possibilities outside. Sometimes it was so light that we could even read our old comic strips.

And sometimes we relayed the events of the day to each other to see if we could make them more fun. Once I must have said something really amusing because my brother laughed so much that he lost control of his balancing act and fell down with his bum in the hole and got stuck there. Then I laughed even more. And neither of us could stop and every time we laughed he slipped a little further down the hole, so in the end you could just see his head and his feet squashed together. He started to cry and said that it hurt. I tried to pull his feet up, but then it hurt even more. He really was stuck there. I have never been in such a good negotiating position with my brother. I could have made him promise anything there and then. But stupidly, I ran to fetch grandmother. When she'd finished laughing she tried to pull him up, but also without success. Grandfather came out to see what had happened. Even he laughed. But then my brother started to cry. Finally, they managed to release him and move him to the bath-house where my grandmother had to warm the water and take a long time cleaning him up. That was another way of making the summer night last longer.

Lavatory humour must be something peculiar to our family. What happened that same evening is proof of it, I'm afraid. My uncle had got strangely excited after our long silence. Mostly because he had his own lemonade bottle. It was Saturday night, as I said, and Bus-David had delivered a parcel to Nilsson and it was all happening in Småland, even if my uncle's 'happening' was limited to hammering away at his summer house.

But suddenly he decided that the house should be painted!

'We're going to give her a helluva surprise when she pulls up that blind again,' said my uncle, and promptly proceeded to put his words into action.

And we started to paint in the middle of that summer's night and actually managed to finish the house. There it was, red with white corners, with the birch trees nearby, rocking slightly to and fro as if in trance. Now and again uncle disappeared up to the kitchen to refill his lemonade bottle and he rocked from side to side when he walked – more than the birches even, to be honest with you. He was incredibly pleased with his finished result. Again and again I had to repeat how fantastic it was to have a summer house of one's own – until an uncomfortable suspicion started to dawn on me. Maybe he had imagined that I wanted to live in there?

Anyway, we didn't say anything that night about it. We shook hands and crept upstairs for a well-deserved rest after our hard work. When we got into the kitchen he gave me a glass of milk. I sat by the kitchen table while he disappeared into the bedroom. They muttered something in unusually loud voices in there. Then he came out to me and said that he had to remove the paint from his fingers before he was allowed into bed. And that's when things started to happen. I expect he was tired. I was more than tired. That's the only excuse I can think of. First he combined two things by having a smoke and a think while sitting on the toilet, then he must have come to the conclusion that things were happening too slowly because he called me and asked me to get a bottle of white spirit from under the sink. I got the bottle out without looking too closely at it and handed it to him. He sat there with his trousers down and his pipe in his mouth and I didn't think of closing the door. I just stayed in the doorway. It was a long-winded business getting the paint off. He soaked the toilet paper completely in white spirit first, then wiped the paint off and threw the paper in the toilet. He was suspiciously awkward in his movements, I thought, and I was beginning to worry that he might use up the whole bottle. I needed to get my paint off as well. In the end the small bathroom stank of paint remover, which was coming from the toilet paper. At that point, his pipe went out – and as if it was the most natural thing in the world, he lit a match and when his pipe was properly lit, he leaned forward to drop the match into the toilet.

Now, how can I describe what happened?

I must have been as surprised as Moses when he saw the burning bush on the Mount of Horab.

Flames rose from my poor uncle's bottom at such terrific speed that I thought they'd burn holes in the ceiling. At first he was paralysed with fear, but then he shot up with a ghastly scream. My heart almost stopped. If there were any death messenger beetles under the floorboards, as Mr Arvidsson claimed, then they must have died of fright on the spot. My poor uncle was like someone obsessed. He jumped up and down because his trousers prevented him from running. He hopped with both feet together into the hall, where he curled up in pain on the floor. And that's where he was when auntie came rushing out. It was she who had the presence of mind to close the lavatory lid and flush down the toilet paper.

But she screamed too. How could my uncle be so incredibly stupid as to use her nail polish remover to take off paint, and how could he throw burning matches onto inflammable paper?

I began to wonder whether perhaps I should flush myself down the same toilet too, as it was me who had fetched the bottle after all, but I never got round to it. My auntie put on her coat, gave me instructions and ran out to borrow a telephone. And uncle got into the bath like an obedient little boy and there he lay on his tummy, or tried to, and I took the hand shower and started the rescue work. God, how he suffered. Ice-cold water on his most precious bodily parts in a never-ending stream.

He had to lie like that for over an hour before the ambulance came to pick him up. It howled through the village telling everyone where the interesting accident had taken place. Luckily, the village was still suffering from its Saturday hangover. Nobody woke up and nobody came to have a look. Auntie had gone back to bed. And she had turned the key to protect her little Erik from his irresponsible father. The two ambulance men lifted my uncle out of the bath and hurled him across to the stretcher. They covered his backside, which looked more like a monkey's bottom than one of those commonly found among glass blowers, then they struggled downstairs with my uncle. I tried to explain the whole pathetic story as well as I could, but it was hard to sound convincing. Not until we got quite far down the stairs did they grasp what had happened. But then they started to roar so much with laughter that they dropped the stretcher with my poor uncle on it. He got so angry that he limped out to the ambulance on his own, shouting at them to come after with the stretcher.

As I was his next-of-kin I sat down beside him.

We drove through the summer dawn with the shrill laughter of the two ambulance men ringing in our ears. My uncle looked at me with a pitiful expression on his face and told me never to bother with women. But I didn't actually understand what he meant by that. Luckily, he said nothing about nail polish remover.

The burns on his back weren't too bad, really. But it was the day of our Cup Final. They just gave him some ointment in the hospital. We took a taxi back and the driver was very inquisitive, wondering why my uncle was kneeling and looking out of the back window all the time. When we got back, I paced up and down in the hall asking him now and again whether I should run over to the captain and tell him to cancel the match. But uncle just mumbled something in his pillow and said that he'd be all right, as long as he could have a rest before the match started.

It didn't go very well.

Despite all the ointment on his buttocks – which really must have greased him properly, you might think – he didn't move any faster than a pregnant cow. That's what the spectators shouted at him anyway. And I couldn't very well run round the field telling everyone what had happened! Oh, how I suffered! It was awfully embarrassing.

My only comfort was that he didn't bother to finish the inside of the summer house straight away. I was allowed to stay on the convertible sofa in the living room.

Then the holidays came. The idea was that we were all going to visit Göte's brother in Jönköping, but my uncle's scorched backside raised objections. As a compensation, I was allowed to go with Göte on his milk round instead, because he didn't bother to take a holiday.

Göte was my uncle's best friend. He drove the bus for Bus-David and devoted most of his time to a hopeless love affair with a girl called Greta who worked in Majken's café.

If anyone needed friends in this world, Göte was certainly one of them. He wasn't exactly the cheerful type and he wasn't very handsome either. He was tall and boisterous and had big boils on his neck. Auntie was the only person who could help him. I thought it was quite interesting to watch when she squeezed the pus out of those blue and yellow and green carbuncles.

He was almost as maniacal about those carbuncles as he was about Greta. He had this idea that they'd heal up in the sun. So whenever he jumped off beside a milkstand, he checked where the sun was coming from and made sure that he always had the sun on his back while he was putting the milk churns on the van. After just three days I was getting bored going round with him.

Suddenly everything seemed to bore me. The days were as stagnant as the oily patches on the mill pond. They stretched out on the dirt roads like fine pollen. They ran away in the stream which looked more and more like a trickling artery. They disappeared into long warm summer evenings with my uncle and Göte on the porch of the schoolhouse. There we were joined by the schoolteacher and occasionally that fat clergyman who could never say no to a drink. Göte was a bachelor and he rented a room on the top floor of the schoolhouse. It was his sad longing for Greta that made him get those bottles out almost every evening. I sat on the bottom step of the porch and listened to them talking. My uncle preferred to remain standing. The clergyman sat in a rocking-chair which creaked every time he rocked. With the help of the rocker he managed to lift his weary hand with the dram glass in it to his mouth. When the glass was empty and he thought Göte took too long to refill it, he started to rock back and forth in an irritable sort of way. Göte would refill the glasses. It was not just the carbuncles on his neck which hurt. He wanted to talk about life. It sounded as monotonous as croaking frogs. In the beginning, he sighed mostly about women's lack of understanding and in the end, he'd sing about lost happiness. I stayed there just to help my uncle back home. Since that unfortunate fire in the toilet, I wanted to take care of him. My auntie felt so humiliated by the event that she almost wanted to move. It was lucky they had little Erik between them in the double bed, I think. Although he was in the way, he still kept them together.

But most of those vacant summer days I just strolled around trying to get rid of that creeping feeling of nervousness. I sought out some quiet places in the forest and down by the lake and suddenly I realized that I was talking to Sickan.

I missed her terribly.

And nobody told me how my mother was. Somewhere beyond the lakes and the forests she was sitting comfortably, breathing air which was rich in ozone, making little silver jewellery, knitting or reading books about interesting people who fell in love, died for a cause or fought noble battles against falsehood and lies. I had to keep an eye on my uncle and auntie,

Göte, the clergyman, Manne and Berit and everyone else in the village. Otherwise I would not have any stories to tell her when I got back home. I had to make her laugh and cry with my stories so she wouldn't need to read any more books, just listen to me instead.

Then one day the Stockholmer arrived and I forgot about everything else. I had never seen a live Stockholmer before, except on newsreels, that is. So no wonder I stood there by the gate staring at the Franssons' house to get a glimpse of him. The Stockholmer was just a year or so older than me. He was staying with the Franssons because their daughter was his grandmother. She was looking after her old father. And her big secret was that the Stockholmer had not had any maternal grandfather. Obviously, he had had a grandfather at some point in his life, but not the kind who stayed and got married.

My Stockholmer was interesting in quite a different way. He was not only my first Stockholmer, he also had a racing bike with three gears and a racing saddle instead of a normal one, a fantastic handlebar which pointed almost straight up in the air and a sawn-off mudguard so he could bicycle on the back wheel only, if he wanted to.

And that's just what he did the whole first day in front of our gate without as much as looking at me.

Next morning I rushed up to inspect my own bike. It looked incredibly corny. It had been sent on by train after much nagging from my side. Now I'd rather not look at it. I couldn't possibly cycle on something like that now. The closest I could get to a racing-bike look was by attaching a piece of cardboard with some pegs to the carrier at the back and to the front mudguard, then tying a piece of string from there to the handlebar so it rattled when you pedalled and the string was taut. But that was just child's play compared to the Stockholmer's racing bike. I sneaked out through the garden gate and down the path at the back to ask Manne's grandfather if he could help out. We obviously needed help from an inventor!

Manne got jealous, but I promised that he too could have a look at the Stockholmer so the two of us managed to persuade his grandfather to help us out. It was not so very difficult. We made a sketch, then he used his thumb as a measure and welded the frames on both our bikes to give them a nice curve. He sawed off the rear mudguards, covered two wooden boards

with some fabric and shaped them so we could put our obliga-
tory racing saddles there. Gears, on the other hand, were something he could not make. Instead he made a couple of extra
levers on the handlebar which he then straightened out. He
suggested we pretend they were top gears. They were much
nicer than ordinary ones.

It took a few days to complete. Then we sped down the road
in front of the Franssons' and our house. And there was the
Stockholmer, cycling back and forth on his back wheel. We had
forgotten about that little detail, but now we had something to
show him after all. We skidded to a halt in front of him, said
hello and asked him if he had any overdrive. 'No, how amazing', said the Stockholmer.

On the whole, he used some pretty odd expressions and had
a lot of silly ideas about 'his' country, as he called it. To him 'the
country' was just something which existed in the summertime
when the Stockholmers needed it.

Anyway, we got friendly with him and soon we could cycle
around as well on our back wheels. And one day the Stockholmer suggested that we should go away on a cycling holiday
further into the countryside.

He suggested Öland, but we were not allowed to go there.
The Stockholmer's grandmother and my auntie became almost
paranoid as soon as we started to talk about that place. To them
Öland was a place where farms were burned down at regular
intervals. We tried to tell them that it must be the safest place in
the world to be as they had policemen in practically every bush
looking for that arsonist Göran Johansson. But nothing helped.
We were not allowed to go to Öland whatever happened. Full
stop.

But at that point Göte came to our rescue.

He suggested that we go in the other direction to his brother
who lived by a lake. Göte could drive us there one afternoon.
And then we could borrow his old tent and cycle back in our
own time.

My uncle and aunt hesitated for a long time. In the end they
gave their permission for me to leave. An old quilt was remade
into a sleeping bag. Auntie cut out a piece of oilcloth and sewed
the quilt into it. Food parcels were also prepared. Unfortunately, Manne could not come with us because he was
actually going to Öland to look at Hagby. Manne's grandfather

92

was interested in the arson attacks from a purely technical point of view. He said that the police had organized car parking facilities and extra camping sites near the famous Öland farm.

The upshot of it was that the Stockholmer and I threw our bikes on top of Göte's lorry one Friday afternoon and set off. Göte was in a good mood. He thought my uncle would be allowed back in the team again after the start of the next season, but I didn't. There was no point in making him miserable, so I kept quiet about what I knew. We travelled through an area where all the glass works were closed for the annual summer holiday; we travelled right to the centre of this province; we travelled for hours without having a clue about where we were. And suddenly Göte stopped by the side of the road and said that now we were as far from Öland as we could possibly wish, so why didn't we get off there.

The Stockholmer and I must have looked equally surprised, because he laughed and said he thought we'd wanted a cycling holiday.

'The thing is, you see,' he said, 'I have no brother, but I quite welcomed the idea of a little secret expedition myself. Now that I have helped you, I wonder if you'd like to help me too?'

He gave us a map, pointed out the road which led home, past a few lakes where we could stop for a swim, and drove off, but only after we had promised not to say anything to anyone. The Stockholmer asked where Göte was going and I told him the little I knew. Presumably he was going to look for Greta who was also on holiday, but who had disappeared. I could have explained about her disappearance too, but I didn't bother. Anyway, he was so worried that he burst into tears. And the sky must have been affected by his steady stream of tears because suddenly the rain started to pour down.

We had no other alternative but to pedal on.

And we pedalled and pedalled. My seat was beginning to chafe; we got soaking wet and it didn't seem as if the Stockholmer would stop crying until we had a relatively safe roof over our heads. I suggested we try to stop at the next farm and ask if we could stay the night in the barn, and he thought that was a good idea. The only problem was that the next farm we got to looked more like a mansion. He refused to cycle up to the front door and ask, but I pedalled into the gravelled courtyard and knocked at the big heavy front door. Meanwhile, the Stockholmer was hiding behind a tree in the avenue leading up to the house. The rain continued to pour down. And nothing happened. I knocked once more, but regretted it as soon as I'd done it: maybe the place was haunted? This is just how all ghost stories begin! Lonely wanderers who arrive at a deserted castle and the door creaks!

I ran down the steps. Too late. Behind me I heard something rattling and I had to turn round once the door actually opened. Luckily, the person in the doorway didn't appear to be a servant with a hunchback. Instead, it was a woman in a black dress with a little white apron. She beckoned to me to come forward and wondered what I wanted. I told her the whole story. I asked her if I and my friend could possibly sleep in the barn. She nodded and asked me to wait, closed the door and disappeared. I ran up to the Stockholmer and told him to pull himself together and in the end we both walked up to the main entrance where the lady was already waiting. She invited us in and said we could use one of her guest rooms on the first floor. I was so flabbergasted that I hardly noticed anything except the wide staircase we were climbing. Then we went along an enormous corridor with pictures hanging in a long row. Most of them were of old men but there was also the odd woman, dressed in some strange clothes. Their eyes seemed to stick out to inspect us so we hurried after the lady who told us that she was the Domestic.

'You don't have to make up any beds, Miss Domestic,' I said. 'We have brought our own sleeping bags.'

She laughed and said dinner would be served as soon as the young gentlemen had changed. Then she left and closed the door behind her, leaving us to find out what she really meant by 'getting changed'.

'I don't know,' I said, and sat down carefully at the edge of one of the beds so as not to sink into the white quilt which looked more like a gigantic white loaf of bread.

'If she said that we should change into some other clothes, then we'd better do that,' said the Stockholmer.

Quite right, too. I suggested that we swap shirts to start with and so we did. The Stockholmer's shirt was just as wet as mine. We combed our hair and dried our faces with the towels which were hanging in front of a washstand with a hand basin and a water jug. To be on the safe side we also washed our hands, because you never knew whose hand you might shake.

Ready for inspection, we stepped out into the corridor and went down the big staircase. To the right of the stairs, we could hear a faint crackling noise from the fire.

We went through the double doors which stood open and entered the room. But just to be on the safe side again, I knocked on the doorpost first.

'I have been expecting you, gentlemen,' cried a thin, sharp-nosed lady who was sitting all by herself at an enormous table.

She pointed with one finger to the other end of the table. Obviously, that's where she wanted us to sit. We could have played table tennis between the lady and us without any trouble at all – but we had to remove the candelabra and all the candles first, of course. We wondered whether we ought to go up and say hello properly but as she kept pointing we sat down. The Domestic pulled out the chairs before we had had time to touch them even. Like a shadow she glided forward and pushed the chairs in again. The idea was that the seat should end somewhere around the back of our knees, but in our case it ended much further up. We had taken our shoes off. Now we shot towards the table, first the Stockholmer, then me, and we almost ended up in a lying position, with our faces just above the table-top. The old lady started to laugh and asked the Domestic to fetch some cushions to prop us up. We laughed too just to test the climate. And that must have appeared immensely funny to the two ladies, because after that the ice was broken.

The old lady told us that her name was Florence and that she was under a guardian just like us.

'Can you imagine! I am just like a child and I can do what I like!'

That was difficult to believe. But what do you say to an old person who thinks she is a child?

We let her talk on and we ate what was on offer. She seemed quite harmless but rather confused when she talked about princes and directors who had cheated her of everything she possessed. It was a little difficult to believe when she was sitting there in her mansion, but when she said that she was the daughter of a king the Stockholmer kicked me on the leg, licked his finger and put it to his temple. I agreed. The old lady was definitely a little overheated. The food was also a bit strange. First we got some soup which tasted all right but looked like water with greasy spots. Then we got a whole fish each. It lay there all alone on our plates without as much as a potato to keep it company. We touched it a bit and tried to work out what Florence was doing with it. It wasn't too difficult. You just took a small spatula and opened the fish with it. Then there were a lot of mushrooms inside it. It all tasted very nice. But when the Domestic turned up with the next dish which had at least half a chicken on it, we nearly choked. For dessert we got pears with whipped cream. Naturally we fell asleep at the table – bloated and full up. Florence kept talking all the time. When we were eating our pears she started to cry. Not much. One little dignified tear fell down just like a real princess.

Slowly it rolled down her dry cheek and she didn't seem to realize that it contradicted her smile as she said that we were probably the only guests who wouldn't cheat her.

'What sort of punishment do you think all these managing directors and princes and their accomplices will get? What punishment could be worse than my declaration of incapacity? I have a life sentence. One day I suppose they'll just have to pay a fine!'

We nodded in agreement. Fancy people cheating her! The greatest lady we had ever met. That's just bloody monstrous!

I got so worked up that I rose from the table and started to swear. That was probably the first time she had ever heard any bad language in her life. She actually started to laugh again and looked really happy. She was just about to clap her hands, but forgot herself and stared a bit oddly at me. I thought someone was standing behind me so I turned round. But there was no one there. I looked at her again.

'But my dear child, you're quite frozen!'

Yes, I was, actually. Both the Stockholmer and I were so cold that our teeth were chattering. Our freezing shirts didn't help. The Domestic took us by our hands, dragged us upstairs and ordered us to take our clothes off. Then she dragged us naked across the corridor to an enormous tiled bathroom where the bathtub was standing in the middle of the floor on curved legs.

'We'll have to get a lot of hot water from the kitchen,' said the Domestic, and ordered us into the bath. I examined the Stockholmer suspiciously, because I don't like sharing my bath with anyone else. It's an old habit of mine. But he looked fairly normal, I suppose, except that he kept covering his prick all the time with his hand. We jumped into the enormous bathtub.

And soon after, the Domestic arrived with one jug of hot water after the other and our frozen bodies slowly thawed out and we got drowsy all of a sudden. The Domestic must have put us to bed in the end. I don't remember how we ended up underneath those enormous quilts. I only remember that we woke up when she rang a little bell and arrived with the breakfast tray.

That is the first and only time I have eaten oatmeal porridge on a silver plate.

Florence wasn't feeling too well, we were told. We bid a warm farewell to the Domestic and got the address from her too, because we intended to write to Florence. The Domestic stood there on the steps for a long time waving at us as we cycled off down the avenue. Our visit had done her mistress good, she said.

That whole day we cycled homewards. Both the Stockholmer and I were quiet and thoughtful. In Nybro we decided to buy a postcard for Florence.

'What shall I write?' asked the Stockholmer.

What do you write to a countess? I wondered, because I assumed that's what she was.

'I'll write "Thank you for a wonderful night",' suggested the Stockholmer.

I thought that sounded good too. We posted the card and agreed not to talk about it, for Göte's sake. He had been really decent to us, after all. We cycled home in the summer night, hoping to find new castles around another corner. But nothing else happened. We did get back to the village in the end, however.

It was embarrassing. The whole village was buzzing with rumours, but I didn't say anything, my uncle didn't say anything, and when we were finally on our way to see his real brother in Jönköping, Göte looked as if he'd swallowed something. We all sat there dead quiet trying to be cheerful.

In Jönköping they have something called Taberg, a kind of small mountain which we climbed and had a look at. Göte's brother was busy taking part in a gliding competition. We hadn't exactly come at the right time. We stood there on top of Taberg, looking at Göte's brother and all the others who kept circling round forever, or so it seemed anyway, that Saturday. When he finally came down again, we drove out to the field where he had landed, which was more fun. He let me sit in the glider. He even promised that I could go up with him. I was so excited that I jumped up and down in their flat all evening. In the end they got tired of my bouncing act so they asked me to jump into bed instead.

The idea was that we were all going to sleep on the convertible sofa in the living room: little Erik, me and auntie and uncle in the two beds. The others were still in the kitchen listening to Göte's brother telling them about 'thermics'. That's a lot of air that goes up and down. And the more he talked, the more anxious I became. I could just imagine how we all might disappear into a hole in the air.

The worst of it was that those holes weren't clearly visible. With my usual bad luck I supposed the last day of my life had arrived.

I tried to imagine that I was weightless, crept into the toilet and jumped carefully from the lavatory seat, but I soon realized that it was hopeless. In the kitchen they were laughing and drinking as if nothing had happened.

Farewell and good-bye!

You only get an offer like that – to go up in a glider – once in a lifetime. I couldn't very well refuse. So I went into the kitchen and asked if they made parachutes for thirteen-year-olds. But Göte's brother laughed and said he'd just pulled my leg. He wasn't allowed to take any small children like me up in the glider.

'Hurry into bed now and I'll bring you some ice-cream,' said my aunt.

That's the first and only time I was actually happy that someone had pulled my leg. I ran off as fast as I could and took a big jump into the sofa. I was going to live after all. It was a jubilant leap, but unfortunately not very weightless. I fell right through the bottom of the bed and the sofa lid slammed on top of me so that my legs got stuck underneath. Erik woke up with a scream. Everybody came rushing into the room. They pulled and pushed and screamed, worse than little Erik even. Göte's brother turned up with a hammer and started to hammer at the hinges from behind. Impossible. He ran to fetch a crowbar. Something in there had got stuck. He forced the lid open from the back and in the end I got unstuck and little Erik was picked up while I crawled out and had to find comfort where I could.

The lifespan of that sofa came to an abrupt end. But as my own lifespan had just been extended, I didn't worry about the sofa at all. The owner of that glider had been punished before he realized it.

That was my reasoning.

But nobody else's, I'm afraid. The grown-ups stopped talking about thermics and started to discuss insurance policies instead. As far back as I can remember I have heard about public liability insurance, but I have never managed to work out what it meant, except that it is the finest thing you can have, I gather. It's a funny sort of insurance: the whole point seems to be that you become a public liability, otherwise there is no point in being covered. Anyway, you can't get any money from the insurance company unless you break other people's property on purpose.

Göte's brother got stubborn and angry. He said with absolute certainty that I was a public liability. My uncle defended me and said that I wasn't and my aunt said that it didn't matter anyway.

It was very embarrassing. We re-made the beds, or tried to, and drove home in silence the following morning, although we were supposed to stay there for several days. And after we got back Göte walked past now and again and asked how 'the public liability' was. My uncle was so angry that he promised to pay for the sofa with his own money: that's how he managed to get rid of Göte in the end. But he shouldn't have done that. Göte shouted that he knew for sure what would happen to the goalkeeper. My uncle was going to be dropped from the team, forever – as soon as the season started again.

That affected my uncle so badly that he resumed his work on the summer house. During the rest of the holidays he stayed in there, painting and papering and playing his old gramophone records all on his own. I didn't dare go in, but through the little open window you could often hear the tunes of 'Oh, what a lovely bunch of coconuts' and 'I do want to be beside the seaside'.

Karl Evert was a funny fellow. Now and then Manne, a few other boys and I would cycle up to where the road bends, to go and work in his factory. Karl Evert was an encyclopaedist. If you mentioned a letter in the alphabet to him he'd reel off everything that started with that letter in the encyclopaedia. He was too clever to go to school, Manne told me. Everything he learned would come out in exactly the same alphabetical order. In the end, the authorities got fed up with him. They let him stay at home with his father and muck about in his factory. It was built of thin boards and measured fifteen by four metres. He had not bothered with any windows as light seeped through the cracks everywhere anyway. He had built a second storey up in the ceiling and that was just one and a half metres wide by two metres high. It looked like an enormous oblong box. We were going to insert a square lath into the two holes in one of the gables. Two men pushed it in, another two sawed it into pieces of thirty and forty centimetres each, two men nailed the pieces together and then two men nailed on the wheels – while Karl Evert stood in the far corner dipping his toy engines in a pot of paint and hanging them up to dry. That was his American-style toy factory. He had worked it out according to the assembly line principle, because it would be quicker that way. But most of the time, production was at a standstill. We got fed up after half an hour or so. And that was lucky because Karl Evert's father had to burn all the engines afterwards. People around the glass works said that he had the highest fuel costs in the whole of Småland, but it didn't really worry him because he was a farmer and as rich as a sheik.

The reason we were working in Karl Evert's factory at all was that he had promised to drive his one-wheeler across the road as soon as he had finished practising on top of the roof. He had stretched a wire up there and managed to support himself against the walls of a makeshift box whenever he was in danger of losing his balance. But sometimes it didn't help. He came crashing down in the middle of the production line – disturbing the whole assembly line principle. It didn't matter, though. We spent more time looking at the ceiling anyway, because we expected him to come crashing down any minute.

But he improved all the time. He even managed to balance things on his head. At first he used a log, then he added an axe to the log. It was more exciting that way, he said.

'Like playing with death,' he roared, and dropped the axe so that it almost cut off our toes several times.

We became more and more excited. The number of people working in his factory increased every day. If we worked for two hours we could watch one of Karl Evert's balancing acts with three logs and an axe piled high on his forehead. The odd glass worker turned up as well on Sundays and sawed a few locomotives just for the hell of it, before Karl Evert climbed up on the roof. And one day a rumour spread that Karl Evert was going to have a go at the real thing. One Sunday he actually managed to get a wire fixed to two tall pine trees on either side of the road, about five metres off the ground.

For the modest fee of one krona per head Karl Evert was going to perform his intrepid balancing act with his one-wheeler, three logs and an axe. Everyone rushed to the spot. Karl Evert was so excited that he reeled off rivers and mountains backwards while getting into his leotard. We had never seen him in that get-up before, so we were rather surprised.

He was wearing a sleeveless jacket of green silk with some Christmas tinsel sewn to his back. The trousers looked more like the sort of bloomers girls wear under their skirts in the winter. His skin was as white as a sheet underneath the jacket because he never went outdoors in the summer. He spent most of the time in his factory – that is when he wasn't on top of the roof, of course.

He climbed the tree with his one-wheeler, turned towards us and waved.

'Ladies and gentlemen, may I ask for absolute silence, please.'

We applauded and watched with excitement as he mounted his one-wheeler and started to put the logs on his head. Everything worked perfectly. Everyone held their breath when he placed the axe with the handle vertically against the logs. Some people whispered that it wasn't going to work, once he started on the tightrope. The wire wasn't as taut as usual, but he moved forward with perfect balance. A collective sigh of relief could be heard from all the bystanders.

But unfortunately, the road he was crossing led to a glassware shop which was open on Sundays to sell seconds. Just as he was crossing the road on his tightrope a car wanted to drive past. The suspense was so great that no one wanted to let the car pass. The passengers got impatient and the driver started to blow his horn. Karl Evert probably took that as a sign of encouragement, because he tried to wave to them and fell down on top of the car roof with a terrible bang.

At that point in the proceedings half the audience fainted because the axe was stuck in his head.

And those who didn't faint then did so when he got up and stood on the car roof, pulling the axe out and bowing as if nothing had happened.

When everyone had recovered, Karl Evert fainted too. There was complete uproar all round. Everybody was bumping into each other, the driver was furious and tried to pull Karl Evert down from the car roof. He was helped by some other people who had recovered by then and together they carried off the tightrope dancer and put him on the grass. He started to scream and fight. He didn't seem to be too badly wounded, after all.

'Say a letter,' I shouted.

Someone said 'I'.

'I for Islands, see page 3620,' he rattled off.

He was quite normal again.

But we took him to hospital and had him stitched up.

The doctor said he wasn't quite right in the head. I think he was. The axe had fallen in such a way that it was the car that had been most damaged. When Karl Evert realized what had happened he pulled the axe out and held it close to his head, just to keep the suspense up. He hadn't really fainted. He just pretended. But the performance didn't make him very rich, because all the money went towards repairing the car.

'Whatever you do, you must keep the suspense going,' he lectured for weeks after, as he walked around with a great big bandage on his head, checking our engine production in the factory.

But we didn't enjoy working for him any more, because by then we knew what he could do and we didn't get paid for our work.

I went to the office at the glass works and was given a time-card. They asked me to look after it, seeing that I was still under-age. Every week the master glass blower had to write his name at the bottom of a page to certify that I didn't work more hours than him. It was an excellent system, much better than getting confirmed, which I was too young for anyway. Immediately I felt just as strong as all the other men at the works. I could just imagine my grandfather smiling and nodding and saying it wasn't one day too soon either. The holidays were over. Now the real stuff was beginning. As an approved under-age worker with my own blue time-card I sneaked away to the glass works on a dewy path at the heels of my auntie and uncle.

They went off in their direction. I had already been given so many warnings that I had stopped listening to them all. As soon as I felt tired I had to go home at once, I was told. And all I needed to remember was to listen to everything Master was saying.

I nodded and disappeared into the forge, and was told which team to join. Master didn't say much. He just pointed to a wooden pole which looked more like a small pitchfork. The idea was that I should use it to catch the glass when he pushed it off the iron-sheathed bench where he kept turning his pipe to make the base of the glass. Suddenly he attached an iron clamp which he'd dipped in water; it sizzled, the pipe jerked and the glass was on the floor.

I stared at my wooden fork where the glass should have been. But the glass was in pieces on the floor and I was not on my way to the cooling belt as expected. Master pushed his specs up and stared at me for a long time. Then he pointed to the various workers in the team and said that I was the most important link in the whole chain.

What was the point of them working their guts out if I didn't carry the glass off in the end?

And I should stop that bloody snivelling in the presence of grown men. And if I couldn't learn to catch the glass after three attempts he'd give me something to cry about all right.

The rest of his team laughed. I sobbed and tried to catch the glass as it came down. The base must not be damaged on any account. I must remember to hold the fork high up in the air, give it a jerk and a twist and make sure I keep pace with the Master, then the glass will land safely between the asbestos-covered prongs of the fork. The third attempt was a success. Master shouted cheerfully and all I had to do was run up to the doors of the cooling belt and press my foot down on one of the floorboards, which in turn opened the door. The heat streamed out from the noisy glasses in there. I said good-bye to my glass and sent greetings to my uncle with it. And already the Master was crying out for his next glass!

I could never have imagined that something which looked so simple could be so difficult!

But I soon got into the rhythm of things and worked in unison with the others. In the end I even managed to whistle and sing while I worked. Depending on age and temperament, we crossed each other's paths with 'King Creole' or 'The street where you live'.

But this sense of security only lasted an hour or so. Then I had to change with someone else who had been cooling the moulds in a water-bath. I plonked myself on top of the box. On either side I had a cut-off barrel which was used as a water bath. When Master brushed past the tip of my nose with his glowing molten lump of glass, one of the moulds had to be in place, open and ready. He stamped his foot, I leaned forward, pressing and squeezing the mould with the help of the two handles. Sizzling steam and the smell of burnt wood rushed up towards my face and penetrated my ears. The pipe was turning ten centimetres away from my nose, Master's legs were jerking, and he stamped his foot and shouted 'Mmmm!' Carefully, I opened the mould – and inside was a glass spinning round! A real glass cover which Master and I had made together!

I was glowing with pride. The flames from the ovens made fluttering shadows on our faces. Everything was fine. My back was aching and my eyes smarted. The Master stamped his foot again. And I wanted to become like him soon. In the first coffee break I ventured up to one of the ovens, snatched a pipe and stuck it into the molten glass running inside the crucible. I blew a little on it as I had seen others do. Then I covered the hole with my thumb and let the air work itself through. I puffed a little again – and there went my warm breath like a clear bubble, conquering the thousand degree heat!

But it was a boring job carrying the glass from A to B. I had to walk back and forth forever. After a few days my thoughts started to roam and bounce back from the walls of the furnace. I was singing or dreaming.

I was everywhere except there.

We were always waiting it seemed, and the whole summer had almost turned into autumn before Göte appeared one day in the yard in front of the post office with the eleven o'clock bus. We waited for what seemed another eternity before Göte pushed the door open to let himself out of the bus.

Suddenly it turned very quiet after all the noise earlier on. The bus engines were switched off, but in the distance you could hear the throbbing of the mopeds, keeping time with our heartbeats, and we hung firmly on to our bikes, afraid of falling to the ground or flying up in the air for that matter. That is how curious we were. Without batting an eyelid, we stared at Göte's wheezing bus door.

But first two elderly men appeared, apparently quite oblivious of their carrier bags, as if the bags had attached themselves to them by chance. In other words, they had done their necessary shopping in town between the first and the second bus. Alternatively, you could fill in a form with your request and hand it in at Nilsson's store and you'd get your stuff delivered the next day. But the two old men probably thought there was too much paperwork involved. Even my uncle who didn't have a care in the world found it a bit cumbersome. People preferred going into town and getting what they wanted themselves. There was always someone who didn't have anything better to do.

And one shouldn't 'aggravate' oneself, as my uncle used to say.

Manne got worried and wondered whether the old men would be able to drag themselves out of the bus before the football season was over. I got the creeps too. What if the Great One decided to stay inside the bus until the season was well and truly over and our club had had it?

I wondered whether perhaps there was a back door on the bus, which we hadn't seen yet. It was meant as a joke, but Manne was taking everything seriously that day, so he spat on the ground and told me not to talk such crap.

We strained our necks and stared through the dirty bus window. We should be able to see him now. He ought to be on the bus!

But we couldn't see him.

The two old men had left the bus ages ago, and the seconds were ticking away. All we could hear was the dull sound from the glass factory; it sounded almost like a giant's song. You could hear it day and night, it was always in the air we breathed, it was something we could tune our silence to. If we heard that dull sound, then we knew that it was quiet around us and that our hearts had probably stopped. My face felt strange and got stiff with disappointment: here we were, two devoted ball boys with a brilliant idea that hadn't come off. We had come to meet the Greek off the bus because that was his only means of transport and he wasn't even on the bus!

Göte must have noticed our disappointment, because he asked if we were waiting for someone.

'In that case,' said Göte, and looked into his back mirror, 'I can tell you that people like him don't travel by bus. And if he'd tried to, I certainly wouldn't have let him.'

That I could understand. And yet I couldn't. The fact that Greta had rejected Göte even though he had chased her halfway across Småland was one thing, but that was no excuse for putting your private life before the future of your football club!

Göte was still staring into his back mirror. We leaned across our bikes and didn't know what to do. But in the end he suggested we ask Greta.

'She's going into the café across the road just now.'

He sounded like some wild bird crying across a lake in misty weather. His voice died away and the bus door wheezed to a close again. We mounted our bikes and went the short distance across the road, skidding to a halt beside Majken's tatty fence in front of the wooden house in peeling yellow where she had her café. Majken's second name was Nilsson, the same as the grocer and the same as the man who owned the petrol station. Strangers to the village used to go bananas when they were asked to go to Mr Nilsson and always found themselves at the wrong Nilsson's. But we knew there was no connection between them. On the contrary.

We rushed into Majken's café to talk to Greta.

And as usual, Manne turned completely red. He claimed that Greta was every man's ideal woman, that she was like Jayne Mansfield. But I still preferred Berit, even if our engagement had been a short-lived affair. Berit was the devoted kind who always got deceived. Greta, on the other hand, was always strutting about with her coat half unbuttoned, making all the local bachelors slaves to Majken's wretched coffee. In order to pluck up courage to speak to Greta, they always diluted their coffee with some stronger stuff which they kept in a bottle in their inside pockets. Just look what happened to Göte who'd almost become hostile to my uncle – who in his turn was even more unhappy than Göte . . .

Manne and I stepped inside to ask Greta some questions about the Greek. First Manne wanted to put some music on the juke-box. He put the pressure on me until I gave him twenty-five öre. Then he put on 'Such a night'.

Greta was standing behind the counter with her back to us.

'I'm buttoning my coat. You mustn't look now,' she cried. Of course we walked round the counter to catch a glimpse of something under her unbuttoned coat. First she turned towards me and screamed 'Oh', then she turned towards Manne just to be fair and screamed 'Oh' once more. That is the way she was. If there weren't any other bachelors around, even we would do. She meant well, but she just couldn't stop herself.

I didn't catch a glimpse of anything, and I'm sure Manne didn't either. He rolled his eyes as if he had and whistled.

'Now you can't be confirmed,' said Greta.

'It was worth it anyway,' said Manne.

He'd heard others speak like that. He could never think of anything original to say. And that's why everything went quiet after Elvis had done his duty for twenty-five öre.

Manne and I didn't get a better view than the unbuttoned place where the breasts bulge out. A big fly suddenly flew up from one of the windows. The loud insistent buzzing noise bored into us. Everything else was still. And we didn't know how we were going to put it to her. But Greta helped us by asking what we wanted.

We told her about the problem – that the Greek had not arrived with the bus.

'Didn't he?' said Greta.

She looked about as self-confident as those cream cakes that Majken carried into the room. But she wasn't as sulky as Majken, because Majken always started to have a go at us as soon as we got there. Always.

The juke-box nearly killed her. She may have earned twenty-five öre on it now and then, but there was a helluva lot of noise in there. And all those kids dragging in sand and muck and playing their Elvis all the time!

Majken got all worked up. We decided that we'd better try and escape her torrent of words. Once outside we watched Greta buttoning up her coat and Majken moving the cream cakes from her tray to the counter, just like in an old silent movie. The words continued to flow out of her. Greta was obviously dreaming about her Greek, because she just smiled and unbuttoned and buttoned up that same button again and again.

I thought it was interesting. The next time I was going to ask Majken why she was so short-tempered with children.

Being religious and all, I mean. Why wouldn't she let us come into the café?

But we couldn't stand there forever. The match was soon going to start. We pedalled up to the football field, disappointed at not having seen the Greek. I had been in two minds about it for quite a while by then. One part of me thought it was awful that my uncle should be sacked from the team, but the other part thought it would be exciting to have a look at the famous Greek. In the end I had silenced my conscience by saying that uncle had injured himself after all. He hadn't been himself that time when he was playing with all that ointment on his bum. Maybe it was just as well that they let him go and grow old without risking breaking his neck. He could still sit down in a rocking-chair and dream about the times when he was really fabulous.

When we saw Lindgren standing by the firm's car it didn't take long for us to put two and two together. The managing director was actually a great supporter of our club, greater than any of us even. He had cut the first turf when we made the football field in the first place, and he had expressed his hope that we should all feel like one great big family. What could be more natural than that he'd put his car at the club's disposal?

We were both on the verge of a nervous breakdown, so we threw our bikes on the gravel and rushed forward.

'Away from the field,' cried Söderkvist, the coach.

'Yeah, yeah,' we shouted.

And there we were, at a decent distance from the goal so we weren't in the way but still close enough so he could talk to us if he wanted to . . .

'Look how he moves,' whispered Manne.

'Like a tiger in a cage,' I said. I have seen that once. They stalk up and down, up and down, and they are completely crazy from beginning to end.

Manne stared at me. Sometimes we didn't speak the same language, he and I. He even seemed to think I was mad, the way he sized me up like that. But the thing is, I can't stand it when it gets really exciting. I've never understood why people scream and quarrel. Every time they do I just find it strange or funny. I can't keep up with people when they want things to move really fast. I just want things to keep still. Anyway, we followed every movement that the Greek made. You could tell at once that he was inspired. That was important. I had told Manne that inspiration is the most important thing. And you look that sort of thing squarely in the eye.

The Greek had played second goalkeeper the summer before, when my uncle was at his peak as first goalkeeper. Then the Greek had fallen in love with Greta. But Greta was in love with Göte. But then she fell in love with the Greek too. At that time the Greek was working at another glass factory where they didn't have a goalkeeper, so Greta was more smitten than ever with the Greek of course, because she thought it was very exciting to go away sometimes to see him. Göte had thought of committing suicide for the Greek's sake, but he hadn't got round to it yet, because he was always busy driving either the bus or the milk-cart. In the end, Greta had grown tired of the Greek, who saved all his money for his family so they could come to Småland too one day. Göte thought his chances would improve once the Greek was gone from the village.

That was the situation up to date and everything would have been fine if my uncle hadn't burned his bottom like that. That's when the whole community started to think of the Greek again. Everybody talked about him. The more they talked about him the more fantastic a player he became. In the end he was as good as the whole Brazilian team put together. What was the difference anyway between Brazil and Greece? One foreigner is as good as the other, they thought.

But how could they persuade him to join our club now?

While the village was in a kind of daze because they thought they'd lost the Cup, Greta suddenly became the key person in this whole drama. She had obviously listened to the talk about her ex-boyfriend, the Greek, so she secretly went to the director of the glass works to ask him if they wanted her to try and get the would-be hero back to the team. In negotiations like that, the director was never impossible. To tell you the truth, my uncle used the same bargaining technique. He was probably a better goalkeeper than glass cutter when he first came to the village.

The secret leaked out of course. When Greta went off to fetch her Greek, Göte was driving round Småland looking for her.

That's how it was and that's what happened.

And that's why Manne and I were there now behind the goal. And the ball was round and the grass was green and inspiration was something our new hero seemed to have in excess.

It was only I who felt a slight longing for my uncle. Maybe that is why I couldn't really reconcile myself to what was happening all round me. I began to wonder what was going to happen if the Greek wasn't as good as everyone thought and I asked Manne about it.

'Nothing will happen,' said Manne.

'What if we tear him to pieces?' I wondered.

But then Manne thought I was getting a bit overheated and told me to stop thinking for a change, and to cool down. I did and looked at Göte who was backing up on one side of the field, letting the away team out of the bus. They had just been to the changing-room in the glass works. Our players were having massages. They swapped liniments and talked a lot of crap. Greta came hobbling along on her high-heeled shoes at the head of the crowd. All the spectators started to crowd in on both sides of the field. There was the director and his wife. In fact, the whole community was there.

The linesmen and the referee ran out onto the field. The referee whistled for both the captains to come forward and toss for ends and then the game could begin.

Our club had the sun on their backs. They jogged with feather-light steps under a cloudless sky. It got off to a good start. Even the mosquitoes seemed to be more interested in the game than in sucking blood from us. But maybe there was no blood to be had. Maybe it dropped into our shoes as soon as the opponents' outside right fired a crack shot at the left goalpost just after kick-off. The blood subsided and we held our breath when our inspired goalkeeper didn't seem to notice the ball at first, but then he hurled himself over it like a tiger.

The only problem was that he hurled himself in the wrong corner.

'What happened?' cried Manne, white-faced.

'It was a goal,' I explained.

'Idiot,' said Manne, still white in the face.

He didn't get a chance to recover. The same thing happened again next time there was a charge. Our great Greek hope managed to let in three goals in the most extraordinary way. At half-time people were practically in a lynching mood. Greta crept away. We heard that the Greek had tried in vain to explain that he had the sun in his eyes all the time.

But he couldn't have had, because the sun was coming from the other direction. Our manager had won the draw and sensibly enough he'd chosen the right end.

The Greek improved after half-time, but our team could not struggle past the three goals even though they fought like animals.

Yes, they almost ate the Greek whole after the match, when he tried to say that he'd had the sun in his eyes again.

'Yeah, yeah,' they said, 'I hope you don't get the sun in your eyes again when you take the bus from here tomorrow.'

There was something wrong about it. There was something that didn't quite tally. Throughout the night I kept wondering how he could have had the sun in his eyes when he'd had it on his back! When I closed my eyes I could also remember how a reflection of the sun had travelled up and down the net all the time. How could that be possible?

In the morning, I cycled alone down to the eight o'clock bus, and skidded to a halt in front of the Greek. His head was drooping when I asked him what he was going to do now.

Then he laughed and said in his broken Swedish that his mother wouldn't have let him marry Greta anyway! I thought he looked grown-up enough to make up his own mind about that, but I didn't say anything.

'They aren't worth it anyway,' I said, without really understanding what I meant.

The Greek waved and got into the bus. Göte turned round in the yard and disappeared behind the factory. And just as the bus disappeared in the distance I was dazzled by his rear mirror. I got the sun in my eyes even though I had it on my back!

But no one would have believed me if I'd told them what Göte had done to get rid of the Greek so he could propose once more to Greta himself.

And I didn't volunteer the information either.

Even a summer must come to an end. I sneaked into it like a puppy exploring a house full of bones. And now and again I dug around a bit among my memories to reassure myself of my riches.

From my summer wages I bought a spinning rod with a reel. My uncle and I took a taxi to Örsjö. I didn't get on the train until he'd promised that I could come back the following summer.

He said that was all right. I could come back any time I liked.

My uncle looked a little strange when he said it, but I didn't think any more of it.

The rail joints throbbed forward and home!

I was on my way. I was on my way home to the Great Wall of China and Happy Heights again. My faithful dog Sickan would probably be waiting for me in the hall when I got home. My brother would probably be home too and my little sister was sure to be back – and my mother simply must have rested enough by then. She was probably perfectly well again!

But there was no one to meet me at the station.

I didn't bother to pick up my registered luggage. I just took my small bag and my fishing rod and started to walk home in the late hot August afternoon while my legs felt heavier and heavier and soon they didn't know whether they wanted to walk at all any more. There was a fine layer of dust above the barracks square where the stables were. My throat felt dry and suddenly I found it hard to breathe. I could hear the horses neighing in the stables and I remembered everything I'd learned in there. We used to go there to groom the horses and every spring when the circus came to town we got a certificate to prove how clever we were. We used to wave that piece of paper in front of the circus manager who'd then give us a horse each which we led through the town. Then he used to suggest that we should walk home again. Always trying to cheat us, he was.

There we were – a bunch of unhappy souls who had carted things around for them all day in the hope of getting a complimentary ticket at least. But the man who had promised us the tickets never turned up on the night. The solution was to hang on to your horse, not let go of it for a moment from the time you'd been asked to lead it through the town until that exhilarating moment when you could rush up to the arena with the horse and then squeeze past to find a seat somewhere at the very back.

That seemed to be a fundamental truth – that you should never let go. There was always someone who asked me to run and fetch something, but when I came back it was inevitably too late.

At home, it was as silent as in a deep cold well. Sickan wasn't there wagging her tail. My brother wasn't anywhere to be seen, my sister had gone and the door to my mother's bedroom was closed.

I knocked carefully and opened the door.

She looked up from a big book. She was lying there in her nightgown with the loosely knitted cardigan over her shoulders and her handkerchief stuck in her left sleeve as usual. Her long black hair with the thick curls made her face look almost translucent and I realized then that she had not been outdoors all summer and that Sickan must still be at the kennels and that I was obviously the first person to come back and that I posed a problem to her as always. The flimsy light summer curtains were half drawn. A narrow ray of sunlight shone on her thin hands, the pale red knuckles clasping the back of the book.

'Are you reading?' I asked, stupid as always.

She was reading all the time. As soon as she put a book down it was my turn to try and grasp what it was about, what was so much more interesting and exciting than me. She was always sitting in the living room with the glass door closed and locked behind her. I'd stand outside in the hall looking at her until she made an impatient movement with her head and looked at me with eyes that were always asking why she couldn't be left alone. Then I'd run away of course. I'd leave her alone. I would creep into the bedroom and find another book, sneak past the door with the glass panes and go into my and my brother's room to lie down on the bed next to the living-room wall. And there we'd be, reading away with just a wall between us.

She waved to me and put her book down. I sat down carefully on the edge of the bed, got my fishing rod out and started telling her things.

I talked and talked, my whole summer danced around in her bedroom like a golden clown. It got more and more fun, more and more things happened – and finally she had to laugh a little after all.

No, she was coughing. Her handkerchief flew out and I stared intently at the wall because I didn't want to see. I have noticed that you can stare at a certain spot for as long as you like and make it the most important thing in the world so you don't have to bother about things around you. A table-top, a table-cloth, a wall. Anything will do. I glanced furtively at her hand and started telling my stories all over again. I stared at that hand, didn't get any further with my gaze, saw her thin fingers, the knuckles, the hem of her cardigan, the handkerchief which was full of dark and light red stains. And while I went on talking I could see how she slowly opened her fingers and moved them up and down and I couldn't understand why.

'What are you doing?'

'I was just remembering a song.'

She was thinking of something else, a tune which she was playing with her thin translucent fingers.

She had stopped listening to me ages ago.

Chapter 5

1959

We were soon like a little family with our regular habits, Auntie Auntie and I. We didn't have any trouble getting on, because we were both sort of redundant. At night we'd lie there in our beds nattering away like a couple of old parrots about our happy childhood memories. After all the unspeakable things which had led up to our sharing the same bed, it felt good to spin a yarn about the past. Auntie Auntie was really terrific at the past. She could dig back so far that I wasn't even thought of. I think my grandmother and she were about the same age, because they talked about their way to school in the same way. All old people remember their way to school, because it was nearly always fifty kilometres and they had to walk it in all weathers in their wooden clogs which were always filled with straw. In those days there was no public transport and there were no school dinners and no sputniks in the sky. But runny noses and blisters on their feet were something they had in abundance. And Auntie Auntie could tell me things which made my stay at the children's home seem like a holiday for well-behaved upper-class children. Her happy childhood memories beat mine by a long chalk. I got so worked up about them that there was hardly room for my own. Just as well really, because I always get scared when I think of myself.

I admired Auntie Auntie's relationship with God. It was terrific. There was not one difficult or unjust event in her life that didn't turn out to be a blessing in disguise in the end. I was of a more rebellious spirit and I saw myself as a crusader fighting against injustices – in other words, if someone hurt me I wouldn't hesitate to chop his head off.

But a normal day would actually look more like this: at the crack of dawn Auntie Auntie and I would step out of our beds and venture out on the ice-cold linoleum. She'd throw a few logs on the stove and I'd get dressed quickly while I thanked God for abolishing those buttoned vests in the autumn of 1953. It couldn't have been a very big decision for him, but for me and my friends life changed radically thanks to that. Without one of those garments, getting dressed was child's play. Auntie Auntie couldn't keep up with me, because she had a bodice. They call it a corset if you're fat and use it to pull your tummy in and a bodice if you're thin and let it all hang loose. Both are pink, sort of piggy pink, if they are ladies' garments. I'll tell you more about corsets another time 'cause I have a personal relationship with them.

After getting dressed really quickly we trudged out into the winter darkness to join my uncle and aunt and little Erik who insisted on sleeping in my old bed. On the porch was my school bag, unopened just as I had left it. Then we had a big breakfast, served by Auntie Auntie. And after that those who were engaged in worldly affairs came tumbling downstairs: uncle and auntie trudged through the snow to the glass factory and I picked up my school bag and set off without any straw in my shoes all the way to the crossroads where the school taxi, laid on by the council, would drive me to Algutsboda church school. On the way to school I always tried to figure out the problem with the local council's savings campaign. How could they afford to lay on this school taxi just to take me to Algutsboda school and back every day, but deny me a new recorder on the pretext that they could not make any new purchases under the present economic climate? I must have cost the council at least ten recorders a day!

Why did I have to sit there with a broken recorder?

The way the council do their sums is one of life's great riddles to me.

Every day I sat there at the front of the class without having done my homework or learned a single note. It was not necessary. The way our organist teacher tested us on our homework made it quite unnecessary to learn anything in advance. He might ask us, for instance, why it was that America, which was one of the world's richest nations, managed to give Europe financial help after the Second World War? And then he wanted us to answer that it was because America was one of the world's richest nations! See what I mean? Clever answers like that were sure to satisfy him. Apart from Mathematics and Music, I managed quite well without putting in too much of an effort, but I never really got friendly with anyone in the class. My first day with those angelic recordists and then me as a window-breaking vandal had left a respectful distance in our relationship.

My school day always ended with a twenty-minute private lesson in the art of playing the recorder. I got those extra twenty minutes because my school taxi didn't turn up until twenty minutes after school was finished. I never understood why that was, but people's fate is often determined by various timetables. There must be a gigantic timetable somewhere, a counting machine that puts all our journeys together in such a way that they never match. And just the thought that the journeys may not tally makes people insecure. They can't hang on to themselves, they go so far that they prefer to stay behind and pass the time playing the recorder instead. Or they might cross the road and go to the café and fall in love with someone there. And then they go home to hang themselves, but, by coincidence, the eleven o'clock bus happens to be early that very day so someone who shouldn't be there according to the timetable arrives earlier than expected and saves the person who was going to hang himself – if you follow me. That's how life is – all the time.

When I got home I threw my schoolbag down on the first step and ran upstairs to eat as much as I could of Auntie Auntie's food. She was happier the more I swallowed, and as she really was in need of a little more happiness now that she didn't have Mr Arvidsson any more – I did my best to satisfy her modest demands. Even when it was getting difficult to speak, because the food was covering both vocal cords, I made a valiant attempt at forcing down a little more food.

Consequently, I waddled like an over-fed duck into the darkening winter afternoon to see what it had in store for me. I don't know whether the events during that winter and spring all stemmed from the Nybro bus arriving just as I came waddling past, but if that was so then it must be true that everything is determined by timetables.

If I grow old I'm going to spend all my time at a big bus stop where lots of buses keep coming and going all the time. Then I'll play with the idea of stepping on this or that bus and wondering what might happen if I do, but I won't really get on a single bus because you never know – you might intend to take one bus and then change your mind at the last moment and you might bump into someone you'd rather not see. Hang around, that's what I say. Soon enough what will be, will be. Just like when Saga got off the bus that time and waved to me and asked what I was doing. I had actually decided to avoid her altogether after that snub in the attic, but she seemed genuinely happy to see me so I decided to go with her when she told me that she was going to the ice-hockey rink to check if they'd hosed it down.

They hadn't. But we stayed there for a while looking at the Greek who was hosing it as we arrived. It wasn't the same Greek as the goalkeeper Greek, but it was the goalkeeper Greek who had brought him there – together with another couple of families. Göte wasn't so worried about Greta at Majken's café any more. The goalkeeper Greek had brought his own fiancée with him. He'd also brought his old mother and two cousins. It was the Greek's cousin who was now hosing down the ice-hockey rink. He was wearing a thin pair of shoes and he didn't have an overcoat on. He tried to keep warm by putting one hand inside the blazer and he put the hose under the other arm so he managed to stick that hand into his pocket. And then he turned round slowly, probably dreaming about great fortunes. A few years previously the members of the local football club had built the ice-hockey rink in their spare time, but now there was no one who even wanted to hose the place down without being paid. They didn't have the time, they said, because first they had to polish their first, second or third car, as my uncle put it. He was always complaining and he was jealous too, because he'd always dreamed about buying a car himself.

Suddenly the Greeks seemed to do everything around where we lived. Everyone liked them. First the Hungarians came with a few families, then the Greeks. They were a happier lot on the whole. They sang in the factory and did all the jobs that no one else wanted to do because they weren't paid well enough. They must have been a terribly hardy lot too, because they were all dressed exactly like the Greek who was hosing down the rink. It is really cool wearing just a blazer and an open-neck nylon shirt in the middle of winter, I think. I tried it once round the house and realized at once how cool it was.

Both Saga and I got fed up hanging around there. She suggested that I come back with her. It would still be a while before the ice was ready to skate on, and did I have a hockey stick anyway?

I had to admit that I didn't. And I wouldn't be able to save up for one either, as long as I had to compete with the Greeks for the jobs that were going round the village. I could just imagine my job at the factory going to some strong Greek the next summer, someone who could juggle the glass without getting tired, then carry on to cut the grass on the football field after work and chop the wood for our managing director's winter supply, and early the next morning he'd clean all the bachelors' cars with the same water that the Greek's mother had used earlier to wash the team's football clothes in . . .

But Saga just looked happy when she realized that I didn't have any hockey stick. I put it down to her budding breasts. She probably had problems on the ice as well.

As a consolation I told her about my boxing gloves. She got very enthusiastic at once so we ran back to fetch them. They were made of green canvas and the reason I got them is really rather a sad story. I get furious just thinking about it, really.

At first, Saga was disappointed because they weren't real leather, but then she said that her father could get hold of another pair. We ran over to her place and crept up to the attic. After a quick calculation, we came to the conclusion that we could build a whole training camp with a boxing ring up there.

My real name is Ingemar Wallis Rutger Johansson. It is no joke. However much I twist and turn those names around they are a pest. Rutger Johansson with specs, that's who I'd be if I hadn't lost my specs, that is. If I wear my specs the name fits because I am small and spindly. I've already told you what I feel about the name Wallis. Only Ingemar remains then. But neither my parents nor I knew that I'd have to live down the measurements 89-184-184-109-86-42-43-19-61-41-25-34-38 which, taken in that order and translated into centimetres, represent the weight-height-reach-chest-waist-biceps-neck-wrist-thighs-calf-instep-fist and under-arm measurements of quite a different Ingemar Johansson, a man who, in the previous autumn, had stunned a whole world by beating Eddie Machen at New Ullevi in Gothenburg after just two minutes and sixteen seconds, and who was now expected to play the title match against Floyd Patterson.

My own measurements are nothing to write home about. I have been on the look-out for my biceps for several years now, but I haven't found them yet. With Saga as a sparring partner maybe I'd have a future as a featherweight boxer.

She wanted to be Floyd Patterson of course. He looked such a nice chap, almost like Pelé, she thought.

'Let's just use one glove each and keep the other hand behind our backs,' I suggested.

119

'Daddy says it is a typical Negro sport. But he is going there anyway in case it becomes a white man's sport again.'

'Going there?'

'Yes, why not? Mummy is going as well. Daddy is going to try out the American market.'

I thought she was having me on and I shouted that the bell had gone.

'First round between Ingemar Johansson and Floyd Patterson. Ingemar's shit hot after a perfect training programme devised by his trainer Nisse Blomberg.'

'Whitey Bimstein! You don't know anything. He must have an American coach, of course.'

She obviously knew more than me about it. And she started handsomely with a perfect left hook, her right elbow just covering her solar plexus. A perfect guard position. She turned her torso round a bit and kind of danced towards me. My God, what had I entered into? I stretched out my right fist and made her stop. She let her guard down and asked in a surprised tone why I'd used a right jab first.

'I don't know,' I said, and that was the simple truth.

But at the same time it was a huge exaggeration, as I hadn't put any arms first. Most of the time my arms don't want to obey me, they just hang like rotten old tree branches along the sides of my body. Earth's gravity is concentrated in two simple points just under my hands. The right jab aimed at Saga must have come at a moment when gravity was on holiday or something.

Actually, that happens quite often when I am about to drink something in the presence of people I don't know. Quite unpredictably, my arm just flies up into the air and throws back the contents in my face. I start by carefully lifting the glass, feel a kind of paralysing stiffness creeping up as a forewarning. Then I know that gravity has gone on holiday all right and I try to lean forward to slurp up the drink, but without success. After that my arm just pops up with a jerk. It's always been like that. I don't know why. In the end, I didn't even get the dish-cloth in my face when mother got angry with me. But that was probably because of a wholesale dealer in herrings who came from Ystad. I think he saved me from her worst hysterical outbursts. And that was quite a relief. That herring man was the grandfather of a friend of mine in the Great Wall of China. He used to sit in their kitchen on a simple stool, spilling over the edges: his enormous stomach looked as if someone had tried to camouflage a zeppelin with a tartan waistcoat. He wore a chunky silver chain with a silver pendant representing a fish stretched across his stomach like some latitude across the globe. He'd sit there sort of kneading his thick fingers. And suddenly he'd point at us and growl:

'Do you want some juice, lads?'

We said yes, of course, got some juice and were just about to drink it, when his index finger would point at me:

'You've got really high cheekbones. You look like a little Mongol. Is it in the family?'

Mongol? I got so scared I threw the juice in my face at once. Mongoloid and Mongol—which was which? Mongoloids must be the people and Mongols must be the funny ones. My God! What if I was a Mongol?

But the herring man stared at me in an odd sort of way for a while, then asked if I was nervous.

I'd never known that children could be nervous so I shook my head vigorously, although I know I was nervous once when I was ill with mumps. That time I got injected with female hormones. It was my brother who told me that it was female hormones. I could just imagine them chasing each other through my body, then meeting up around my prick in order to dismantle it and make a hole there instead. That time I was really nervous, I can tell you, but since then I've simply not had the time to worry about that sort of thing.

At any rate, the herring man got so angry that he took my hand and brought me home, then closeted himself with my mother. I could hear what he said. He was very fond of children and he couldn't stand seeing nervous little children who threw juice in their faces – even if it was just a way of attracting attention as my mother claimed. When the herring man came out he blew his nose and gave me a krona and said I could ring him any time I liked. I never did, though. There is something fishy about kindness in the extreme. I have never been able to stand it.

He'd made an impression on my mother, though. She cried the whole day and said she'd been put to shame. It was mad to throw juice in my face like that. Didn't I understand that I must not make her more worried than she was already? She was worried enough about her own health and her own nerves. How could she possibly cope if she had to think about my nerves too every day? She'd get completely hysterical if I didn't stop shaking my arms like that immediately. Didn't I realize that she couldn't become well if she lost her temper and had to waste her efforts on me? Or be put to shame in front of strangers again?

She got so hysterical just thinking about it that she hit me extra hard with the thing she had in her hand. It happened to be a coat-hanger, but it was so ridiculously small that she had to go on hitting me for quite a while. And she cried and screamed so terribly that I had to take her hand in order to comfort her. I thought it would have been stupid not to do that as I suddenly got the feeling that she was smaller than me and that it was more important that I understood her than that she understood me.

But I never succeeded in curing those strange reflexes in my underarms. Nor could I force myself to become a good boxer. So Saga had to comfort me when I told her the story about Mongols and hormones. We laughed until we both got cramp. Then we decided that we should build a training camp in her attic.

'I'll ask mother. But it doesn't matter. They're both going away anyway.'

'Are you going to be on your own?'

'Mrs Lindmark will be working for us.'

'You can't live on your own. That's not allowed.'

'Oh yes, it is.'

She did a bit of shadow-boxing around me, in narrowing circles, and suddenly she lowered her left guard and circled round me with her arms, held on to me and kissed me right on the mouth!

I could see her tongue slide far into my head, licking a lot of things on my brain, I am sure. It must have stretched like a wriggly snake and touched a switch button somewhere without my realizing quite how. My tongue started to explore things too and found its way into her mouth and made an investigation of her throat to see if she still had her tonsils there. While we were all fused together like that, slowly drowning in our frothy saliva, I tried to get one hand out to do what I hadn't done earlier. Unfortunately, it happened to be the hand with the boxing glove on, so I couldn't feel her breast very well. Instead I sobered up. My God. There I was, Ingemar Johansson kissing Floyd Patterson!

I got out of her grip and told her that kissing and cuddling had nothing to do with a training camp whatsoever. If she was interested in such below-the-belt strategy then she could carry on without me. I was going to take my boxing gloves and leave. I didn't trust her.

There was a strange carelessness about her, as if she was capable of breaking something or someone and then letting others tidy up after her.

She tossed her short dark hair and glared at me while pulling off my glove.

'I promise! Provided it's just you and me who practise!'

I promised, relieved and confused at the same time at the sudden change of tone. I could still feel her tongue swirling about, her sweet smell, her breath pulsating with mine, my brain slowly dissolving and trickling down towards the midriff region where it filled the bowl in my pelvis. A dull weakness spread over my whole body, signalling a lot of things which had nothing to do with my fiddling down there. Of course I had wrestled with it before and it had certainly raised one or two questions – like what kind of madman was I who amused myself by pulling it back and forth when nothing happened – but now it was waking up after the kiss. And that was something quite different. Suddenly I was very scared that it wasn't only my arms that would end up with strange reflexes. My head, my torso, my back, everything was ground down into a centrifugal movement. The whole of me was pressed down into that bowl in my pelvis. It was as if I had turned myself inside out and now I was forced to look into a boiling sea from the high vantage point of my unbelieving eyes. And the sea was me and that was how I actually looked. And there was no denying it.

All the same, I did.

That spring there were two burning questions being asked in Sweden: was a cat without a tail allowed against expenses and would Swedish Broadcasting stick to their stupid guns and bar the live transmission of the World Championship match between Ingemar Johansson and Floyd Patterson?

The chairman of Swedish Radio and the Governor of Gothenburg City thought that as a compromise our U.S. correspondent Arne Thorén could relate the match afterwards like a good storyteller. And for that suggestion angry licence payers promised him a place at the bottom of Gothenburg harbour encased in concrete. And in the middle of it all there was the question about the cat without a tail. Honestly, not too many people were interested in that question. It was mainly Mr Holdst who got worked up about it and he didn't agree with Gustav Knutsson's trip to the Isle of Man to study Manx cats. I thought if a writer wanted to go to the Isle of Man to study cats for his books then surely it was up to him, but Mr Holdst agreed with the people from the Inland Revenue. They had moved that the proposal be rejected, although Gustav Knutsson was probably the only person in the world who really needed to make a study of tail-less cats.

That was the kind of climate I lived in. And that's how immutable Mr Holdst was, except when it came to corsets and music. Because then it was quite a different matter.

It was Auntie Auntie who suggested that I should call on him and ask him to teach me to play the recorder. In the end, I gave in and knocked at his door. Mr Holdst sat there, straight-backed in an old dining-room chair, staring with his pale yellow eyes at a distant spot where he saw things I couldn't see. He was almost blind.

I can't say that he was particularly happy at the prospect of becoming my music teacher, especially when he heard my tentative notes which fell like seagulls' droppings against his highly polished floor. But I told him how things were. I was a whole term behind the others in my class and I needed his help. He stared right through me and finally came up with a suggestion which would mean that he taught me a lot more than just music. If I promised to read the newspaper to him one hour a day, then he'd make sure that I could play the recorder just as well as the other prodigies when the time came to play in church at the end of term.

'Let's skip the notes. You'll never learn them anyway,' he said. 'Just tell me where those dirty marks are on the black lines and then I'll give you a letter and you just fill it in above.'

The method was foolproof.

I was better at letters than notes so I quickly learned where the A and the C were on the recorder. Mr Holdst drummed the time on the table while singing the tune to himself. It was mostly hymns. His gruff voice quivered and my ethereal recorder notes had a slight tremor as well when we ascended towards heaven with 'For those who perish on the sea'.

But in no way could you call him religious.

All he cared about was politics and corsets. While I am on the subject of politics, he let me read a boring paper which was about something called SERP. He was crazy about this thing SERP. He even promised me I'd get it when I got old. First I'd gain a lot of points and then I'd get a lot of money. But I won't retire until after the year 2000. And if the council can't give me a recorder in 1959 I don't see how they'll be able to give me something so much later in life – never mind the points I might manage to collect in the meantime. That's what I said to him. I also got hold of some other magazines at Saga's place. And that's where I read about Gustav Knutsson and Ingemar Johansson and King Frederik of Denmark's birthday and about Brita Borg who sang 'Augustin' in Cannes. She was Sweden's voice in the world and Ingemar was our clenched fist!

Now, whereas Mr Holdst would have perhaps three pieces of furniture in his flat, Auntie Auntie would squeeze in twenty-three pieces in the same space. I may exaggerate a little but sometimes it was a bit of a relief to see Mr Holdst on his one and only straight dining-room chair by his table in front of the window, without as much as a geranium on the windowsill. I used to sit on the floor in front of him. To the far side of the tiled stove, in the same place as in Auntie Auntie's flat, he had his bed and above it hung his old cornet. He said he could play all kinds of instruments, but that the cornet was his chief instrument. 'I used to be a wind player amongst wind players!' he sighed, sounding worse than an old horse.

He sighed just like that one evening when he leaned forward, breathing down my neck as he looked at a double spread in the *Weekly Journal*.

'What's that?'

'An advertisement for corsets,' I said, almost suspecting that he had some eyesight left after all. But it is not called a corset. It is called a girdle.

'Read,' he said. 'I want to keep up with the latest fashion.'

And then I read a little to him about RIBBONS in black which pulled you in at the waist with the help of the incredible elastic latex wool and the special ribbon front which got rid of all superfluous ounces. And then I read about CHEERS with its concealed nylon threads which shaped the bust in a special new way and which was available in delicious gossamer-thin nylon lace and nylon marquisette with A and B cups. And then I had to turn the pages back to VASSARETTES with its BANLON which hugged the body and had a detachable crotch as well. And so on.

All those things I knew by heart because for a time in my life I lived with garter belts and brassieres up to my ears. I was practically reared in a plywood box full of small bits and pieces, which if seen together could turn into all these miracles.

When I think about it now, it was a wonderful if short period in my life and it came to an abrupt and dramatic end. My mother's sister used to work at home as a dressmaker and she looked after me whenever there was some trouble in our flat. When mother fell ill, I mean. You probably wonder where my brother and sister went then? I think they went to our grandparents who lived in the same block of flats as us. But I spent most of the time in that big box full of pink and white and black lingerie. As soon as I climbed into it I was told off and was lifted out of the box again. But I outwitted my aunt. When she put that box outside the front door I climbed into it quietly and pulled the flimsy tissue paper over my head. My faith in lingerie was seriously challenged though when I happened to go to sleep in the box once and was carried off. The box was picked up by a big strong chap who didn't notice the difference between ten kilos or three kilos. So I ended up in the factory. It was a terrible experience to wake up in the middle of the night locked up with a million girdles around me. A night watchman found me in the end, screaming my heart out. In return, I bit his hand.

I must admit, I had had more than my fill of women's lingerie that time.

But Mr Holdst didn't seem to have anything against being immersed in women's underwear, judging by the way he sighed and talked about his bachelor days when he was in the brass band and they were playing waltzes and things.

'Oh, the girls I knew in those days!'

In a way it was lucky that Mr Holdst lived on the other side of the stairs. Otherwise I might have forgotten how to read. Before I had read in order to catch up with and talk to a very special person, but Mr Holdst gave me quite a different perspective on the matter. He amused himself by twisting and turning events round until they were in their right place, according to him, that is. Sometimes his reasoning was very strange, though, I must admit.

'If you only do what you're expected to do, you're just a sheep among other sheep. Sometimes you have to do things that are not expected of you in order to become the person you are destined to be: a wolf in sheep's clothing. But never a wolf that gets lost and never a sheep that gets eaten by a wolf! Everything depends on the balance!'

That's what he said. And I agreed with him. It is so simple it almost scares me.

Auntie Auntie was always knitting something or other. One evening she'd finished her knitting and she sat there with a ghastly huge pile of knitted pieces of a sickly green colour which almost seemed fluorescent. Around something, which I slowly realized must be a collar in brilliant yellow, other pieces gradually took shape. But while she was knitting I was overcome with tiredness and my head was buzzing and crackling like the fire in the tiled stove. We had had a hard training session that day in Saga's attic and afterwards I'd had a short recorder lesson and after that I'd been reading forever for Mr Holdst from an old newspaper. According to that paper and according to him, our whole country's welfare was at stake because of that SERP-thing.

It didn't bother me, though. To be honest, it was quite tiring reading and listening to him all the time. But Auntie Auntie's quiet occupation with her knitting needles, combined with the crackling sound from the stove and my own thoughts which circled round and round before settling down in the end, all helped me forget all the trials and tribulations in my life. I dozed off and was far away in another world where I heard Auntie Auntie say something about the Brazilian football team. I neither understood nor wanted to understand what she was talking about. It wasn't until she woke me up with a cry about the sweater being finished at last that the whole truth in all its gaudy colours appeared before my astonished eyes and I realized that she had knitted that sweater for me, and me alone. And it wasn't just any old sweater. It was a sweater in fluorescent green with an equally striking yellow collar. And everything was knitted in a loose and casual style. In my half-awake state I had a vision of at least ten Brazilian players who suddenly ran off in different directions all at once. In a flash I realized that knitting had never been one of her strong points. And at once I suspected that I was not entirely blameless myself. Hadn't I after all said yes to those very colours the summer before when she had shown me a few balls of knitting wool? Surely we'd come to some agreement in terms of colour and style?

So I let myself be led into the sweater willy-nilly. I turned round in it and felt how it followed me cautiously after a slight initial delay. I raised my arms to beam at Auntie Auntie and to give her a big hug. That is a reflex action of mine. I don't know where I get it from. It has always been harder for me to handle other people's failures than my own. I'll do anything to take on their failure myself.

I lied like a trooper to my Auntie Auntie and her uncertain expression soon turned into warm embarrassment. We were both intoxicated by my grandiloquent lies, but at the same time it was clear to both of us that the sweater was too big for me. It was terribly loosely knitted and it was floppy and shapeless like a fagged-out fishing-net. It was only the big collar which had turned out all right. In the mirror I could see how, in a strange way, it seemed to take a strangling hold on both me and the sweater as a whole. Much further down, roughly around the knees, my spindly legs emerged from the sweater.

Now, if I had been a horse-dealer I would have cut the sweater in two and used it as a horse-blanket. But what do you think I did? I hugged Auntie Auntie and promised to wear the miracle every day, year in and year out, in all weathers. And I immediately asked her to knit me another one, to have in reserve, in case I should wear this one out. Happy as a sandboy, I lost myself more and more in the mesh of the sweater until there was no point of return. It belonged to me and would remain with me forever and nothing in the whole world could make Auntie Auntie change that fact.

And during the following night I had a nightmare. At first I didn't know what it was about. I woke up with a perfect defence attitude, ready to do a right hook and a left hook, and my jaw muscles were tense and taut. Then the dream appeared before me again. Deep below the surface, like faint reflexes on running water, I saw a sack of something sinking to the bottom of the lake. And then I saw it was me inside that sack. And yet it wasn't me. It was Sickan and me at the same time. I was a dog and she was human. And we grew together and became one growling mouth snapping at our own air bubbles. But at the same time everything was completely silent. A roaring thumping silence descended on us while we tried to bite our way out of the sack. I struggled down there, my neck muscles stretched in desperate effort, my jaw muscles grinding away. But I was sinking and sinking and the air bubbles became fewer and fewer and in the end the silence settled inevitably among the stones and the seaweed. Some surprised shoals of fish scratched against the insufficient air holes in the sack. But the holes were large enough to let in the eels. They managed to slide through and sink their sharp teeth into my flesh. After a short while they'd made a meal of it and they were delighted at this godsend that had come their way. They stared fixedly at my heart and then they came racing from every direction.

My plan was to wear the sweater up to the crossroads and then change into something else on the way to school. I could always bring something to change into, I thought.

But it didn't turn out like that.

I was prompted by the driver's surprised look and his sudden lack of interest in the road to keep it on. It would have been impossible to do anything else. Anything else would have been like a betrayal against Auntie Auntie.

And in that way I learned that you can stretch the limits a long way when it comes to conformity and kinship. After some exhausting struggles the sweater gave me a new kind of freedom and a bigger world to live in. Suddenly, I was right at the bottom of that vertical line of liberated madmen that I mentioned earlier on. I had simply become a loony in a long row of other loonies. Not that I did much more than walk around in my sweater, despite my aunt's protests, but that was enough. I took two steps, waited for the sweater to catch up with me, then took another couple of steps. It was wonderful, absolutely wonderful. And I had a very nice friend to talk to called Ingemar who happened to live in the same sweater as me . . . and meanwhile the people at the factory got used to regarding me as a nutcase.

Now I am exaggerating again. The only thing that actually happened was that I felt the PULL. The truth was that I suffered agony in that ghastly green sweater, but at the same time I saw the road to freedom beyond the frontiers of conventionality. But it is true that I got used to thinking of myself as two or several people, just to have some company. And all sorts of images and noises made a big impact inside my shell sometimes. Sudden feelings of vertigo and dreams which seemed much more real than petty problems like sweaters and other things became my real companions. I couldn't understand why. But it felt nice not to be completely yourself all the time. Like a Red Indian I could have laughed at my own imminent torture. And if someone had hit upon the idea of asking me why I laughed I could have answered that it is impossible to torture someone who isn't there.

Images, yes.

The Artist had persuaded Berit to pose for something he called 'a group'. And although we had broken off our engagement she still asked me if I could come along as a chaperon. She didn't realize how much pride I had to swallow in order to do that. But it didn't matter because I reckoned I might have a chance to see her breasts. For Saga's and my sake I wanted something to compare with hers.

So one evening we marched along the lonely road to the Artist's cottage which was renovated and extended. The large lit-up roof lights showed us the way. At first he wanted Berit to come in the daytime, but she didn't want to do that. God knows what people might have said then! Strangely enough Berit cared a lot about what people said. But she never realized that everyone at the glass factory knew about our evenings, for instance. The gossip about her modelling spread alarmingly quickly and I don't know how many requests I had from various people who wanted me to be on constant guard. My uncle wanted a report from his point of view and my auntie from hers. My uncle even suggested it would be better if he came along too but he wasn't allowed to.

Everyone was jealous and curious. They wanted detailed reports and descriptions of every second, preferably told with photographic exactitude.

This plus Berit's words of warning rested heavily on my shoulders when we crossed the threshold of the Artist's home.

'Now, remember this: you're to see that everything is done artistically.'

That's what she said and I nodded and walked along behind her. First came Berit, then me and finally my sweater came trailing behind through the door. We'd all arrived. But the Artist wasn't too happy when he saw me. He pointed at me and asked her what 'it' was.

'A sweater,' I said, because I found it hard to imagine myself as 'it'.

Then he laughed and said I was the smallest little existentialist he'd ever come across. I didn't bother to ask what he meant by that. You can't know everything about football, can you?

Besides, the Artist was in roughly the same boat as me. Whatever he did he'd always be the Artist. He wore an invisible sweater and people expected him to behave differently. When you came into his studio directly from the narrow forest road, it was like entering a glowing enchanted Aladdin's cave. His pale eyes shone with intensity from his pure oval face which was outlined by his black hair and beard. He ended up with two ovals – roughly the shape of two eggs; one slightly below the other. His mouth was big and wide and he opened it when you least expected and grinned at you in a happy sort of way. He didn't say much, but he seemed to be measuring us in order to mix us into some witches' brew. He'd probably chop us up into small pieces and mix us with cement and water and make us into those strange sprawling figures that were scattered all round his room. And I knew that we would be only too glad to be of assistance to him, because his power of persuasion was incredible. Despite all the fuss and all the resistance down in the glass works he was actually about to turn the clock forward for us. Every day new stories were told about his innovations. He stirred up a lot of feeling. People showed admiration, surprise, dislike and pride all mixed up. He belonged to the glass works. He was the Artist.

But when he described how he wanted Berit to lie I'm afraid her enthusiasm waned. She said good-bye and pulled me up, ready to leave.

And when the Artist's arguments had run out, he finally despaired and cried:

'Did you think I was going to paint you like Lorraine Petersen on those packets of raisins?'

'Sun Maid,' I said, in order to say something, but also because I wanted to explain to Berit what he meant.

I hadn't come along to look at her corkscrew curls exactly.

Then Berit hesitated. She had never really thought about the woman on the back of those raisin packets. But that girl came from Småland originally, said the Artist, when he saw Berit's questioning look. And now she was a symbol of Californian dried grapes. Who knows what Berit might be a symbol of one day!

The Artist had the answer to that one: 'The Mother.'

And then he described how he envisaged his picture. In a sunny warm meadow lies a woman who's just had her first baby.

It looks as if she's just lifted the baby out of her womb and now she is holding it up in a curve towards the sun. The child is babbling with joy at being alive. It is ready to embark on its journey of life and the mother is holding it up.

It sounded so beautiful that I got a lump in my throat and Berit too must have realized the greatness of this image. She of all people was going to symbolize Motherhood. She started to undress at once. The sculpture was going to be called 'Woman having her first baby' and when it was finished it was going to stand in a town square. I could just imagine the Artist and I walking around a reclining naked Berit and I was quite convinced that I would take just as professional an attitude as the Artist.

But I deceived myself, I am afraid.

Berit must have had misgivings about my professional intentions, because she suddenly asked what they were going to do with me – without letting me disappear altogether, mind you. I was allowed to listen, but not to look. How could I see if everything was done artistically then?'

'But I had an A in Art,' I protested. It didn't help.

The Artist suggested that I should sit on the other side of a curtain, quite near but still at a safe distance. And that's just how Berit wanted it. The curtain was drawn and soon I could hear the condensed silence on the other side. Sometimes the Artist muttered that Berit should lift her arms or knees a little higher and more often than not she told him that it was very tiring to keep that position. But I was the one who found it most tiring. Besides, I had certain obligations to make reports to other people. And what did I really know about what was going on in there? There were probably many people in the factory who wouldn't accept my eye-witness report if I stayed behind that curtain all the time where I couldn't even see what they were up to. What if Berit's honour was at stake, for instance? And maybe she didn't understand the full implications of it herself?

I sneaked out slowly and soon found a way up to the roof. Once up there I moved across to the large roof light, inch by inch. The Artist had swept the snow away in order to let in as much light as possible. He had even put a ladder beside the window for his own – and my – convenience. So when I rested on that I believed I was safe. I recovered my breath and eased forward a bit more to be able to see what I wanted to see at last.

But unfortunately the same old curtain was in the way again.

All I could see were Berit's feet. I tried to stretch across the window. Impossible. I crawled towards the ridge of the roof in order to lower myself to the upper edge of the window from there, and I realized at last that I could lie on my stomach and hang on to the other side of the roof-ridge with my feet. In that position, I didn't have the slightest thought of retreating. I only had one goal: forward, not backward!

So I lay down on my stomach and started to slide down slowly. Everything went according to plan. There was Berit all naked. Her arms were stretched upwards – towards me in fact. Her legs were a bit apart. She was smiling happily and seemed to whisper COME! And I hung up there under the stars in heaven for one brief second before the law of gravity pushed me forward with all its might. Without being able to do anything about it I started to glide across the window. I must have looked like a degenerate version of Batman against that dark sky. Berit had a completely blank expression on her beautiful face and I understood exactly how the cow must have looked the summer before just when she caught Manne by her horns. But Berit was not a cow. Least of all a cow, I would say. She reacted immediately and rolled away from the glass splinters that rained down just before I came crashing down too with a bang on the draped bench where she had held out her tempting arms a second earlier, beckoning to me with her naked body.

Luckily, neither she nor I was badly hurt. I fainted for a moment, just to make sure that the Artist wouldn't kill me, but when I woke up he just stood there laughing with the corners of his mouth pulled up to his ears.

And he laughed even more when I, in my stuttering way, tried to explain that I'd been asked to see that everything was done artistically and decently. This was the first time in his life he had heard that artistic and decent were supposed to be one and the same thing. I got angry and one of my knees was aching and swelling up.

Berit just said that I had obviously been a little too inquisitive for my age. She had forgotten all about our engagement. While she got dressed, I was allowed to see the Artist's sketches of her. And then we walked home in the night. I limped beside her and thought of those sketches which didn't look at all like Berit. But he explained all that to me later. What he was after was the actual linear quality. And as a consolation he even allowed me to help

133

him with that. As soon as he'd fixed new glass in the window he wanted to see how a babbling child would look in his mother's arms. But we'd have to do it without Berit. And I was allowed to keep my clothes on too. He fixed up something with scarves and hooks in the ceiling and then I'd hang from there staring down at a spot where my imaginary mother was supposed to lie. The idea was that I should look weightless. I was going to rest on her warm hands.

I think he was pulling my leg.

But when Berit and I walked home that evening something funny happened. Jesus who'd burned his hands in an acid bath wasn't the only God-fearing man in the village. On the contrary, there was no shortage of people of all sorts like him. The summer before, one open-air religious service followed another. But Jesus wanted his own parish, which was to be twice as holy as all the others put together. My uncle would probably be the last man to join it because the first condition was that you should give up all carnal relationships – except for breeding purposes, if that is what it's called. The only person so far who'd put his name down for this sect was Stuff-the-hole Hardy. Mind you, he was a loony and he'd got engaged to Ava Gardner by proxy, so it didn't matter to him, anyway. He met Ava when she and Frank Sinatra visited Småland on their Swedish tour. And he claimed that it was love at first sight. Anyway, these two oddballs suddenly turned up on the road that evening when Berit and I were walking home. I don't mean Ava Gardner and Frank Sinatra, but Jesus and Stuff-the-hole Hardy. Berit jumped and squeezed my hand which she had just taken because she wanted me to be as afraid of the dark as she was. They frightened the life out of us when they started to shout about all those devilish punishments which awaited the Artist and me. Jesus waved his long arms about and from the black hole that was his mouth gushed forth a sulphurous stream about the horrors we could expect in hell.

Berit gripped me and started to run. She pulled me past the two figures. My knee was burning like fire and I tried to make her stop but she just kept on running right up to the streetlights on the main road.

'Remember,' she said, panting, 'you are my witness that it was all done in an artistic manner.'

'And decently,' I added.

Then she said that I was so wise that I would probably never be confirmed.

Around the time when the snow was melting Mr Holdst became quite obsessed with what he called our choice of destiny. Every day when I was reading the paper for him he got more and more worked up about it. But one night he changed his tune completely. He wanted me to accompany him to the glass factory where the managing director was about to make a speech. I don't know how he found out about things like that. I had no idea that the managing director was going to make a speech but Mr Holdst insisted that it was now or never, as he put it. We had to show up and make our contribution. I should have asked someone, I should have told Auntie Auntie, for instance, that he wanted to go out, but when he said that I was to be his guide-dog at the most important moment in his life, it sounded so exciting – and anyway, it was I who was finally going to benefit from it with SERP and extra money in the year 2000, as he pointed out.

So I gave in and helped him to get ready. It wasn't difficult. Most of the time he was just wearing a pair of thin trousers, a vest and an old cardigan without any buttons. His jacket almost made him look respectable, except that his vest was showing. I suggested he use a scarf to cover it up. I gave him mine, wrapped it round him once and led him off to a small mirror. He stood there for a moment while I gave him a running commentary on his appearance. And as I didn't like what I saw, he appeared absolutely wonderful, of course.

Who looked after him then? And who was he?

Well, he was an old man who lived in the flat opposite us and every day he taught me to play the recorder, and in return I used to read for him. As a rule both he and the flat looked quite clean and proper. But sometimes his dim yellow eyes, his sad long face and stiff body made me feel so sad that I wanted to swap with him. It would have been better if I was him, I reasoned, and saw a kind of temptation in swapping with him. Like taking one great leap through life and ending up in the waiting-room where nothing could surprise you any more.

Every day my body rushed away from the past. I was split into two people. The person I recognized as me was pushed further and further away into a desolate landscape that became more and more unattainable as time went by. In front of the mirror where

Mr Holdst was staring at himself with a glazed look I saw one single big eye which became everybody's eye. And that eye only wanted to see the me wiped clean of memories, that eye was my uncle and my aunt, it was everyone who wanted what was best for me. It was everyone who pretended that life went on regardless. Nobody wanted to say anything about the people who were missing. Time heals all wounds.

I lied like a faithful dog to Mr Holdst and wondered what he'd say if I told him the truth. What would he have done if I had shown him that I felt sorry for him?

I wallowed in kids' lies. In a few years' time I would be able to advance to a senior level. My shining armour was just a shell waiting to be filled with dung and excrement. And I could even kid myself that it was possible to skip life right up to the comfort of Death's door. Mr Holdst was standing there with burning cheeks before the night's adventure and there was no visible sign of him cooling down either. On the contrary! He asked me to take down the cornet and get my recorder out.

'Now it is time for battle,' he said, and explained that we were going to practise a piece of music which would silence both the managing director and his yes-men. All I needed to do was to note down the letters on a piece of paper and just follow him. Surely I could remember that much after a little practice?

I wrote the letters down. We rehearsed the piece a couple of times. It was as boring as a hymn and I must say that I found it a bit difficult to understand how the managing director could be silenced by such a boring tune. Besides, I was getting a bit worried about what the others might say, but Mr Holdst was quite clear on that score too: as soon as we started to play, everyone in the glass factory would start to sing in unison.

'We can't sit on our backsides waiting for that Königson,' he said, as if I knew what he meant by that.

Anyway, we marched towards the glass factory together. Mr Holdst took a firm grip of my shoulder and hid his brass instrument inside his jacket. Once we were in the warm, dimly lit hall my pulse suddenly rose to fever pitch. I realized then that Mr Holdst had talked about something very serious. Everyone looked serious, in fact. The place was filled with people. I caught a glimpse of my uncle's surprised face as we squeezed past, but he didn't say anything. Nor did anyone else. It felt strange to see so many quiet people lining the walls. Only the very boldest – a few master glass blowers and some young boys – sat on the work benches close to the flames which made reflections in their eyes. And Mr Holdst was going to play for those people! And I was going to make my debut on the recorder in that gathering!

I started to sweat, even though we were standing at quite a distance from the sweltering heat of the furnace. Mr Holdst sniffed like a lost retriever, although still on a lead. He could not stray very far from me, however much he wanted to. The bright reflections from the fire which lit up the dark room and cast shadows all round made him look more than usually handicapped. I hung on to him. In the end, some old glass workers came up to say hello to him, surprised to see him there at all. On the whole, they all said the same thing. They said it was a bloody business and they said they didn't believe it. And they said that one thing had nothing to do with the other. And slowly I realized that the glass factory was going to be sold. It was going to be sold to another factory which, in its turn, owned several other glass factories and the workers were afraid of coming under new ownership.

In the end, when the managing director stood up on a stool and started to talk, I must have nodded off. His sentences were as long as rattle-snakes and had the same pattern. But even I knew that Mr Holdst and I were on a losing wicket. Everything was going to be hunky-dory. Those SERP points couldn't be given away free. So I nodded, anaesthetized by the managing director's long speech. But suddenly I felt a violent tug at my shoulders. It was like being woken up by an eagle's claw. Mr Holdst hissed his NOW and produced my piece of paper with all the letters on it. Not one of them had stuck. I had to revise before I could play!

But Mr Holdst had no time for revision. He started without me. He let go, blew his first bar and marched straight on in the direction he thought the managing director was standing. Unfortunately, his hearing must have been back to front. I tried to follow him, but my legs didn't want to go. With the recorder stuck in my mouth I stared at Mr Holdst and I stared at all the others in the room. It wasn't just my mouth that was gaping. I could have walked round inspecting all the teeth in that glass factory. That is how flabbergasted they all were. And not one of them made a point of singing, as Mr Holdst had promised they would!

No. People just stared transfixed at Mr Holdst who marched straight up to one of the furnaces with quick jaunty steps, eagerly blowing his cornet. Just in front of one of the tunnels he bumped into a bucket of water. He climbed right into the bucket and turned round in surprise, losing his foothold at the same time as he took the instrument from his mouth and shouted:

'Recorder! Join in!'

But I might as well have had a huge cork in my mouth. I was silent. I was silent and I started to feel ashamed as I was meant to help him.

Mr Holdst must have been furious at my lack of response. He shouted something about everyone's wretched weakness, opened his arms as if about to make a speech, but then he banged his fist against a tin screen beside the furnace, screamed in pain and lost his cornet into the bargain. I was very surprised to see it ending up in the furnace after a perilous journey through the air.

At that point people started to react at last. The site manager rushed forward and seized Mr Holdst by the lapel before he could fall and get badly burnt.

And his lovely instrument melted away in the furnace. Mr Holdst was stiff as an old dinosaur when, strangely enough, I was assigned to take him home.

How would I ever be able to thaw him out and get on friendly terms with him again.

I got the idea that everyone else in the room had been gradually convinced by the managing director's speech. He had not been too keen about that SERP thing, but the rest of his speech had been one long promise that the glass factory would live on in perpetuity. Why did Mr Holdst have to contradict him then and why did I have to carry the burden?

When we got back I put the old man in his usual chair and pulled off his shoes and socks. Everything was soaking wet, even me. His feet looked like old blue-white porcelain. His narrow face with its dim yellow eyes had got fixed in a grim expression which I couldn't do anything about. I decided to steal away and leave the old man to himself. Old people are too odd to mix with. I was almost ready to say: You old devil, before closing the door behind me. But just then he suddenly looked in my direction. And his face collapsed at once and became smoother than mine even. He seemed like a helpless child with his yellow eyes which were covered by a layer that wanted to break into tears. But not one single tear fell down those dry cheeks. Instead he said in a serious tone and with a great sigh:

'I used to be a wind player amongst wind players. Can I tell you about it one day?'

'Of course,' I said. 'And afterwards I'll read about those corsets.'

Then he smiled. And I knew that I'd hear a lot more about how much better life would be with SERP and extra pension money, and what a rough background he'd had, with straw in his shoes and all that, and a long distance to school of course, no food in the house and off to work at the age of five, and how his father had been a soldier and drunk a lot when he was young and spawned thirteen children, before he went to America, never to be seen again. One of his sons became a millionaire, five died and one became a wind player amongst other wind players and the rest built a glass factory with their own hands and lived happily ever after.

I know those stories well. Auntie Auntie keeps telling them too. It's no fun listening to them. One thing I can't understand is how they could be so badly off when everything was so much cheaper in those days.

As soon as Saga's parents went to America and she was on her own, she wanted me to move in with her. That was out of the question of course. But I ran up to her house every evening. Her Mrs Lindmark cooked for at least fifteen people before she left. Saga and I had plenty of everything, but Auntie Auntie was a bit worried all the same. I didn't tell her anything about my double life of course. All she noticed was that I was losing my appetite. But my God, how we ate at Saga's! She had persuaded Mrs Lindmark to make 'TV-dinners'. We sat in the living room in large armchairs with the TV on, munching our chicken pieces and watching those quiz programmes at the same time. That was the first time I had seen any TV, apart from the odd test picture, that is.

'Judge for yourself' was a fun programme.

So I was pleased as Punch being my own little Nero – thumbs up, thumbs down – on those evenings with Saga.

But one evening I got a slightly uncomfortable feeling that there was someone missing in the household. I knew her father wasn't there, but it wasn't just her parents who'd left. That stupid tail-wagging boxer Oscar had also disappeared. Where could he be? Why couldn't he take part in our fantastic TV-dinners too?

He, if anyone could do with some enlightenment, I should have thought.

'We had him put down,' said Saga when I asked her, and she munched away happily at her chicken thigh as if it were the most natural thing in the world.

Oscar!

A rather stupid dog with a big bare uninhibited wagging backside and protruding eyes . . . He didn't look like a proper dog, of course! But he was still a dog. And fancy putting a dog to sleep just because he was in the way!

Where would it end? Judge for yourself!

I must have looked like Oscar's ghost, because Saga interrupted her eating and asked me if I didn't know that it was common practice to put dogs to sleep when they could not be looked after any more. No, I didn't know that. I had never had a thought like that. I had learned that people kill animals for food, but to kill a dog in cold blood just because he is a nuisance, that was news to me. Why couldn't they do what we had done with Sickan? Oscar would probably have been very happy in the country and he might have come to the end of his life in the middle of a feeble attempt to catch a rabbit perhaps – happy even when breathing his last with the rabbit between his teeth. Why aren't dogs allowed to live according to the law of the jungle, at least towards the end of their lives? Småland must be full of suitable farms – even for a dog like Oscar!

Saga's voice didn't have as much as a tremor in it and her piece of chicken had not rebelled and flown up in her face and killed her rotten words. Couldn't God think of any punishment for her? Was he completely blind or was he also sitting there like me, forgetting the world for a quiz programme on TV?

It was part of the game that Saga ruled supreme in her palace. My admission into her home was dependent on her whims. Before I had time to say anything about Oscar she jumped out of her chair, put the plate on the floor and suggested that we should practise as soon as I had cleared up the dishes in the kitchen.

The slave Ingemar Johansson had to wash up before he could become the world-famous challenger who, thanks to his own determination and some help from Edwin Ahlquist, his trainer perhaps, had reached the perfect physical condition needed for the title match. My slave hands rummaged around among the gnawed-off chicken bones which fell into the rubbish bin, but suddenly everything seemed so misty and far away. It was only when I heard myself sobbing that I realized I was crying for Oscar. I couldn't understand why. That stupid idiotic dog! Why was I lamenting the death of an unknown dog? Through floods of tears I could see his basket in the corner of the kitchen. The blue-and-red check blanket was still there. Everything was there. Just as if Oscar would come tramping in any minute with that sheepish expression on his face. But instead he'd been shot through the head. I felt faint, my body collapsed towards Oscar's old basket.

And there I was, immobile, curled up in a position that even Oscar could not have imitated – when suddenly I heard happy voices and I realized that the other members of our training camp had arrived. Obviously, our training camp had not remained a secret in the village. Apart from my best friend Manne there was a muscular guy called Tommy. He was always dragging a hopeless girl called Karin behind him. But he claimed that it was she who followed him around. Anyway, I saw their grinning faces through a kind of haze when I peeped above my dog's basket. I barked a couple of times and growled in a menacing kind of way. They obviously enjoyed it so I bit Karin's leg just to show them that I was serious. Her shrill voice became shriller still when it slid from laughter to screams of pain.

'He's got rabies, he's mad!'

Tommy saved his Karin by kicking me somewhere in the region of the stomach. Some sour bile swished about in my mouth and I had to let go of Karin's leg. With a tremendous effort I got up from the animal kingdom and progressed through billions of years to join my fellow human beings again. I finally surfaced with a self-congratulatory laugh:

'I bet I frightened you just now. I was just pretending to be a dog.'

Karin looked doubtful. She was really quite different from Saga and I couldn't understand why Saga let her join our training camp at all. But maybe Saga was so tolerant because Tommy was the captain of our football team. And Saga's breasts were growing at an alarming rate just then. It was one of my more pleasant duties to wrap them in bandages to make her as flat and hard as before. My vow of silence was unconditional. I got plenty of food. And Saga and I lived with those two budding breasts as if they were poisonous boils.

No, now I'm lying again.

Of course it's not true. In our secret handling of those bandages there were as many question marks as in a swarm of mad wasps disturbed from their nest. Without any warning at all, Saga would suddenly decide that we should repeat what had happened that first evening. So in the middle of all that wrapping and mucking about she might suggest that we should do it again. I don't know why I did it, but I did it anyway – again and again.

Ask me how a martyr feels when dying on the wheel. One thing is for sure. He knows there is no way of escape. And he knows there is not much enjoyment in it either.

Since that first kiss Saga had cut out all expressions of intimacy. I had to walk over to the door while she went to the window, because she wanted a big distance between us. The only person who was allowed to peep at our strange goings-on was the famous centre-forward, Kurre Hamrin, who looked down from his picture on the wall. What we did was this: we both took our clothes off quickly, then stood there looking at each other. That is, I tried not to look at her and she kept staring at my unhappy dick which seemed to rise of its own accord, first somewhat hesitantly, but then with greater determination until it pointed straight at her.

'There you are, you see,' she said triumphantly. 'Don't think you can get out of it for much longer!'

There was nothing I could do about it. I tried to imagine her light red opening – which was barely covered by a few strands of hair – as the entrance to some tunnel which ended up in a yard where a police patrol was waiting for me, the man condemned to death. But suddenly her body underwent a change. It became like Berit's but still not quite like hers.

And judging by Saga's contented 'There you are, you see,' I knew that the last thing I was thinking about was a razor-sharp guillotine that would strike me with the speed of lightning. No, if I had been thinking of that, I know I wouldn't have had any problems keeping it down.

Saga was like a fourteen-year-old Boot-Carlsson: it was impossible to avoid her, but it was dangerous to get too close to her. In the end something was bound to happen. But I didn't know what and how.

Never mind. Tommy, Karin and Manne soon grew tired of me as a dog. They disappeared into the attic. Far away in the distance, like in another world, I could hear their noise and laughter.

Manne was even more of a weakling than me. He preferred to walk around with a stolen cigar in his mouth pretending he was Cus D'Amato and saying that he'd do anything for money. I stayed in the dog's basket, wrapped in my sweater which everybody had stopped commenting on by then. It felt good to be a dog, but a bit insecure perhaps. My body was completely relaxed, but at the same time ready to attack at a moment's notice.

But there was nothing to attack at the moment. I didn't need to defend myself against anyone. What I wanted most of all was to get my teeth into more shadows.

I didn't want to see Saga any more.

The worst thing was that I was beginning to feel restless as soon as she was around. I longed for her even though she hurt me. It was time for Ingemar Johansson to put his boxing gloves on the shelf.

That is exactly what I had in mind to tell them when I finally got up to the attic. But as soon as I crossed the threshold someone put a glove on my right hand. Saga stood there stiff and strange with her left glove ready. Her face was paler than usual under that jet-black straight hair of hers. Manne walked around, snorting. That is all he could do. Tommy tied the glove around my wrist and made a contemptuous face:

'She won't hit you anyway. Guess why?'

'No blows below the belt,' snorted Manne, and blinked as if he'd cracked the joke of the year.

Had they discovered that Saga was strapped in perhaps? Or worse still! Did she think that I had grassed on her?

I couldn't think of anything to say. Anyway, it was too late. Saga started to glide forward in my direction.

'Ingemar's right fist will go straight through the wall,' yelled Manne encouragingly.

He didn't realize that a wall can resist a blow. I circled round to avoid a confrontation with Saga. What had they said? Her face was as closed as a refrigerator door and it was probably as cold inside. We'd agreed to feint a bit with our gloveless hands and then hit with the other one. I am a typical right-hand boxer without a left jab to follow up.

In the distance I could hear the roar from the crowd.

I decided to aim a couple of jabs at her breasts. After all, it was

143

the breasts that had ruined everything. But Saga sensed what I was up to. Before I had got anything resembling a guard position organized she landed a pure beauty on my chin and I fenced around in complete darkness. I felt like a parachutist at a height of 5,000 metres going down at full speed towards enemy country without a parachute! Tommy called me an eggshell and they all disappeared down the stairs. Everything became silent and I decided never to get up again.

I enjoyed dreaming about how I had just beaten Floyd Patterson and how I was interviewed by the world press. I told them that there was a meat-ball cooking mother behind every male success. Great men never become greater than their mothers. So that's why I'd like to say hello to my mum in Gothenburg.

Then I heard someone sobbing. At first I thought it was the journalists who were moved by my speech, but then I realized that it was Saga. She was sobbing and beating me at the same time to wake me up. I must say that the real world isn't at all like the cinema. On the screen they usually beat the prisoners before torturing them. But it is a very dubious method, I think. I fainted again while wondering why no one had stopped the match.

When I woke up Saga was gone. It can't have been many seconds that I lay there on those dirty boards in the attic, but it felt like light-years and I was all alone. The red juniper branches which held up the clothesline around our boxing ring danced before my eyes, and I wondered quietly whether to cough a little blood while the lights were being switched off and I was left to find my own way home. I wasn't even worth spitting on.

I only hoped the village wouldn't find out that I had been knocked out by a girl!

One thing I kept thinking about was God's mercy. Now, if I were Jonah for instance and God asked me to wander off to Nineveh to warn the people there that their wickedness would not go unpunished, I'd agree with Jonah that that was a pretty meaningless task, especially if I believed in God's mercy, that is. Why shouldn't the people of Nineveh enjoy His mercy too? I go along with Jonah when he said: 'Why don't you go on those meaningless expeditions yourself!'

I am sorry. I shall make myself bald as a vulture and cut off my hair if ever I dare speculate again over things that I don't understand. I just wanted to make the point that there are things which are incomprehensible. Of all the people that Saga knew, she had to pick Stuff-the-hole Hardy to talk to that evening when she knocked me out. She rushed down to the glass factory when she thought that I was never going to wake up again. Stuff-the-hole Hardy found it a bit hard to grasp when she told him that she'd killed Ingemar Johansson, but he still let her cry her heart out in his arms! And those arms weren't bad, you know. He'd saved them for Ava Gardner, after all.

And at that delicate moment in the proceedings, Jesus turned up and misunderstood the whole thing of course. He got quite wild and spat fire and water over them. Stuff-the-hole Hardy had taken a vow of celibacy now that he was a member of Jesus' sect and everything.

Saga ran home and locked the door behind her, but Jesus' tongue could not be locked up. Oh no, the story spread all over the village and each new version was wilder than the previous one. Auntie gave a composite picture of all the gossip when she said that things like that ought to be reported to the Social Services Department.

That was quite amusing, actually, because Saga's mum was a committee member of the Social Services Department.

But I was too tired to laugh at it. I recognize a perfect break-down in myself when I see one. Saga was like a glass with too much tension in it. A lot of unhappy atoms which want to escape make the glass suddenly explode. You can't see it until the explosion is a fact. And you can't do anything about it either.

It's got something to do with the seasons. Suddenly everything was peace and quiet again. I practised the recorder, read to Mr Holdst and ran around with the spring dust tickling my throat. Sometimes Manne and I thought of a way of passing the time, but on the whole, nothing at all happened.

Every second was like an unruffled surface of water which reflected the past. But oddly enough, it doesn't seem to be like that for grown-ups. They seem to enjoy uneventful peaceful living conditions – as if life is one enormous long queue that you have to work yourself through. Soon enough you'll reach your goal. And never turn round to see what has already happened!

But when they talked about how well I had settled in and how well I was getting on with everyone in the village they didn't know that I was walking round like a kind of receptacle. Inside me everything was splashing about in great turbulence. I didn't want to stand in the queue, I thought it was pointless because I knew what was waiting for me at the goal. I wanted to think back, but I couldn't. Panting away while chasing something was my only means of escape, my way of forgetting things.

So I walked around in my sweater and tried to talk sense to myself. I told myself not to be childish any more. I told myself that I had to grow up now. I told myself that I had in fact grown up already and the proof was that I had forgotten how to cry. And yet this uneventful existence was like a quagmire that tried to rise up through my throat.

I had wanted to be a child when I came to my uncle's and aunt's and I didn't want to grow up. But I hadn't realized how time would rush along day after day.

In the end, Saga's and Stuff-the-hole Hardy's episode was forgotten. It was only Jesus who ran around telling everyone, and Hardy himself who went round saying that he was innocent. For the sake of decorum Mrs Lindmark moved in for a few weeks. Then everything was back to what it had been before. But something was different. I avoided Saga like the plague. It was only Karin who went up to Saga's house. The rest of us stayed away. So we were taken completely by surprise when Karin finally presented Saga to us. Saga had been transformed; from having been a hard-hitting boxing champion in trousers and dirty jerseys, she was now a giggling girl in a dress and that's how she looked when she invited us to a party the following Saturday.

Some of her friends from the grammar school in town were also going to come. Did I want to come too?

I hadn't been to a party for ages. In the Great Wall of China we were always having parties. I have never had one myself, but I was quite popular and was always invited to other people's. The whole point with these parties was roughly the same as when Little Frog and I built our huts. At first we'd have cake and soft drinks, that was the formal side of the party, and then we'd close the door and pull the blinds down and throw ourselves on top of each other in one great big heap. That was the informal side. When someone wanted to change partners your name was called out in the dark. I was passed round more often than anyone else because I was so popular. But that's because I never did anything with the girls. I never had the time. Every time it was my turn the

146

girl would gasp for breath and say that she needed a rest. And I, being such a decent bloke, understood, didn't I? So most of the time I just sat there like a nice, kind idiot in the semi-darkness trying to imagine what was going on around me. My kindness really was a liability at times. I was being used. But I learned to tell lies afterwards. My descriptions didn't differ from any of the others.

It's always been like that. Even when I was eight years old I was the type girls wanted to marry and my brother was the type girls wanted to screw. It is a terrible fact of life to carry around with you.

But even so, I decided to give myself another chance. If only I could stop being so damn kind, someone would probably fall for me.

The children's home had supplied me with a set of clothes at least. There was no shortage of money at the home. In fact, that was the only thing they had, it seemed. The clothes were really meant for speech day but it never happened because I spent my speech day with my legs in a parcel in hospital. At the children's home everything happened in wholesale. Everybody had to do everything at the same time. That's probably why I haven't grown very much since. It was so embarrassing coming from a children's home and marching in a line through the town to the men's outfitters that I tried to crawl under the tarmac. I did a funny walk just like Donald Duck. That's what we called the fellow with the webbed feet. The two of us matched each other really well. He waddled beside me in his strange crawling fashion and I think it must have been around that time that I stopped growing. Experiences like that can handicap you for life.

Don't misunderstand me now. I really don't mind people with webbed feet. I even think it's quite a practical thing to have because I am not a very good natural swimmer. But our Donald Duck stinks. I don't mind admitting that I've had earth between my toes too sometimes, but this fellow managed to get whole dung heaps between his toes in just a quarter of an hour. Even though he'd just had a wash he'd still stink when it was his turn to try things on in the shop. And I was ashamed. And then I felt ashamed because I was ashamed, if you follow me. My soul was like a marble in the lap of the gods. DING DONG! I was sure to land in a hole somewhere without gaining a point. Somehow, I must have stopped growing. I was almost thirteen then and now I'm getting on for fourteen and I haven't grown one millimetre since.

The positive thing about the new clothes we got at the children's home was that it was the only time I'd been in a situation where the final bill didn't seem to matter. You just took what you wanted and they just added it to the bill.

So I bought a dove-blue blazer with faint stripes in it. It had long slits at the sides and looked as if someone had sprinkled silvery pine needles on the material. Then I picked a mustard-coloured shirt with a button-down collar. And instead of a tie I chose a black string which I tied with a bull's head in gilt metal. The trousers had to be light grey of course and very narrow at the bottom in order to make the maroon-coloured shoes shine in all their pointed glory. Keeping in mind my future life as a dwarf I chose the shoes with the highest heels I could find.

The only time I wore those clothes was at a Midsummer party with my betrothed, Berit. Those clothes don't smell of the children's home. Maybe of hay and barn, but those are masculine smells. And with an outfit like that it was really time to produce a broken cigarette from a crumpled packet, fix it to my razor-sharp, cruel-looking lower lip and light it with a cigarette lighter of real gold, then walk into the night, looking tough and bitter.

But instead, I nervously wandered through an evergreen Småland, up towards Saga's house where I was welcomed by a sweaty Karin. She giggled and tied a scarf round my eyes, then put something in my hand which felt like a knife. She asked me to walk straight through the crowd of laughing people. Suddenly there was a bang. My scarf was removed and I saw a broken balloon before my feet and several other balloons were floating around in the room. With obvious delight Karin picked up a note from one of the balloons and told me that I was to escort Louise to the table. The balloons contained pieces of paper with girls' names on them. The balloon you prick and so on. Very funny. It was so silly that it could only have been Karin who had thought of a thing like that. And I must have done something very silly too because Saga's face darkened ominously. She and Louise were complete opposites when it came to character, but to look at them you might think they were twins. Louise had the same short straight hair, although hers was fair. Her eyebrows were completely black though. They looked like two straight lines above her serious ice-blue burning eyes. I suddenly understood why the Italians thought of Anita Ekberg as a combination of ice and fire.

When I was with Louise I was very self-conscious. She had exactly the same taut body as Saga, exactly the type of tension we always tried to achieve when we made longbows from the material that we stole from the building sites around the Great Wall of China. My grandfather would have been happy if he could have seen how I, like an arrow in a horizontal position aiming at an imaginary target on a vertical line, now wanted to rest against her bow. I think I must have got that feeling from my mother. The slight limp in her left leg made her hip protrude like that of a three-year-old. Her arched back in those flimsy summer dresses she used to wear, her high-heeled sandals at the end of her long legs, must have been the linear view that my eyes were most preoccupied with – and in case it might disappear I made mental pictures of it in my head, like having a secret photo album.

With a name like Ingemar Johansson you always try and think of a good way to start a conversation. Something easygoing like: 'Don't be afraid, it's only hired muscles . . .', but Louise's exploratory look just made me speechless. I drifted around with a stupid smile, at the same time realizing that I wasn't the cruellest guy around there. As a matter of fact, I was probably the youngest because most of the others came from the grammar school in town and they'd just heard that Saga was having a party with no parents around, so they came along. Somebody put a glass of something in my hand and I sneaked away to finish the contents outside. But Louise came after me to see what kind of fellow I was. Fiasco. I could already feel my right arm cramping up. And what was in the glass, I wondered. Could it really be liquor? My arm signalled a warning shot. After one attempt I had the stuff in my face. I leaned over the glass and inhaled the raw aroma of the liquor, carried up by the bubbles of Babycham. Louise wondered what on earth I was doing.

'Nothing. Skål,' I said, and threw my first precious mixed drink over my shoulder, to be on the safe side.

Her eyebrows fluttered a bit like birds' wings before I managed to stop them by telling her that I wasn't too keen on the hard stuff myself as I was an active sportsman. Then she stopped moving those eyebrows, but they stayed in a slightly higher position than usual. She could talk with her eyebrows. For the moment they seemed to show some interest. The drink was gone. It was now or never. I felt really wicked and I took her hand and pulled her through the room and up the stairs. I was definitely not going to be the nice guy.

If I could keep quiet, everything would be all right.

But I lost my bearings when I got to Saga's room. She had taken down the football pictures from the wall and put Tommy Steele there instead. He looked just like the horse she'd put up beside him. But the worst thing was that Louise jumped up on Saga's bed and patted the place beside her and said:

'Do you know what? In half an hour everyone will be pissed out of their minds and then all they'll be interested in is snogging. But in here we're safe!'

I started to scratch myself around the crotch like I've seen Sven Hansson do. He must have felt just like I did at that moment and what's more natural than grabbing hold of something familiar when you feel at a loss? Her eyebrows fluttered again and sent out some signals before they froze and she pouted her lips and repeated her sentence once more.

What went on in the house could be divided up into two worlds, one aboveboard, and one underworld. And guess where I wanted to be! But Louise kept fluttering those eyebrows in such a determined way that I had to jump up on the bed and sit down beside her.

It wasn't too bad after all. I discovered that I loved her and that I didn't have to do anything. We soon drifted off on our safe little island. Time passed and she talked as if she was quoting from a scientific book about the problems of womanhood.

'I'm sure you don't understand what happens to us, but neither do we. Women are actually surprisingly unaware of their impulses and innermost motives in life. We don't know why and what lies behind our actions. It's not at all the same for women and men. You've almost got two kinds of lives. With you it's the head that rules, not instinct. We, for instance, have a kind of built-in clock which tells us when it's time for motherhood. That's why I feel so sorry for Saga. Her clock has stopped, you see. Do you understand what I mean?'

'Yes,' I said. 'But we're not that old yet. Surely we can wind it up again?'

Louise arched her eyebrows in a way which just spelt contempt.

'So you're going to muck about with Saga then, are you?'

She jumped out of bed and closed the door before I'd had time to answer.

Why did everyone want to change Saga? Was it because she was the best football player around? Or because she was stronger and better at fighting than anyone else? Or because she didn't care what the other girls thought about her? She was a strange bird who flew past the traps everyone set for her. If freedom was denied them, why should she have it?

Who had made her put that dress on and who had asked her to lay on this party? Was it Karin or Louise who had masterminded the whole show?

Just thinking of the whole miserable scene made me want to get sloshed so I could forget everything and be like a child again. I sneaked downstairs and went into the kitchen to look for a drinking straw. But I need not have worried about my nervous reflexes. The living room and everywhere else down there had changed into an area for games in the dark. I crawled around slurping half-filled glasses while quietly wondering what Mrs Lindmark would say if she came in at that moment. Or maybe they'd locked her in the coal cellar? The grammar school boys were in the process of depleting father's drinks' cupboard altogether and I did what I could to help them. Most of it was sweet and sticky and it rose to my forehead like a fomentation. In the end I was convinced that all the worries in the world were over and I was just about to stretch out on a pleasantly moving carpet. Then I felt something pulling my hair at the back. Of course, Oscar's dog basket! That's where I belonged.

Perhaps it is a custom they have in Småland, kicking their dogs, I thought, when I woke up and found Karin standing over me, kicking me in the ribs with her foot.

'Wake up, we're going to play truth or trick!'

She looked so pleased with herself that I ought to have bitten her foot off there and then. People like her shouldn't be let loose. They have a kind of inner rabies. I scrambled after her into a well-lit room. The girls had got fed up with struggling in the dark. The grammar school boys looked a bit worse for wear. Tommy and Manne were sitting in a corner giggling to themselves. And Karin had had a report from Louise about my behaviour. You could tell. And Saga was nowhere to be seen. Maybe she'd got fed up with her own party. It couldn't have been her idea in the first place, after all.

151

What had taken place while I'd been asleep in Oscar's basket?

'It's only you and Saga left. Truth or trick?' asked Karin with something like triumph in her voice.

'Where is Saga?' I wondered.

'In the attic,' someone cried out.

I slunk after the other lemmings to the attic. Ruling a mob is not my strongest point, except when I have a vested interest in it. The mob from town was already laughing at our boxing ring. It was still there. But most of all, they laughed at Saga who was now standing in the middle of the ring, perspiring all over, her thin straight lips firmly closed and her nostrils quivering. She had given up. She was practising in order to get away from herself. And she was wearing a pair of brand-new *leather* boxing gloves!

And I hadn't even strapped her breasts in.

They were burgeoning underneath her thin dress – however much she tried to conceal the fact.

But strangely enough, Saga managed to win the others over. Suddenly all the fellows wanted to borrow her boxing gloves and everyone forgot about 'truth or trick'. My boxing gloves turned up as well and soon the war was in full swing. Saga walked around like a Bimstein, instructing everyone and impressing all the fellows by being able to skip longer than anyone else. It was only Karin who didn't like it. She saw her perfect party turning into a filthy training camp.

I was more than pleased, as long as nobody had the idea of measuring their strength with Ingemar Johansson. Most of the time I lolled about like some soft and disgusting jelly-baby. If someone had hit me in the stomach I would probably have thrown up various samples of liquor in one huge go. The vomit was splashing about in my stomach, bouncing off the various corners and just wanting to get out. I kept worrying about how I could throw up. That's why I didn't notice the sudden silence in the attic.

'Is it true?' asked someone, breaking the silence.

'What?' asked Saga.

'Good for Ingemar. Floored by an old man, eh?'

It was Karin who had been spreading the rumour about Stuff-the-hole Hardy. So now everyone started playing a game that we all have to play sooner or later. People kept jeering at Saga and she felt more and more isolated. Time cuts through one's life like a razor-blade. Suddenly all games hurt terribly, but you have to carry on and look unruffled, however much it hurts. You can't defend yourself against the masses. You just have to forget the anger that made you fight for yourself and your world. You have to put yourself on the shelf. It works. The art of life is not to show anything. When you're grown-up you probably walk around like a safe with all your valuables locked up inside you. 'Surely there is a mine for silver and a place for gold which they refine. Men put an end to darkness and search the farthest boundary for the ore in gloom and deep darkness, and the thing that is hid he brings forth to light,' as Job said. Very well said too, if you ask me. I often imagine that I have some kind of silver and gold in my own mine just like any other person.

But Saga didn't want to play. She couldn't put herself on the shelf.

'The person who spreads those kinds of stories must stand up for it too!' she said.

Saga was furious. The older boys thought that a boxing match between the two girls was a brilliant idea. Karin was caught at once. Only Tommy tried to object, but everyone else thought Saga was right. They gave Karin my green boxing gloves and pushed her into the ring where Saga was already waiting for her.

'Like Cus D'Amato says: those who haven't bought a ticket must stay outside.' That was Manne of course. He had got his cigar lit at last and felt just as rotten as me. Behind the blue-grey smoke I caught a glimpse of a face which was as green as his hair.

I was appointed referee. (You're supposed to laugh here!) Saga obviously had it all worked out. I realized at once what she was up to, of course. She let Karin warm up with a bit of impulsive fighting while she just aimed a few short straight jabs at Karin's breasts; never too hard, so Karin pretended that it was nothing. But she started to blush and at the same time the people were roaring with laughter all around the ring. Karin got clumsier and clumsier while trying to protect her breasts.

At that point I interrupted the match. She was just about to hit me instead, even though she'd suggested I be the referee. The boys cried with disappointment. Some of the girls joined in the chorus too. I tried to mediate.

'Not below the belt.'

'The belt isn't up there, surely?'

What should I call the breasts then? Aboveboard? I asked for two scarves and suggested that we strap their breasts in. Then we could call the scarves out of bounds. Karin agreed gratefully after Tommy had whispered something to her in her corner. The noise got worse. I tied the scarves round their breasts. Saga wanted to carry on. Karin felt the pressure from the crowd and had no alternative but to carry on too. Both stuck to the rules of the game. And I, stupidly, made the game even more dangerous by tying those scarves round them.

Saga was not able to tease Karin in the same way any longer. She had to box properly now and Karin got angrier and angrier and didn't want to give up. Suddenly Karin got furious. She did everything to reach the elusive Saga who finally started to punch Karin with left and right upper cuts.

I tried to stop them both, but it was impossible. Everyone screamed with delight when Karin, in one of her furious fits, managed to get Saga down against the rope which promptly broke. Saga was surprised. In all her life up to then she'd always knocked down those who disagreed with her. This time she knew that it didn't matter. You couldn't beat down Karin's gossip. As soon as the others realized how superior she was, they would support Karin. Saga had swept the floor with Karin. But why? You could tell that she intended to make Karin fight until she was exhausted.

But when Karin punched Saga in the face with an open glove which made a gash on Saga's cheek, I thought the game had gone on long enough. I tried to stop the match by coming between them. At that point Saga lost her patience. And for the second time I was punched in the face, and for the second time I collapsed in a heap on the floor and everything turned black all round me.

It was becoming a dangerous habit of hers. I was not fourteen yet but already punch drunk. I have no idea how the fight between Karin and Saga ended. For me, the fun was over anyway. When I woke up, the house was empty as if there had been a gas explosion. Saga dragged me down to the bathroom and washed off the worst mess. We didn't utter a word, but she helped me to get home because I was swaying like a hypnotized cobra.

Saga pushed me through the front door at Auntie Auntie's, who got out of bed and came up to me in her pink nightgown, moaning about her dear little child.

In a way, it was an advantage having an older brother. I didn't have to think up an excuse for my wretched appearance. I just pinched one of his. Auntie Auntie got a cock-and-bull story about three rotten fellows who'd laced my Coca-Cola. First I got drunk for five minutes, then I was sick for three hours. She was so moved by my story that she dug out a bottle of Arvidsson's Special and offered it to me. After I'd washed and undressed, I was given a glass on the spot 'to clear away the poison'. Instead my head spun even more as I climbed into bed.

Auntie Auntie leaned over to tuck me in and suddenly, without realizing what I was doing, I crept down beside her. I grabbed her scrawny body in the warm flannel nightgown as if I was clutching a knotty tree trunk on a precipice, in the middle of a raging storm. Auntie Auntie melted in my arms. She disappeared right through me when I tried to strangle all the tears which kept coming out: I couldn't run away from my mother's death any more. I wanted someone to say something to me. I wanted someone to tell me it wasn't my fault.

Chapter 6

1958

When I think about it now, it wasn't too bad, after all. Worse things happened in the autumn of 1958. Just think how tragic it must have been for the boy who had to go all the way to Boston to get a new kidney. He became famous and had his picture in the papers, but he died all the same. Or think of Miss Anna-Greta Stjärne who was killed by gangsters in Ethiopia when she was going about her business as a missionary, trying to convert the heathens to the Christian faith. She was only thirty-two. Or think of that train which crashed into another train at Grycksbo. Six dead and fourteen wounded! Schoolchildren as well. That could have been me. Or I could have been one of those 4,638 inmates in various prisons around Sweden, put inside because I hadn't done my homework. Or I could have walked diagonally across Johanneshov's sports ground on the night of the 28 August, like Bosse Larsson, and been hit in the chest by a javelin. He probably died because he was totally flabbergasted. You just don't expect to die from a javelin, do you? But it's like I always say: don't take any short cuts. Soon enough the inevitable will happen, anyway. I keep track of other people's misfortunes too. Not just my own. I mean, you have to have something to compare with, don't you? In actual fact, I am a specialist when it comes to feeling compassion. I still can't forget that terrible story about Laika, the poor Eskimo dog passenger in Sputnik II who was so brave while there was still some food left in the rocket.

But what happened after that?

Did she starve to death?

Just think of that! Laika didn't even have enough food to eat. She circled round in space for five and a half months and they didn't even have enough sense to give her sufficient food supplies.

I use these sorts of things for comparison when I think about my return to the Great Wall of China after that summer in

Småland. There was mother in bed, and everything was as quiet as a dried-up well.

Just thinking about it is an enormous effort and I've come to it in a roundabout way. It's like when you want to get to an island in the middle of a lake and you waste all your energy running round the lake wondering which end you should swim out from. If only things could be as they were when I was six years old and the family was on holiday. My father swam out into the lake with me on his back. The water was almost black and the sun was just setting. The shadows grew heavier and heavier, and his strong arms looked almost yellow in the water. They were like hard pistons, indestructible. They moved silently and rhythmically. And the water got blacker and blacker and he promised to swim across the whole enormous lake. I pressed my legs around his waist, held my arms around his neck and felt the surge, the terrible black silent thing down there. But we were safe. Dad wasn't even short of breath. I was deliriously happy. With combined efforts we'd conquered something more than just the lake.

But this time I was alone. Just as lonely as when I came home from my summer in Småland, expecting to find a healthy and happy mother there, but no. I wasn't completely alone. My brother and I cried and wept for Sickan. Why wasn't she there to greet us when we got home? She was just as much part of the family as we, after all.

In the end we had to accept the inevitable. Sickan was staying in the country where she was well looked after. You can't move a dog around any old how. We could choose between having the dog back and our mother in hospital or do without the dog and have our mother at home. So we shut up. My sister didn't seem to care one way or another. She'd turned into an elusive shadow.

We tried to forget about it. After all, we were home again at last. It was wonderful to be back in that madhouse again. Mother coughed up her demons from her bedroom and threw them at us. I ran around, waiting for the next crack of the whip. I knew of nothing better. That's how it should be.

But our various home nurses didn't agree, of course.

A home nurse is a council person who is as old as my grandmother, but who wears a blue-grey costume, has short hair, a red nose, thick glasses and a shrill voice. Home nurses make a lot of disgusting food which no grandmother would ever do and which

157

no child wants to eat either. And everyone in the block of flats can see when they come and go and everyone knows that the people she goes to visit cannot look after themselves. That is the first step towards the children's home. The nurses come for three hours every day and are always angry because they don't like their job.

My brother and I managed to get through one of those people a week.

The record was three days. But it is fairly easy to get rid of a home nurse. They disappear on the spot if you don't show them you're grateful. But we just couldn't understand why we should be grateful to them.

They were paid to do a job after all, weren't they? It wouldn't surprise me if they even got free uniforms.

Every time one of them left, saying she refused to work for wild beasts like us, I had to go into the quiet dark bedroom to get some money out. Talk of going to the gallows. The half-drawn curtains made my mother's face disappear in the gloom. She was like a transparent white vase with a clear blue flame inside her. Sometimes it was like a hissing welding flame, but most of the time it was a quiet flickering hesitant flame.

What did we think we were up to?

Did we try to breathe some life into the flame perhaps? Didn't we realize that every time she got one of those attacks she needed more fuel? Didn't we realize that the fuel would run out in the end?

Oh yes, that was the worst part of it.

She gave me some frightening bedside lectures: my brother and I were a couple of little hangmen, destroying angels chosen to push her to her grave.

She fiddled nervously under the bedcovers as if her hand didn't want to produce the purse with the household money. The home nurses were a luxury we wouldn't be able to afford soon, but vital if we wanted to stay on at home. So why did we make their lives such hell?

Maybe because we so desperately wanted her to get up and say that she really wanted us.

I figured out that she'd definitely not wanted me from the start. The first thing she did was throw me out into the world. I know it's called being born, but with a start like that I am of the firm opinion that she didn't want me. I was bound to have misgivings about everything from then on. My first unforgiveable mistake was probably when I latched on to that egg in my early days as a sperm. I ought to have choked or drowned, got flushed out or ended up outside the womb. And I figured all this out by myself, because I never dared ask her about it. Asking mother about such fatal things was something I'd only do when I was so big and strong that I was sure no one could take me away. I dreamed of a house with a porch in summer with white birches standing like peace pennants outside the windows, and she and I would understand and respect each other at last, like two sensible adults. I must have read about that sort of thing in a Russian novel somewhere.

But this is the way I see our family story.

My father was a Swedish soldier during the Second World War. He was posted on a minesweeper in the harbour of Norrköping where it was safely moored. In the general hurly-burly, the minesweeper had been so badly fitted out that the propeller fell off just before coming into harbour. There was never any time to get another propeller. The minesweeper was moored in the harbour and was fully manned as a sign of our good military preparedness. And that's how it came about that my father was always telling us about a restaurant called The Grape in Norrköping. He spent the war there, you see. The commander of this minesweeper was the director of a sweets factory in civilian life. For a long time it was a favourite joke with my father, although we couldn't understand how he could talk in such derogatory terms about a director of a sweets factory.

During the exciting period when the country was in a state of alert, mother had worked out how she'd be able to have the greatest adventure of her life, but I turned up, just like Wallis, and stopped her from doing anything. My mother really wanted to be a singer, but she couldn't because of her lungs. She was the brightest in her class but got behind because she had to go to hospital for almost a whole year after they operated on her hip. She was not allowed to carry on at school after that. They didn't have any money, so she decided to be a photographer instead. She bought herself a second-hand Leica, took a job in a photographic studio and started to take photographs for a newspaper in her spare time. Soon she managed to open her own studio. And when my father turned up on the scene, she was ready to conquer the world. I am sure he was very charming, five years younger than her, with a sense of adventure which appealed to her and her idea of the future. Then she got pregnant. That was my brother. But when the war was getting closer to Sweden, she wanted to do something useful. She wanted to get up in the air, like a female Biggles. She wanted to fly and she was actually promised training as a photographer in the air force. So the studio was sold. Grandmother promised to look after my brother, provided the family moved into the top floor of my grandparents' house. Everything was carefully planned and prepared in advance to enable mother to set off on her adventure. If I may be so bold as to express my opinion in the matter, even though I was not present at the time, the preparations were not bad. Even my mother-to-be was on the verge of throwing herself into a battle of fire. Her only weapon was a camera, that's true, but still.

Then I came along.

I came with my father and I came with peace. With a steadily swelling stomach she got anchored on the ground. And once I'd been chucked out, they didn't want her in the air corps any more. No cannon fodder was needed there. She was free to go home and look after her Wallis.

I reckon I was lucky that she had sold her photographic studio by then. Who knows, she may have thrown me into the acid bath otherwise!

Peace came as I said – but not for us, I'm afraid. First I arrived. Then my sister. Suddenly one day she just appeared and I loved her above everything because with her around I saw a chance of sharing my burden of guilt with someone. Everything was a wonderful chaos. It was very hard for my mother to learn how to cook, but my grandmother helped her. And grandmother certainly made up for mother's deficiencies in that field. So when mother went on about the greatest mistake of her life, at least we knew there was always room down at my grandmother's – and the food was always nicer down there anyway.

In the legend about myself I had always done a disappearing act. Once I crept into a larder and ate bananas until I fell asleep, and I was reported as a lost person to the police. The bananas came from my father. It's odd, really. He always came home with some fruit, then he set off again, like when you visit someone in hospital and you always take fruit with you.

It is a terrible thing to say but I think I hated my mother because she wasn't a proper mother. I hated her because she insisted on trying. I really wanted her to float about in the air instead of taking photographs of me all the time with that old Leica. I sat there with my pretty curls grinning at the frozen eye of the Leica, and I knew that the woman behind the camera was busy taking pictures so she could take my soul and send it off as a postcard to my father who was somewhere on the other side of the globe. She was a volcanic island and I tried to become the sea around her pain. That was all I could think of doing at that time. I desperately wished I had never been born at all and that's the most desperate wish I've had in my life. And then this terrible feeling of shame at having all this hatred pent up inside me made me even more invisible. Maybe I am unfair now but I actually believe that she killed me. She was a friendly angel who killed me and she was the only thing I had. My father was always somewhere, loading his bananas. Even before I could walk, I loved her and told myself that it didn't matter that she was killing me. I understood her all right. It would have been stupid not to. One day we'd both be reborn again anyway.

But I got more worried every time I had to go into the bedroom to ask for money. That way I was making sure there would never be any reconciliation between us. My only solution was to become a home nurse myself!

'Don't worry, mum. I'll fix it.'

What a terrible lie!

Why do small children always have to be so dirty? Why do children always have to break things? Why did I always fall into the canal? Why did I sit on that rubbish dump, why did I lose my glasses, why did I cut my fingers, why did I need to eat, and why can't children look after the electric mangle in the basement by themselves?

Is dust created out of nothing? Is it harmful to people with lung disease? Can the vacuum cleaner suck the dust out of the air? How does a child prepare a sauce?

I'd have to ask Little Frog these questions. She lent me a hand. We became a double set of grandparents to ourselves, that's how sensible we were. To her it was just a game, to me it was deadly serious. She comforted me tirelessly when I realized on my way back from the dairy that I wasn't as big as I had thought. Even though I tried to be my own father and mother too, I was still just as small. That meant that the milk bottle always broke on the first step on the stairs. It's no use crying over spilt milk, people say. They don't know how spilt milk can turn into a nightmare which

161

grows daily. The first step was relentless. Crash! I had done it again. Life on the way home with a simple bottle was such a nightmare that I'd rather not think about it.

What was my brother doing in the meantime?

I think he was down the cellar, smoking most of the time. Like he said: he belonged to a lost generation anyway.

Sure enough, the day came when they took away my mother in an ambulance. She didn't even have the strength to say that we had won again.

The high clear autumn air seeped through the narrow chink of the kitchen window. The ambulance men were not in a hurry as usual. I was standing where they couldn't see me, but I could still see out of the window. They were so slow in their movements that the whole of Happy Heights managed to witness our defeat. The family was split like an atom. Some small kids were hanging around on their bikes, trying to look into the ambulance. Now, if I'd had my brother's air gun I would have shot them down, one after the other. I completely forgot that I used to chase after ambulances and fire engines myself because I liked looking at really gory accidents.

Once I saw someone who'd lost his head. Literally, I mean. They just swept up the pieces and poured the leftovers into a bucket. I really felt sorry for that guy. Both my mother and me were still in one piece after all. And she was quite pretty too, because I had helped her comb her hair and put a cardigan on.

I pretended we were all taking part in a film. She was like Greta Garbo, pale and beautiful. She tried to lift her hand to wave at me. I walked away from the window because I didn't want to be seen. The door closed. The ambulance did a U-turn and disappeared. It neither flashed its lights nor used its sirens, but it drove so fast that nobody was sure where they were going. Honestly, I don't understand how the ambulance got there. I had just got home by chance two hours earlier. 'By chance' is not the right expression, perhaps. I was sent home with a long letter which explained that I would need special treatment if I didn't listen to reason. I knew that's what it said, because I read the letter as soon as the ambulance had left. It wasn't the ideal time to hand over a letter like that to my mother. She'd only have worried and that would have been silly.

The letter was about an accident that had happened to Monkey, my best friend. We called him that because he was so good at

162

making funny faces. The two of us had hanged ourselves in the gym after writing farewell letters to our teacher: 'Sorry, but we are no good at apparatus.' Our teacher rushed in and fainted almost at once when she found us dangling there from the wall bars. It looked quite real, you see. But you must not joke about death like that, of course. We certainly could do with some special treatment.

I sat on my mother's bed and read the letter again and again, but there was a lot in it that I didn't understand. My head was emptier than a squashed punch-bag. I was obviously a good candidate for special treatment. Sooner or later it would come out. I might as well hang myself for real. Or move into the attic at least and hide there to avoid special treatment – not to mention the children's home!

It really was time to pack my belongings.

I got up and paced about a bit, but couldn't make up my mind what to do. And suddenly I found myself standing there looking into a box of necklaces and other trinkets. I held a necklace up to the mirror. Brooches, silver jewellery and other bits and pieces in the box; they were mainly things she'd made herself during previous visits to the sanatorium. And there were the drawers full of her secret clothes. At last I could find out something about the person who was my mother!

Her clothes were hanging in the wardrobe. I inhaled the smell from them, moved about inside, stood in the wardrobe and felt the clothes against my burning cheeks. Her underwear was in the chest of drawers. Slowly, I pulled them out. In the first drawer on the left there were some letters from my father. Did he say anything about me? The underwear was all jumbled up. White and pink. And suddenly the tension made me feel sick. My hands trembled and my stomach made some violent leaps towards the palate. Before I knew what was happening my back arched as if a giant had taken a firm hold of my neck and pressed it down towards the drawer. I threw up into her underwear. Her letters were covered by a yellowish cascade.

Oh mother! I couldn't stop. Again and again, my body bent over in violent pain. And my sick covered your secret hiding-places while my tears blinded me and I tried to tell myself now and again to stop, but in the end I fell down on the floor.

I had not cleaned properly under the two beds. The dust clouds reigned there like obstinate proprietors, but I killed my reluctance and crawled in among them for want of anything better to do. Surely I'd be sucked up and carried off as well if I lay there long enough? But what about my deposits in the chest of drawers? And the letter from my teacher? Who would tidy up after me?

I had to clean up before I left.

I actually managed to pull out the drawer and carry it to the bathroom while I closed my eyes and held my breath. I had a stomachache and the stench wafted up to my nostrils. I tipped the whole drawer, contents and all, into the bathtub. It was a long time since she'd taken those photographs of me and my brother in the bath when we were naked and laughing.

Now the same evil-doer was standing there with the hand shower, flushing away his horrible imprints. And as if that wasn't enough I couldn't stop crying, however much I tried. I flushed and squirted and had a vague inkling of someone ringing the doorbell.

Who could it be?

Life is like one of those games where you build up your pyramid and knock it down again. Once it's been knocked down you should stop. I know that, but unfortunately I don't follow my own advice. I get quite obsessed about it and I think everything is going to be all right, if only I can build another pyramid. Now the simplest thing to do when the doorbell started to ring would be not to open it, of course, but instead I thought I could clean out the drawers so I chucked everything into the toilet – the letters were illegible anyway and my mother would probably get new underwear where she was going. So I put the seat down, flushed the toilet and ran into the hall to open the front door.

It was the Manufacturer. I could tell straightaway just by looking at his knee caps when I bumped into them. His muscular hand lifted my chin and raised my reluctant head so he could have a proper look at me.

'Let me have a look at you. Don't be sad now.'

What did he mean by that? He didn't have a clue about how sad I was.

I had to get him out of the flat quickly. If he stayed he'd probably ask me to sing and be happy as a lark. The only thing I could come up with on the spur of the moment was that I had caught it too. We actually had a medical examination twice a year to check if we'd caught TB. That's when they'd tell you if you had a period of grace in this vale of tears. I tried unsuccessfully to warn the Manufacturer about coming into the flat, but he just pushed me further and further towards the bedroom door, even though I put up a lot of resistance. In the end, he got angry and carried me out of the way. I lay there on the floor looking at his back when he opened the bedroom door. He started to shake. What was he doing? Was he crying? Why did he do that?

I was so surprised I almost forgot to be sad myself and I even thought of crawling over to him to comfort him. Maybe I should tell him how Bo Larsson got a javelin right through his chest, but just at that moment water started to pour into the room from the toilet. Despite his height he noticed the approaching flood at once and asked me in typical grown-up fashion what it was. Surely he could tell! At moments like that there is no point in lying. I told him that it was water and I made a quick sprint for the front door. But no joy. His arm was quicker than a lizard's tongue and longer than the arm of the law. His bony hand fastened on to my neck and I was taken into the bathroom where the toilet had overflowed of course. I closed my eyes, but the scene was just as dreadful when I opened them again. The Manufacturer was not prepared for this, I must admit. I think something must have burst inside him. I think he wanted to hit me because he swung round with his long arm as much as the bathroom walls allowed, but then he froze, halfway. It was horrible to see how he froze like that, with one hand raised and the other like a steel ribbon screwed tightly round my neck. The seconds kept ticking away while we stared at each other.

Now if you stare into the eyes of a tiger it always looks away in the end. You've got to establish eye contact before it starts feasting on you. Try for yourself when you next get a chance. I am sure I must have spent hundreds of hours staring at tigers.

I know what I am talking about, even if there has always been a fence between me and the tiger. Maybe it's got something to do with the struggle of will. Civilization against nature. Who knows. Ask Kipling.

The Manufacturer and I soared through time and space while he was thinking about knocking my head off or maybe I was a goner already. I was in the process of formulating the most courageous sentence of my life: I was going to tell him that I would kill him if he so much as touched a hair on my head. But I didn't say it and he didn't hit me. He must have realized that it wasn't worth it, after all. In the end, he lowered his arm and just grunted. I promised not to run away while he cleaned up in the toilet. God knows what he was thinking about in there, but when he came out again he sat down on the bed and said that we had to talk things through, he and I.

'Look at me.'

It's a kind of tiger's trick which is part of the art of taming little children. With open ingenuous eyes you're meant to answer clearly and without guile when spoken to.

I was thinking about the Manufacturer. He was sad and he obviously wanted to be my friend. But I couldn't understand what he had to do with us. So I decided to look at him and ask him straight out.

I should never have done that. He looked so upset that I could almost have sworn it wasn't faked. First I had to promise never to do it again, and that was no problem. Then we promised that we'd help each other. That was a bit more difficult, but I had to. Like Jack London said: 'I'd finished all my matches and it was fiendishly cold. What should I do?' I had two alternatives, either the children's home or I could promise the Manufacturer that I'd improve as a person. He'd let me come home with him because he couldn't just leave me there.

'I don't think you realize what your mother meant to me once.'

That's what he said. And I could have said the same thing about the same person, but I didn't bother. Grown-ups are happy as long as they can tell children about their feelings. He got so carried away that he asked me to sit on his lap. So I did. I wandered over to him and climbed up. Like a parrot without claws, trying to get a grip on his perch, I clambered up on his rickety leg and wanted to try my wings and fly away!

But where to?

He stroked my hair and promised he'd fix everything. I hate saying it, but I told myself: Here is a person you can really trust. And that's how I came to end up in his home.

You have to measure justice in some way. In metres or in money. Before, I hadn't been eligible for school dinners because we lived too near the school. Mother tried to persuade someone, I don't know who, but it was quite impossible. When I lived with the Manufacturer, however, I was suddenly several metres further away so I was granted school dinners for the first time in my life. It was just like a self-service restaurant. The only thing you couldn't help yourself to was the cod liver oil. In fact, that was the condition for getting into the dining-hall. We formed an endless queue outside and passed the table where the person on duty would dish out the cod liver oil. The dining-hall was in the basement of the school and the corridor with the single window was like paradise if you wanted to squeeze a girl's breasts, for instance. It always sounded like a night in the jungle down there. At first there was just the general noise, then a mad scream and after that a completely uninhibited cackling and babbling until the person in charge of law and order got fed up and shouted and screamed at us. That's how it went on while the queue slowly meandered forward and the first victim had to close his eyes, open his mouth and swallow that disgusting cod liver oil. I was beside myself with excitement. The procedure with the cod liver oil was like a shop window, something you could forget about. Besides, I had never tasted cod liver oil before. That's why it was too late to refuse it when it slid down my throat like a rotten snake. The delicious food in front of me suddenly made my stomach turn. I picked at the bits on the plate. Not burned anywhere. That's what I call professional handling of first-class products. My cookery teacher would definitely have marked the plate I had in front of me with an A.

But I had only started eating when people suddenly got up from their tables. I'd finished my milk, but that had only given me a temporary relief. The smell of cod liver oil was at the level of my eyebrows at that point. It made me want to die on the spot and it was incomprehensible to me how children could get well from something so disgusting. I cast some furtive glances around me to see if I could leave my food, but I was surrounded by other unhappy comrades and towering above me was a teacher who asked in a friendly way if perhaps the food didn't appeal to me?

It was fried herring and mashed potatoes with cranberries, and under normal circumstances I would have been happy to have two or three helpings of it. But instead I made a mountain of the mash, built terraces in it and cut the golden brown and fast cooling herring into little squares and laid them out like little houses. I used the small green sprigs of dill as bushes and trees, and made a red lake at the foot of the mountain out of the cranberries. The only thing missing was the sun. Instead, there were hundreds of thunder clouds sailing above the mountain before it was gobbled up. I quickly ran to the toilet and threw up.

The afternoon passed as if I'd been under an anaesthetic, that's how weak I felt. Normally I was quite lively during lessons, but that afternoon even I managed to get an encouraging look from my teacher. She regarded my condition as an improvement. The Manufacturer had a long conversation with her and I was on probation after that. It was the cod liver oil that saved me from the special treatment. All through the autumn I threw up all that wonderful food. I wasn't my old self any more. I would have loved those school dinners, I would have loved to be able to swallow that cod liver oil, just for the sake of it, but I just couldn't.

And you don't push other people out of the way when you're a guest in someone else's house. I was withdrawn when I was staying with the Manufacturer. He had a wife and two children. Funny, because I had always imagined him as a bachelor. There is not much to say about the wife. She was as fat as he was tall. It wouldn't have mattered which way up she'd decided to stand. She was like a clumsy building block that bumped into every-thing in the kitchen. Their children were a boy and a girl, the girl was tall and the boy was fat. That is one of life's ironies. The boy was going to be a manufacturer when he grew up and the girl was going to be a manufacturer's wife. I hope they succeeded even though their measurements were all wrong. Sometimes I feel a little sad when I think about them. Even if I have a memory like an elephant I still realize that they have their problems too and one can't avenge everything in life. The Manufacturer's son followed in his father's footsteps and, like him, started in the cellar. They had their own cellar in their house because they lived in a detached house. The boy was always playing with his enormous model train set down there. On my first day in their home I was allowed to have a look at it. Then he threatened to kill me if I as much as took one step inside the cellar.

But I didn't mind. I have never felt as empty as I did then. I was like a glass jar with the inside greased with cod liver oil. As soon as I opened my mouth there was a stench of rotten fish, so I preferred to keep quiet. I even forgot to ask myself how it would all end. The questions fizzled out on the starting track like cheap little rockets which never took off. They just smoked and died like a silent fart. Life was dark and empty and I cycled from the posh area where they lived across the railway bridge over the canal, past the Great Wall of China and up to the school, where most days resembled any other. I served my time at school. I opened my mouth and closed it again full of that rotten taste of cod liver oil. I tried to distribute the taste with the help of some portions of my school dinner. I threw up in the toilet and I tried to touch some girls' breasts, but without too much enthusiasm – and I crapped like well-oiled lightning every morning and night. In other words, I was slowly disappearing from the face of the earth. My speech was far from sweet, my body was not ivory work nor was my appearance like Lebanon, choice as the cedars – if that gives you an idea of how I looked.

Sometimes I worried about my best friend, Sickan. How was she?

And where was my sister? What was my brother doing? How did my mother feel at that sanatorium?

Because that's where she was, wasn't it?

All they told me was that my brother was crazy. The Manufacturer's son told me that every night just as I'd gone off to sleep. He shook me until I woke again and there I was in bed, staring into his fat serious hippopotamus face which was all wrinkled up with envy as he told me about my brother's pranks in the class. My brother was in the form below his at the grammar school. I heard some really encouraging things, mind you. He kept up the old standard. Now that he was alone in our flat he was converting it into a place for parties where certain daring girls from the girls' school used to go. According to the Manufacturer's son my brother had screwed his way through the whole girls' school already and would become the father of the year in our town before the year was up. It's funny how time flies. It is only six months since he stood there by the dump and was jealous of my episode with Little Frog.

The whole point of those reports was to frighten me, of course, but I only regarded the stories as logical consequences of what I already knew about my brother. I turned over and went back to sleep again, leaving the jealous hippo face behind me.

And the autumn got colder and colder. And I sailed away from people as if they were foreign harbours that I hadn't been very fond of anyway.

It was only the Manufacturer and me who maintained a kind of contact. Strangely enough, he seemed to like me. Sometimes he'd call me into his study and then he'd ask me how everything was going. My monosyllabic WELL made him happy and he immediately wanted me to sit on his lap, so I climbed up. Why bite the hand that feeds you, I thought. Besides, he was some kind of engineer and could have been my Weedon Scott. In theory, at least.

It is quite funny with memories and sights and sounds. You sometimes think you can stop seeing and listening, but memory keeps playing its gramophone records without a break. You cannot close your eyes because the images unfold in one enormous reel after the other. My grandfather would have said that the sound lies in the brain in a horizontal line, like records, while images stand up vertically like film reels. Then they mesh into each other in some wonderful interplay. Sometimes it is only sounds, sometimes it's just pictures and now and then it is synchronized. But most of the time the projectionist is drunk and without judgement. He refuses to work at all for some people and for others he works overtime. He definitely worked overtime for the Manufacturer as soon as I sat on his lap. The trouble was he kept showing the same old reel over and over again. It was just memories from the choir with my mother's angelic voice and him full of admiration for her. He wanted me to understand how beautifully they'd sung together, so he kept repeating the same tunes in my ear until I was hard of hearing. I might as well have listened to him from the kitchen. But as I told you, I sat on his lap and controlled myself while he slowly blocked my right ear with his saliva. It is probably thanks to that that I have escaped life-long injuries from all those hymns.

I sat there thinking about my time as a cowboy. That was the effect the Manufacturer's lap had on me. I sat there remembering the summer when we were all going to have a proper holiday and rent a cottage as far away from my grandparents as possible, as my mother put it. She thought we ought to be all by ourselves for once. We moaned because we loved the summers with grandmother and grandfather, but she got what she wanted. And the summer really turned out marvellously, but for her things were as usual. She fell ill. But my brother and I had a good time anyway. We decided to practice cow-riding in a field. It was all right for the first three metres or so, but after that we fell off. And after three days the cows were so fed up with us that they ran away all the way to Sölvesborg's railway station. Those who didn't drown in the harbour were run over. No, now I am exaggerating again. It was only one cow that died. But judging by the farmer it sounded as if the whole herd had kicked the bucket.

We had forgotten to close the gate behind us, that was the trouble. There was talk of 'public liability' and various insurance policies that time as well, and the atmosphere got worse and worse between the old farmhouse where we were staying and the newly built cottage where the farmer spent the summer. It got even gloomier when we discovered that the chimney was blocked and he refused to do anything about it. The kitchen range was smoking all the time, so my brother and I moved into the back yard where we put up a tent. It was only my mother and sister who slept in the smoky room in the house. We were convinced that we'd wake up one morning and find their bodies in there like smoked herrings.

My mother never managed to get out of doors and that was a great pity. The archipelago of Blekinge was so shallow that it was perfectly safe for children. It was quite impossible to drown around there, however much we tried. We waded between the islands and pulled our dinghy behind us. As soon as we thought that the dinghy was afloat we hoisted the bathrobe on the two crossed oars and shouted that we were sailing, but then we got stuck again because the boat always sank an inch or so every time we jumped in.

That's how it was and I could go on thinking about that summer for a long time, but it makes me just as sad as everything else so I won't bother. I sometimes think of those days as a string of glittering festivities, like one huge fireworks display against the backdrop of the jet black night. It is fun while it lasts, but then everything turns black again. Just as black as when we came home that time and saw her coughing by the wood range and decided to go out again.

It is no good having fun when you have a bad conscience about it. A sort of chemical obsession is engendered in the body all the time. I don't even want to think about it.

Sometimes when the Manufacturer was really in his reminiscing mood he might show me a photo album with pictures of my mother and a lot of other people who had been in that choir. He always flicked past the same couple of pages. I noticed it at once and wondered what he was hiding from me, of course. So one afternoon I sneaked in and found the secret pages myself. There was nothing special about them at all, just my mother and him on an excursion by a lake. She was leaning against a birch tree, laughing; she was wearing a flimsy summer dress. And in another picture they were both standing in front of a car. It was mostly pictures like that, nothing odd about them at all, really. You could tell that they were very good friends. I have seen other pictures with her by lakes and the seaside, in gardens and in front of cars. It is those sort of things that people keep.

The only person who didn't like those pictures was the Manufacturer's wife, of course. Sometimes she was strange and sulky with me. Maybe she didn't realize it herself, but I could sense something in the air which worried me. It went up my nose like a warning which I couldn't understand, but I knew it was there all right. I have a nose for things like that. I plant my roots in other people's nerve ends as soon as I can, in order to sniff around and see if there is something wrong. And the reason why I am still so surprised every time something happens is that I have a great ability for wanting what's best for me.

I soon imagined I was quite well off at the Manufacturer's. It could have been worse.

One day the Manufacturer gathered us all together. It didn't take too long because there weren't that many of us. It looked as if it was going to snow. It was a grey cold Saturday morning and we were all given new clothes before the shops closed. My plastic jacket with reflective bands was exchanged for a blue duffle-coat which looked 'nicer'.

New clothes are not something that come as a surprise, usually. But in my life there was always a reason for new clothes, apart from the fact that children grow out of them, I mean.

The only things about me that grew that autumn were my nails, but that is true of corpses too, I've heard.

Why do I always have such morbid thoughts?

Especially when we travel through undulating countryside where some late autumn leaves are falling in the rich silence, which is the perfect setting for a sanatorium. Dressed up like two dolls my sister and I sit there holding hands while my brother gives us satisfactory reports about his school work. The Manufacturer smiles approvingly. I knew that my brother was making it all up and that he really wanted the Manufacturer to get stuffed, but I didn't say anything. I just shivered in my new duffle-coat which I had chosen myself. All the others wore black ones, but I had chosen a dove-blue coat with black toggles. I thought it looked different.

A sanatorium is a mixture between a prison and a castle. It always lies in such a remote place that no one can catch the disease, except those who are already there. In the summer, people wander about in parks and on terraces, deep in thought like in old pictures. The only difference is their dress. In the winter the same people sit in big rooms and become artistic and intelligent. They make jewellery of silver threads and clay, they make pots on the wheel if they have the strength and they read and talk seriously about life. On the whole, you can meet any kind of person there and that's why you get wiser there than in other places where you only meet people like yourself. In a sanatorium everyone is mixed up together and you can't see where they come from. I know all that because my mother became so intelligent and refined in the end. Every time she came home from one of her stays she brought with her some strange habits. Suddenly she might be eating grapefruit and drinking tea instead of coffee. Just things like that. Grandfather who was still eating with his hands and one knife was mortified when his daughter pointed out, in a venomous way, that he was a hundred years behind his time when it came to table manners. And we've had drawn-out struggles about things like the size of coffee cups. She bought small narrow ones so we couldn't dip our bread in them. My God, we who'd been raised on grandmother's dipping – small white squares of bread and butter floating about in the coffee with double cream and lots of sugar. Was she going to deny us feasts like that in the future? We started to cut the bread up into long narrow strips just so we could carry on dipping them. The struggle got tougher. Guess who won in the end? Nowadays I am ashamed as soon as I think of grandmother's disgusting habits and grandfather's slurping noise when he drinks from his saucer.

That's the sort of place a sanatorium is. If you manage to get out of it again, then you're not the same person as before, anyway. You've been in a crucible where everything is mixed up together under very intense heat. Come to think of it, my father must have been dazzled by it all. Maybe the Manufacturer was too? Why else would he sit there behind the wheel and take on tasks he didn't have to?

The tall long building with the gravel path leading up to the white double staircase which seemed to welcome us with a sweeping gesture looked more like a ship in the forest than anything else. Quietly and with determination it chugged along with its fragile cargo. We dreaded going inside and couldn't understand why the Manufacturer sounded so cheerful.

Did all visitors have to wear a mask, I wondered. Would it help if we held our breath? Were we allowed to touch her? What if she were full of some new crazy ideas? I could just imagine her kissing us on the cheek. We'd die on the spot, if she did.

We walked slowly along the corridor as if we were in some cool silent dream, huddled together, like a ball of fear. Whatever happened we would manage somehow. We were going to at least look cheerful as the Manufacturer wanted us to. Visiting sick people isn't easy. It is an art. When you're with a sick person it's like pushing some enormous beach ball under the water – without letting on that you're doing it. And because you're the healthy one you take on all the trouble. You just skid a bit and the ball comes up like a cannon ball splashing everyone in sight.

Fruit is another thing you must bring. I'd forgotten that.

Shouldn't we have brought her some grapes? I asked the Manufacturer, but got no answer from him. He'd already suppressed all his secrets so much that he didn't have time to think of anything else. He radiated nervousness; it flared up and gave off smoke in all directions when he decided to organize us in order of size on a wooden bench in the hospital corridor while he disappeared through a door.

Perhaps she was in there. But it could have been an office. My brother pointed at the belt on his new trenchcoat and hinted that we should take off our overcoats. I shook my head and looked at the highly polished black and white floor tiles instead. You never know what you might catch if you take your coat off. Better keep it on. The black and white floor squares were swimming before my eyes as if they were covered by water and that water was suddenly put into motion by a slight breeze. It was me crying, of course. I could never stop leaking. I swallowed and swallowed my brother's taunting remarks and my sister's surprised earnestness. Poor thing. She didn't have a clue. In fact, she looked surprised more than anything, as if she had no business there in the first place.

Maybe that was the best attitude. You could pretend you weren't there at all even if my brother couldn't stop teasing me. In a way, he and I resemble each other. The only difference is that he is two years older than me and he is up to all sorts of things which

I hope to God I'll never have to do. I am not beating about the bush. If I grow any older I hope it will be a quick process so that I am back in my second childhood in a flash. I admit it may be a little disgusting with incontinence and all that, but you're spared a lot of trouble that way. There is always someone trained to look after old people too.

At last the Manufacturer's narrow face appeared again. When we saw it, we huddled together even more, but he beckoned to us and whispered urgently that he wanted us to go in, one at a time, and finally we obliged. My brother was the first to go. Maybe it was not more dangerous than going to the doctor's.

I know many of my friends who have never thought of running away from themselves, but when I was waiting there on the bench looking at the grey weather and the snowflakes falling outside the large picture window at the end of the corridor I saw how I stepped out of myself like a spirit and tiptoed away across the black and white tiled floor. The person sitting on the bench wasn't me at all. It was just a copy of me which people might think was the real me. From then on I was going to regard myself as a temporary hotel without any rights or staff to run the place. I let other people mix with this copy of myself to keep it company. God knows where the real me got to.

It was my turn. We exchanged a few brotherly looks which were full of messages and questions when we passed each other in the doorway where the Manufacturer was acting as caretaker.

I had imagined an enormous ward with lots of beds in a row, just like when I was paralysed for three months in hospital, but it wasn't like that at all. My mother had a room all to herself. It was so small that I was almost pushed up against the bed-end at once. As if to compensate, the ceiling was very high, like a kind of lift shaft for sick people. I couldn't tell whether it was going up or down, but I wanted to get off at once. Luckily the Manufacturer's hand squeezed my right shoulder so hard that I almost screamed out loud. I was full of a kind of chummy gratitude and allowed myself to get pushed forward. She took my hand. That alone was really strange and it made me look in two directions at once. .

And then we started to press our ghastly beach ball under the water, but it was mostly she who kept nattering away and I just answered yes or no all the time.

It wasn't too bad, really. She looked more beautiful than I remembered her. Her paleness had given way to a kind of glow.

She was definitely the thin interesting sort. Her large full mouth, painted a deep red for the occasion, her straight bold nose, dark eyebrows with the determined angle which she'd inherited from grandfather; her almost green eyes with yellow flecks in them, her black hair with some grey streaks and large natural waves . . . it was decent of them to make her so attractive for our sake.

After a few minutes I decided that it was possible to breathe normally again and I was even prepared to say something about my new adventures, but I was promptly led to the door by the Manufacturer's firm hand. He didn't let go of me for a moment. Time was running out. What was I going to say? The words were spinning round in my head. What was the most important thing to remember? I knew it could be a long time before I saw her again. Why couldn't I squeeze out a single word? I struggled free, rushed up to the bed again and made a shy circle on her blanket.

'What would you like for Christmas?'

Funny how cogs keep going round in our little world, groaning and grunting reluctantly as if they had retired long ago and now wanted to rest in peace. They balance unevenly and wobble, but soon pick up speed again with a sigh thanks to one single drop of oil.

In the far distance and after what seemed an endless silence I could hear her answer.

'Anything will do. You know what I like.'

And here she held out her hand and together we managed to get those cogs going again. We had a future together. Happy as a sandboy I tore open the door and shouted to my brother that he'd have to give me half his pocket money.

I knew exactly what she wanted!

Funnily enough, my brother was very surly and unwilling when I put forward my proposal. I cycled down to see him one evening after having prayed that our flat wouldn't be too full of filth, but he just sat there quietly poring over his homework like any other anxious half-grown grammar school boy. He must have pulled himself together, as the Manufacturer put it. There was something wrong with him. First of all, he made an effort to try and be friendly in a sulky sort of way, and secondly, he was busy carving a great big hole in the table top when I tried to tell him how happy mum would be if we gave her a toaster for Christmas. Preferably we should buy one of those you see in magazines where the slices always pop up by themselves. Having one of those must be great fun, I thought. But we could also make do with a simpler toaster if he didn't want to spend too much money. What did he think of it?

That's how I carried on. And he made a bigger and bigger hole in the table. It was my table as well, as I pointed out in the end. I looked at the hole with horror because I knew that sooner or later I would get the blame for it. That's how it is when you share a room with an older brother. Nobody believes that a mature and confident grammar school boy would carve a big hole in a table. I sighed and tried to bargain with him.

What if he paid a third, or just as much as he could afford?

He didn't answer. Soon he'd carved right through the table. Maybe it was a practical exercise in Physics? 'If a boy by means of his right arm – used here as a lever – carves a hole with a knife etc. . . .' I got fed up with him and started to mope around the flat. In a way, I was quite proud of him, though. He'd suddenly grown up in one fell swoop and now he was managing by himself in our flat. It is only a three-room flat, but all the same. The glass door to the living-room was locked, as always. We had got used to not going in there. We'd rather stand outside pressing our noses against the glass as if looking through a glass case in a museum. There were the two armchairs, the sofa and the table with a glass top to protect the inlay. Then the bookcases, two of them. I knew the titles by heart. Pride of place was given to Dickens, Jack London, Selma Lagerlöf, Kipling, Strindberg . . . Selma Lagerlöf's books were the most beautiful ones. Leather and gold leaf with supple pages which fell into place by themselves when you opened the book to read one of those scary fairytales where death went galloping after a frothy four-in-hand.

The large heavy linen cupboard which mother never opened when aunties or other fussy people came to inspect inevitably developed into a kind of tug-of-war where mother always ended up the winner. The others were furious because of her apparent unwillingness to understand their curiosity – and now I was nosing around in there just to check what was left of it.

Everything was in order: sheets and pillowcases were folded with the monogram up, the table-cloths were on rolls, if they were of the kind that needed to be on rolls, frilly bits and pieces organized in a way that was older than the alphabet. I couldn't understand why all mothers wanted to look at each other's linen cupboards. Why did some of my aunts voluntarily and importunately open the doors of theirs and force us to peer in as soon as we paid them a visit? And why did mother not want to show them hers? What besides orderliness could you expect to find in a linen cupboard?

There was the bureau where mother used to write her letters, always to my father and always asking for more money. She could account for every penny but it didn't make any difference. It was the actual inflow that wasn't sufficient.

I couldn't see the dining-room table and chairs. I could count on one hand the times we had eaten there.

With my back to the living-room door I was facing her bedroom. I opened it quickly. Silence, cool and dark. The two twin beds looked severe and empty and they seemed to float in the reflection from a streetlamp.

Then there was the kitchen. My brother's housecleaning was nothing to write home about. The dust was already settling in the larder. The bread tin was carelessly opened. The bread would dry up before breakfast the next day and that would upset him. I felt sorry for him. Maybe he could not look after himself. He'd never coped very well in the kitchen. Something happened to his nerves when he was there. He'd mix anything together. Once he tried to cook some shoe polish. The tin exploded and we were short of a home nurse again. She refused to help a family who tried to assassinate her.

I knew my brother wouldn't be able to cope. I realized that and decided to offer to help him. I could move back home and look after the house while he was busy studying. I could become an English butler who always knew what was what, steady as a rock whether in the jungle or the brothel. I would be such a help that he wouldn't be able to do without me.

I stood there daydreaming along these lines with the stale bread in front of me when my brother came out and asked me what I was doing. It was time I went home. I must have stared at him without realizing it.

Home!

'Promise me one thing: forget about that toaster, will you?'

'I'll buy one myself then, you mean bugger.'

He got furious and exploded faster than the shoe polish, shook me and screamed and said that there wouldn't be a home at all soon and that there was no point in buying a toaster.

'She is dying, don't you understand? Dying!'

My brother has always been a great one for lying. He does it to avoid responsibilities. I got out of his grip and went into our room to have a look at the table again. It really was a proper hole. If I put my foot underneath I could see it as if looking through a camera lens. What was he going to destroy next? Could I find a witness? Any time now I'd be accused of doing it. I'd better push off. Anyway, I knew how to get hold of enough money for a toaster. He could keep his money. Pity though, that he had to lie. On the other hand, he wouldn't be able to enjoy that money for much longer. The knife was lying on the table beside the hole and all I had to do was to stick it in his back when he bent forward the tiniest little bit.

It was gory. Pure slaughter. I lost and he won as usual. He knocked me to the floor before I had a chance to touch him with the knife. My arm didn't seem to want to rise. I should have reckoned with that. He took the knife away from me and said I was lethal. Good thing he realized it, anyway.

After that he chucked me out. I warned him. Considering how thick he was, he just wouldn't be able to cope. He even thinks you can eat shoe polish. But then he told me, just before he slammed the door in my face, that there was alcohol in the shoe cream. My poor brother. He probably sat there eating shoe polish every day. How could I save him? What kind of a toaster should I buy? Remembering my mother's nerves I'd better not get the one where the slices pop up. That would probably just remind her of me.

I cycled to the Manufacturer's house mulling over the questions in my mind and I knew that he'd help me. The toaster was my last test. I wouldn't fail this time.

People always lie. It is as if we've got something wrong with our vision. We've had it so long that we can't get rid of it. We'd be completely confused if someone invented a corrective lens for all of us. Just look at the Manufacturer, for instance. He was always telling me how he started out in the basement with two empty hands. Not a word of it was true, though. He just liked the idea of it. In actual fact, it was his wife who started in the basement. And she didn't have empty hands either. She had her hands full of thin sharp slats which gradually turned into Venetian blinds.

They were also full of small children and food and dirty dishes and dirty laundry. And so time went by. Days and nights, whenever she had the time, she made new blinds and she became more and more accomplished and more and more short-sighted. And all she could see in the end were those rustling Venetian slats which she put together herself. What about the Manufacturer then? Well, he went out to sell and fix the ready-made goods. And he was good at it. There wasn't just one Sven Hansson but many Sven Hanssons who wanted to build a lot of fine houses after the war. In all those houses the Venetian blinds were an absolute must. Suddenly no one should be able to look in any more, but everyone should be able to look out, while remaining hidden behind those sharp rustling slats. That's how it was. And at the time of my story the Manufacturer was very big in blinds and his wife had nothing at all to do, because they had employed five people and there were lots of fitters around who all hoped to become manufacturers one day too.

And how did I come to know all this?

The wife certainly didn't put me on her lap, but she did go on about her role in the basement with nostalgia.

Once I actually asked her why they didn't swop roles so she could go out selling and fitting blinds. She was just as handy as he after all, wasn't she? But then she laughed with a funny sort of gurgling noise which I recognized in myself when I don't know whether to laugh or cry.

And I must say this: The truth is that grown-ups will screw anyone as soon as they get a chance. That's why they have Venetian blinds, you see. Or they discovered that they could have a go at it, after they'd bought them. I don't know which came first. But that is the root of all evil, anyway. That's why there's something wrong with their vision. There isn't one single lie that doesn't start with a screw, believe you me. And that is true of everybody, except my mother because she's always been ill. She's simply not had the opportunity. But all the others – the healthy ones – something cracked inside them during the war.

I know I sound a bit like my grandfather now, but that's the whole point. Now there's a person who doesn't need Venetian blinds.

But his kind is on the wane, I'm afraid. They don't make people like him any more.

And how come I know all this about Venetian blinds then?

Well, you see, the Manufacturer's son didn't want to distribute circulars on Saturday afternoons in the block of flats around where we lived. Every Saturday he made a great fuss about it. The Manufacturer wanted his son to learn the trade from the bottom so to speak, but the wife wanted him to do his homework so he could become something which had nothing to do with the Venetian blind business at all. Hippopotamus Junior didn't care one way or the other. He sat there playing with his model train set most of the time. If I as much as dared touch one of the levers, the whole thing would probably burn up completely. He was quite convinced of that. But as I didn't have any really grand plans for my future – all I wanted was a toaster – I suggested that I could hand out the circulars instead. So we struck a bargain. The Manufacturer was so pleased that he almost had tears in his eyes and he talked about me as a shining example. I worked out how many Saturdays I'd have to run up and down stairs and I was satisfied. It was going to be all right. But the wife, oddly enough, got upset even though she got it her way because now she had nothing to nag about any more. Maybe that's why she started to talk about her heroic efforts in the basement, I don't know. But the first Saturday when the fitters came to give an account of their work I added two and two together. They just talked about how many housewives they'd screwed. Up with the blinds, down with the slats, fuck the wife and then off to the next one. That was the Venetian blind fitter's daily routine. It was terrible. I had to keep a poker-face, although I knew jolly well that the Manufacturer's livelihood and our whole security was based on the fact that SHE had remained in the basement while HE had been fitting blinds and her laughter was really hollow because she knew it was impossible to reverse the roles.

The origin of this chronic visual defect in the human race is excessive fornication. It's only my mother who really escaped it all. But, on the other hand, I haven't heard her version of this. I think she must have seen it in the same way as me, though. 'And thereby I have cursed that which cried out to be cursed. And my tree shall be cut down and my heart shall be changed into an animal's heart if I am wrong.' I swear! My toaster, in other words, was practically sewn up. There was just one small thing that got in the way. Their son showed me his new boxing gloves which were made of a light green canvas material. Neither of us could understand what he wanted with a pair of boxing gloves with that heavy body of his, so we agreed to do business. He'd sell them to me secretly. It was his hopeful father who'd given him those boxing gloves, of course, but I didn't mind about the high price. I just thought how supple, quick and strong I'd be after running up and down all those stairs on Saturdays. The boxing gloves were like a mirage and with a name like mine you have certain obligations. But the scandalous price affected my plans for the toaster. What should I do? As my mother didn't know that I intended to give her a toaster anyway she couldn't very well get upset if she didn't get one.

Why did the boxing gloves have to come my way as a temptation?

I was torn to pieces every day. Boxing gloves or a toaster? Why a temptation like that?

And the truth is I'd very much like to know what my choice would have been, but now I shall never know. One day the Manufacturer came, unwittingly, to my rescue. I was the paragon of virtue – the A, B and C of how you bring up a child. Letter one, first paragraph. He offered to sell me a second-hand toaster which they had grown tired of themselves. Unfortunately, he couldn't give it to me because it was bad to get things without working for them, according to his ideas on upbringing. At this point he cast a furtive glance at his son, I must admit. He wasn't that stupid. In a way it was he who was the real object of the whole exercise. I was just a living example.

But the toaster was now almost within my reach. The boxing gloves would also be mine soon. Running up and down all those stairs was also good exercise and the cod liver oil kept my joints well lubricated and supple. I got thinner and thinner and I was actually beginning to believe that I was an indestructible piece of machinery which could tick away inside the glass jar. Everything went like clockwork. But I wasn't present myself.

I don't know whether it was due to my angelic appearance or my unnaturally quiet behaviour that autumn, but my teacher asked me if I wanted to play one of Father Christmas' children at the Annual Festival of Light. I didn't mind one way or the other, but I was glad to have an opportunity to meet Sven Hansson at last. I am sure politicians are quite used to people being sick all over them, but I was going to apologize all the same. The Queen of Light and all her attendants usually performed in the People's

Park on an initiative from Sven Hansson. Our class was taking part and our teacher was so nervous that her capped teeth were clattering when she described our happiness. The girls were rehearsing as Lucia's attendants and the boys as little Brownies. The costumes which were generally of rough homespun were made by eager mothers during cosy evenings in the bosom of the family while their rosy children were making happy noises and the father of the house was smoking his pipe and reading his newspaper and in the background the radio would be playing Christmas carols.

I know how things ought to be, that's the whole problem. And I too would like to live like that. It is only the people who have experienced those cosy evenings who can dispense with them and despise them. It is difficult to throw away something you have never had. Just think, a parade of little Brownies walking across the open-air stage with flickering candles in their hands and thousand of parents wiping away a tear. You can't say no to that now, can you?

The problem was that I didn't have my rough homespun. I thought for a while of asking all the nurses in town to make me a kind of council costume from all their hospital blankets. They were all grey, after all, and could easily be mistaken for homespun. Besides, they should have a certain feeling of compassion for me baked into their training: my long golden tresses must have become legendary with the years and must have helped to strengthen their feeling for their vocation. I dismissed the thought as unrealistic. The Manufacturer's wife had to help me instead. And she was quite happy to, as a matter of fact. She also used the proper material. For an extra special effect I was allowed to borrow a red cord from an old dressing-gown so now I could happily put my name down for the Brownies' parade. The other mothers hadn't made proper Brownie costumes at all. They preferred more colour, more red, so we were a rather motley crowd of Brownies who ended up in the gym where we practised walking on tiptoe and singing 'Tip, tap, tip, tap'. And I can assure you that rough homespun is a sturdy sort of material. As we started tiptoeing around, the material started to chafe and itch all over my body and the sweat was pouring down my face.

In the end our teacher was pleased with us and the day came when we were going to invade the People's Park on tiptoe. The dance hall we used could take up to 2,000 people at least. I think there must have been 4,000 people there. The air was heavy with parents' expectations that morning of St Lucia's Day. As soon as the electric lights were switched off, we were supposed to move forward with our lighted lanterns, singing 'Tip, tap'. Then we were going to stand in a semicircle on the stage waiting for St Lucia herself and all her attendants. It was very exciting. We stood there squashed together in a dark corridor waiting with our lanterns. In my rustic costume, which definitely would have been suitable for a trip to the North Pole by sleigh, I quickly evaporated while someone else forgot their lines. Nobody had a cigarette lighter. Our teacher couldn't very well stand there by the door lighting one lantern at a time with a match. Some more rational method was called for. And guess who rushed forward to solve the problem? Sven Hansson in person!

All the Brownies' candles were lit in a jiffy and we accelerated forward to start our tiptoeing into the dark hall. Here was his great chance at last to thank me for burning that dump to the ground. Everything went very smoothly. I smiled at him and held up my lantern so that he could recognize my sweaty shiny face. We must have stared at each other for several seconds like that. His foul-smelling petrol lighter was flickering before my eyes and too late I realized that my grinning face must have looked really malevolent and he probably thought I was capable of burning down the whole People's Park with Brownies, St Lucia, her attendants, parents and all!

I shook my head vigorously. In front of me the other Brownies started to tiptoe away and their whispering song echoed TIP TAP in my head while he, like a true man of action, pushed me behind the door and held me in a steady grip there.

It wasn't even worth screaming.

Anyway, I couldn't, the way he was pressing me. I was completely flattened.

I should have been the third man from the right in the procession. Those who were really observant would have noticed that my side was one man short compared to the other and those with a taste for history can check with the newspaper which took the photographs at the event.

I was not there.

I cycled home furiously in my costume. Sven Hansson didn't even speak to me. He just let go of the door when everything was over and disappeared. One day the hour of revenge will come, that is something I know for sure.

When I got home to the Manufacturer's everything was upside down. That is, the Manufacturer himself was at home, which was not usual at that time of day. I had already made up my mind not to go to school any more. They could do what they liked, but it had to be without me. First I was going to fix my mother's Christmas present and then I'd be off and away. It didn't matter where to. A Brownie can always manage somehow. Everyone would put porridge out for the Brownies now that it was close to Christmas, anyway.

I closed the kitchen door behind me and got the toaster out. It was mine now. We'd finalized the deal. I had cleaned it up and it was almost like new. The Manufacturer had promised to take it up to the sanatorium and I could come as well, if I wanted to. Everything was wrapped up, as Father Christmas would have said.

That's when I noticed that everything was upside down. The Manufacturer and his wife suddenly appeared in the doorway and his tall body was making strange movements. He didn't seem surprised to find me at home at this time, he just looked at me in a detached sort of way as if he hadn't noticed that I was there before. My heart started to race. I knew what he was going to say even before he had opened his mouth. I left the parcel with the toaster in the kitchen while I crawled after him into his study and climbed up on his lap.

He cleared his throat and told me that my mother was dead.

But I must not be sad. It was all for the best. She had struggled for months and she had suffered terribly. Now it was all over and there was nothing in the whole world that we could do about it.

I hated him.

Waves of hatred flared up in my chest and I almost suffocated. My mother had been past cure for a long time, but they had still let me save up for their rotten old toaster. That was the last time I was going to trust anybody.

As it was a normal schoolday and their own little hippopotamus was still at school, they let me play with his model train set as a consolation. I played with it all day and all evening. And the Manufacturer must have locked his son in the wardrobe later, because he didn't turn up and he didn't kill me as he'd promised.

TOOT, TOOT. I drove up to the Arctic tundra and loaded the

train with presents for all the good little children everywhere.

TOOT, TOOT. I drove down to the equator and fetched bananas for all the sick children.

TOOT, TOOT. I bought a single ticket for myself and disappeared from there.

That night I cried, but I pulled the cover over my head so no one could hear me. I was crying mostly with anger and hatred. And I decided to leave that place as soon as possible. Surely, there must be somewhere else I could go?

Christmas was approaching fast. My father was down by the equator as usual, loading bananas. My brother and I decided to celebrate Christmas with mother's parents. And that's what we did. It was the second time we had walked across the railway bridge on the way to their house where the candles were already lit in the windows. The Christmas before we'd been on leave from the children's home. This Christmas, with our mother on ice, we were free to do more or less what we liked. We trudged through the snow across the playground in front of their house. I stayed in the middle and looked up at the pitch black star-studded wintry sky. If I gazed at the stars I could just imagine for a moment at least that we were Trappers wandering across some arctic wasteland. The main adventure was still to come. The winter of the wolves had started.

I've never in my life felt so lost in the wilderness as that time in the school playground in front of my grandparents' house, the evening before Christmas Eve in 1958. At that moment I understood the meaning of the word SMALL, I also understood the meaning of the word HUGE and I understood what LONELINESS meant, and I wanted to hold my brother's hand, but he just snorted and trudged on. Maybe it was hard for him too. Last Christmas Eve had been a funny Christmas, divided in half. One half we spent with grandmother and grandfather and the other half at the children's home. The people at my grandparents' place were dwindling. The man who rented the corner flat had brought himself a TV. But the reception wasn't too good. We spent most of the time wondering what the flickering snowy-looking pictures were supposed to be. Not much was being said. And that was lucky perhaps, because we didn't know what to say. When we handed out the presents there were the usual grunts from my grandfather. He refused to open his presents in front of an audience so he went into the bedroom first to have a look, then came out and said that he approved. Grandmother was modesty itself. She could never afford anything but soft hand-knitted parcels. She needn't have worried. Once we were back in the children's home everything was bought in bulk. We got all the presents that had been left over. A whole pile of tin motorbikes with policemen on top. We got ten each. And from our father we got a box of oranges. He'd come by and left the fruit for us. Nobody had touched it so we ate oranges the whole night and didn't mind that they were almost mouldy and with rotting skins. None of us could understand why he hadn't called at our grandparents' house. Maybe he'd been to the sanatorium? We munched away and played with our motorbikes, but after five laps they broke. In the morning, at around five o'clock, we both felt ill because of the oranges. My brother shat his pants. The yellow stuff poured through his pyjama trousers. Then I laughed and shat myself too. He ran out into the corridor with his orange shit trailing behind him, and I ran after. We both laughed.

Then we had to clean up after ourselves. It wasn't funny anymore.

And the Christmas at grandmother's after mother's death wasn't much fun either. We sat there quietly like some petrified people in a giant's Christmas crib. The giant's name was Fate. That's what people like my grandmother think anyway. I am not so sure. Without quite realizing it, my brother and I were becoming rivals. I really don't know where my sister had got to. I always seem to forget her. My brother and I struggled on in silence towards the same goal: we both wished to stay with our grandparents.

My brother won.

Both he and my grandfather are the kind of people who can tell the horizontal from the vertical. It's obvious that someone like me made him confused. The decision was made after taking their circumstances and failing health into consideration. However much I tried, they still didn't want me. Or as they put it: they couldn't take us both.

What alternatives were there?

Not for anything in the world did I want to stay with the Manufacturer again.

It wasn't until the funeral when I saw my mother's brother that I knew what I wanted. He was a funny irresponsible sort of chap and he would probably make me into a child again.

There is not much to say about the funeral. My father came home in the end. By then everything was organized so he could go off to get some fruit again. My grandmother sighed so deeply that we thought the whole world was having trouble breathing. The Manufacturer sang a song and the coffin disappeared and my mother went up in flames.

It is very hard to speak about it in detail because at the time I pretended I wasn't there. Nothing more was said about the toaster. I packed it in my bag. I got the boxing gloves too, and I ticked them both off the list with the heading 'Personal Belongings' which was fixed to the inside of my suitcase, then I cleared off to Småland where I was going to forget everything. I travelled by train and arrived there like a stranger.

Chapter 7

1959

Even though I was floored for the second time by Saga's hard right hook, life went on as usual. The story about our decadent party in the sale director's big house had leaked out of course and for the second time Mrs Lindmark was installed as a cautionary measure. She ought to have stayed in the house all the time, said my aunt angrily. But Saga just seemed to do what she liked or else people didn't know any better, as my aunt put it. I was given strict orders not to put my foot in that house again. People started to be wary. Maybe it wasn't such a good idea for me to be in Småland after all?

I heeded warnings like that.

If I didn't behave I'd be exported to – I don't know where. It was time to toe the line, obviously. At least on the surface. I persuaded my uncle to buy a TV set. That wasn't difficult. I talked about Siw Malmquist who was the hostess on Hyland's chat show. That made him buy a set and even my aunt was happy about this new toy, because it meant we stayed at home more. That television was fantastic. The whole world suddenly climbed into your living room. We didn't even need to worry about how to pass the time of day. The vegetation outside turned dark green with envy while we did nothing but stare at the noisy TV screen.

It didn't matter that it was a bit of a lonely occupation at times. I had turned my back on society anyway. At least on school friends. The idiots voted for a six-day week at school when for the first time they finally got the chance to vote. In contrast to Mr Holdst, who was extremely pleased with his Königson, I was deeply shocked at how the children voted in Swedish Broadcasting. But Mr Holdst claimed that everything is difficult in the beginning. One day I think I'll be proved right anyway. I don't know what good that would be, though. The tragedy was already a fact.

I carried my chains, imprisoned in Algutsboda village school.

My dreams fluttered around like birds in a redundant green-house wanting to get out. I found it hard to sit still, I was afraid of decomposing, of becoming a half-withered vegetable.

Oddly enough my organist teacher seemed to sense some of this fear in me. We met up during a practical exercise in Physics and Chemistry which sent us into raptures. We lived in order to abolish death. First we heated the tin above the Bunsen burner, then put the lid on – yes, it was possible to see some purpose in it all, first when it crumpled up as if under a giant's hand and then when it was cooling and the pressure came from below.

Or was he pulling my leg perhaps? Maybe he meant that it didn't matter what rubbish he shoved in as long as it fermented.

I think he realized that I had stopped doing my homework a long time ago. My school bag was permanently anchored on the bottom step on the way up to my auntie's flat. I threw it there when I got home and hurried upstairs to have a look at the Great World Drama on television.

Able and Baker returned safely to earth after their journey in space in the *Jupiter*. It was certainly a better year for monkeys than for dogs.

But it was worst of all for our managing director. He worked himself to the brink of a nervous breakdown that spring. His eager calls across the treetops became more and more frantic every evening. We weren't the only ones who'd bought a TV set. And the managing director had three pet hates in the world and they were: SERP, TV and PV* in that order. Those letter combinations ruined the whole atmosphere in the village according to him. Village atmosphere implies that everyone feels as if they're married to each other. It was family spirit he talked about most of the time when he walked between the cottages trying to persuade people to put in an effort down at the football field. Time and time again he came and fetched my uncle who had no other choice but to go with him.

Nobody understood why we need a bigger sports complex when we could watch sport on TV.

That is how spring and early summer progressed until one day I got a letter. And inside the letter there was a map just like in Enid Blyton's *The Famous Five*.

Manne and I were invited to take part in a treasure hunt.

* An old model of a Volvo car

We left in good time, map in hand, but didn't take any food with us. You mustn't believe everything that they write in books. The silliest thing I know are Blyton's kids. They never leave their front door without boxes of food supplies.

But enough of that. We pedalled out of the village, left the main road and took a winding path which led further and further into the pine forest. The tall trees almost pushed us back with their cold shadows. The gravel scattered in all directions and the tyres wormed themselves onto the bank in the middle of the path. In the end, our legs felt like stiff pistons in a machine that none of us had any control over. And it was much further than we had first reckoned with. Click click! Somewhere around the front fork a bearing was working itself loose. I wanted to turn back. Why chase secret treasures with the help of a map which has arrived by ordinary mail and with an ordinary post office stamp?

But Manne toiled away on his homemade pushbike. His hair was standing on end and his legs worked resolutely with circular movements. I didn't have much choice except to follow him. We travelled further and further along the narrow gravel path. The green grass verges had got a sibling in the middle of the path. We struggled on in the dark forest with the grass bank like a luminous tape in green.

And suddenly a steep slope fell away below us. We screamed out like a tribe of Red Indians. Click click! The handlebar jerked, the air rushed into our mouths, the noise had a deafening effect on us and we went down the hill like two cannon balls, impossible to stop. We were carried away by the speed. We became scorchers who forgot that there were such things as brakes. Manne suddenly lurched and the bike stopped with its back wheel in the air, while he headed straight for the fir trees. I could feel the cool wind in my face. There went Manne, I thought, and let my bike find its own way. There was no point in putting up any resistance anyway.

Then I got to the bottom of the hill. And over to the right of the path was the woodpile, just like on the map. To the left was the footpath and on the footpath stood Louise arching her eyebrows in a pensive sort of way.

'I hope you didn't come alone.'

'Not quite,' I said.

I should have realized that she was behind the treasure hunt. The other girl peering at us from behind the woodpile was a complete stranger to me. Hopefully, she would do for Manne. If he was still alive, that is.

My converted racing bike with the carrier removed, the rear mudguard reduced in size and with a raised handlebar, stopped for a second by itself as if taken by surprise while I sprinted back up the hill to look for Manne. I soon spotted his white face among the fern leaves and said hello to him, but he blinked and hissed that I was the stupidest person who'd ever walked in a pair of shoes and I saw that he was hurt and trying not to cry.

'Does it hurt?' I asked, just to have something to say.

'The wind got in my eyes because of the speed,' answered Manne.

We discussed the way the wind can affect the tear ducts and we came to the conclusion that it was a local shower that had hit him as he went helter-skelter down the hill. Then Manne moaned and wanted to get up before our 'treasures' appeared. I helped him onto his knees and propped him up against a tree. We started to laugh. You do on funny occasions like that. Presumably we were suffering from shock, because we both laughed until we fell about. Manne came to his senses first and asked how the girls looked. Above all, he wanted to know whether his bird had any breasts. To cheer him up I told him that he was going to see breasts that were even bigger than Anita Ekberg's.

He started to crawl through the fern at once. I followed him and together we held down the last fern leaves to study our treasures who were standing on the road, a bit confused. At first, Manne was surprised. He hadn't expected to find Louise there. Then he was pleased when he saw her friend. I may have exaggerated a bit, but not much.

I only had eyes for Louise. It seemed as if she and I were going to end up together despite all the preliminaries with Saga. The first time that we'd cycled into the forest and got lost trying to follow our secret map, no one turned up. But he who seeketh findeth. The sirens of the wood had appeared at last.

I thought Louise was beautiful. The flimsy dress underneath her cardigan was as mysterious as the surface of a forest pond. She flicked her fair fringe out of the way.

'Are you both dead or something?'

'No,' I said, and stepped forward. 'But Manne is wounded.'

They went to have a look at him. Manne closed his eyes. Louise knelt down and her straight back with the shoulder blades looking like wings made me think of the kneeling angel by the suffering Manne. Then her dress rode up. At first she tried to pull it down over her bottom, but then she started to scratch herself absentmindedly. So the idea of the angel suddenly vanished. And that made me happy because we hadn't ridden all that way just to mix with angels. Manne's tormented pale face suited him. Green hair and red eyes are not things everyone can boast about. I scraped my foot impatiently and felt I was getting jealous of him. Why hadn't I been smart enough to make that dangerous passage through the air too? Both the girls were extremely preoccupied with the invalid.

But in a way it was a good thing that we had Manne's pain to focus on, otherwise I suppose we wouldn't have uttered a single sensible word.

In the end Louise took command of the situation. We were going to an even more secret place. The two of them sneaked off and I had to support Manne while they disappeared behind the trees, giggling. I nagged Manne to speed up the walking process a bit and in the end he got going. We hurried after them. We followed the laughter and the giggles and the movement of the branches. Our faces blossomed with the excitement and the heat. Where were they leading us? What were we going to do there?

'Did you see when they bent forward? God, what breasts!'

'How's that?' I wondered.

I wasn't at all displeased with Louise. Her flat front didn't look as frightening as Saga's problematic buds. It was a bit dodgy with breasts, I thought. The friend's tits were far too big for my liking. As a matter of fact, they were twice as big as anyone's I could think of at our age. But I didn't have too much time to worry about that. Suddenly we could hear their voices among the trees.

'Fat lip!'

We stopped and looked at each other long enough to notice that my lips were twice as thick as Manne's. His were just as cruel and thin as lips should be. Mine were fleshy and there was nothing cruel at all about them. They were put there without a purpose as if an absentminded trembling artist had lost control over his water colours. My lips dissolved all over the face. Little Frog used to say that it was like kissing the whole body. That's the reason why she liked me. But suddenly in Småland I realized that I was the Fat Lip of the province. I hesitated. Should I force the issue? I had no idea what indescribable cruelties were waiting for me at the goal.

'You can take a joke, can't you?' whimpered Manne between his razor-sharp lips and walked on ahead of me.

I dragged my feet behind me.

And found the three of them in a little playhouse. We'd travelled right through the forest and ended up at Louise's home. It was her old playhouse. They waved at me from the doorway. Judging by their sign language I should have crawled on all fours across the lawn. But even a Fat Lip has some kind of pride. I walked fearlessly up to them and stepped inside.

'Why did you do that? What if someone had seen you?' protested the friend.

'Great balloons you've got there. Have you blown them up yourself?'

I tried to say it with my mouth closed in order to look as cruel as possible. She pulled in her breasts as much as she could under the ribcage and it was deuce between us. Louise acted the sensible girl she was. She gave us a few fluttering eyebrows and three long cigarettes. Her mother never knew how many cigarettes she had, declared Louise reassuringly. We were welcome to smoke and have a good time.

The playhouse was not big. Manne and I were sitting on one side and Louise with her big-breasted friend on the other. In order to make it more exciting we intertwined our legs and after a few puffs the white smoke lay like a cold mist over our faces. The suspense increased all the time. We stopped giggling, we stopped talking and they were probably feeling as lousy as me. I had still not overcome my Fat Lip status. My facial muscles struggled desperately to obey me and do their job properly, but it was hard both to smoke and look cruel at the same time.

And what were we going to do when our cigarettes were finished?

In my wild imagination I could just picture the playhouse shaking convulsively – like grandfather's rabbit cages when all the rabbits jump on top of each other all at once. Manne blinked through the smoke curtains. In my eyes he looked just like an enormous rabbit. I wanted to get out. I wanted some fresh air. My God. The playhouse would fall to pieces when all our forbidden lust was unleashed. Maybe someone would take the first step in a second's time and start the ball rolling.

'Shhh!'

Louise suddenly raised her hand and lowered it again to stub out a cigarette. None of us had heard a sound, but in our imagination there were at least fifteen grown-ups outside the door, ready to barge in and reveal our rabbit-like behaviour. Manne was in possession of the weakest nerves, despite his cruel lower lip. He was out of that door before I had even put my cigarette out. I saw two giggling faces as I ran away and I had a vague feeling that it was all part of Louise's masterplan to frighten us away when it got to the crunch and we were ready to pounce on them. But I couldn't rule my body with such thoughts. I flew across the lawn and into the forest with imaginary people breathing down my neck.

Manne was already far ahead and gasping for breath. We panted in unison and agreed earnestly that smoking has a negative effect on one's general physical condition. Suddenly we heard their sarcastic laughter again and their light voices crying: 'Fat lip!'

They had cheated us. We'd had it. We had been exploited, but we didn't want to admit it. We cycled home and commented on how close we had been and what strategy we'd use next time. Manne comforted me by saying that I could always have my lips operated on if they grew any bigger. I didn't believe that. I had difficulty in falling asleep that night. I used to worry about my nose being too broad. Small bits of skin were growing right in front of my eyes, practically. When my brother pointed out how abnormal that was – nobody else had anything like it – I spent every night with a peg across the bridge of my nose. In the end I succeeded in pulling out the skin a bit, but it hurt and it was difficult to explain to people why I was always walking around with two red spots on the bridge of my nose. What should I do now about my full lips? Maybe I could fix up some kind of lip brace that would push the lips in?

What if the rumour spread that I had the fattest lips in the whole of Småland?

No problem. In fact, it made me more popular. Suddenly lots of girls were hanging around my uncle's gate, asking me in a giggly way whether I was going to get confirmed. I hadn't actually made up my mind about that yet, but with the summer vacation coming up it was about time I did. There were quite a few of us and we'd cycle to Algutsboda church every day. That was the whole point. You could get up to all sorts of tricks on the way there.

My brother got confirmed so he could have a watch and a dark suit. I wasn't sure it was worth the trouble. I thought it was a bit off-putting pretending to eat Christ's body and drink his blood as proof of one's holiness. Like pretending you're a cannibal just so you can call yourself a Christian.

But the idea of the cycling trips appealed to me. I don't know what was happening to me. Maybe the sap was rising, as some people say. I was even prepared to succumb to my brother. I don't think it's good for you to think too much. The time had come to screw and get confirmed.

And my father had turned up for my brother's confirmation. Maybe he'd turn up for mine too?

I went to the bathroom to be on my own for a while so I could think of God, my father and all the giggly girls who were swinging on the gate. But I wasn't allowed to stay there for too long. My uncle whispered through the door that the girls wouldn't go away. What did I want to do? He was both impressed and worried about my lack of interest in the girls out there. As it wasn't in his nature to ignore such matters, he regarded my behaviour as an insult to the family. He almost volunteered to get confirmed in my place. But in the end the girls and my uncle grew tired. I could leave the house at last. I went to sit down under the flowering apple tree. Soon the term was finished. What was I going to do then?

My uncle came out with his pipe in his mouth and sat down beside me. I looked at him. I was looking at the kindest, finest person I've ever met. I saw a carefree man, I saw a day without worries, I saw life passing by, I saw my rescuer and helpmate. But I also saw that he and I were not made of the same stuff.

Jack London says somewhere that your character is formed by the places you live in. Did I want to be like him?

'What are you thinking of?' he asked.

'Bloody hell,' he said.

Then we sat there staring up at the window in the red house which was now my home and still not quite mine, because I didn't sleep there.

Just at that point Manne arrived and my uncle told him that I was thinking of God and that I was getting confirmed.

'Bloody marvellous!' said Manne. 'So am I!'

We played like little angels in Algutsboda church. My recorder produced hitherto unheard-of sounds and our organist wept with happiness. The speech day went off like a master class in the cool room of the church. His obstinate banging on the blackboard had borne fruit at last. This was a magnificent way of marking the end of his career. We were the last masters of the recorder in Småland and the organist, like my grandfather, was of a dying species.

He'd put me in the middle of the group, of course, so that I was surrounded by more competent recorder players than myself.

But I was part of it all.

And when he spoke to us he must have meant me too. He said that nobody but ourselves could prove that our school grades were meaningless and wrong. I thought it was nice of him to say that. I got lower grades in Swedish and Art. My A in Art disappeared simply because he couldn't see very well. Maybe I should have used more colour. And my Pass in Swedish became Fail. So much for my theory that it was worth giving alternative spellings all the time.

Never mind. I was going to turn into a delinquent anyway and would probably never need to write any more essays. But first I was going to get confirmed. And I wasn't the only one either. Practically everyone was going to get confirmed. The only one missing was Saga. She was missing from our football team too. And she was missing from our cycle tours up to the rectory, where I never got the answers to my questions, and she was missing from our talks about where we were going to spend the Night of all nights. Manne's grandfather said he'd bet his lorry that he could fix the best reception between Småland and Radio Luxembourg. At last his scrappy aeroplane on the barn roof would come in useful. Swedish Sound Broadcasting was sulking and would prefer to block the transmission from Radio Luxembourg. The whole village walked around in a nervous mood. No one really believed that the Swedish broadcaster's voice would reach Småland and no one really believed either that Ingemar would box in Madison Square Garden. It was hard to grasp that the dream had come true.

The two great events were the confirmation and Ingemar's

preparation for the great match. No wonder I forgot about Saga and me. The preparations for the confirmation were a piece of cake. I knew the Bible by heart already. All I had to do was to remain quiet. Our stout clergyman didn't really want to discuss things that I didn't understand anyway. I nodded in agreement. I was a bit like a root vegetable. I was about to put down my roots properly and everything was being put in order around me. I almost stopped thinking – but then Saga turned up when I was on my way to Auntie Auntie's one evening. As soon as I saw her I tried to run away. But she tripped me up and straddled me, just as usual.

Then she accused me of having squealed about her secrets. I hadn't helped her with her breasts as I had promised. I was a cowardly weakling who followed the law of least resistance.

She was probably right. On the surface I was a paragon of adaptability. And if I ever had some kind of inner core, then it must have stopped transmitting signals a long time ago. My only ambition was to be like others. I tried to lie still while she got all worked up with all her accusations. In the end she shut up though. I felt sorry for her. It was probably true what Louise had said, that her clockwork was not wound up properly. I must try and help her with it. It couldn't be good for her to run around like a boy. All my resolutions about not seeing her any more evaporated and I whispered to her that she and I should stay up that wonderful night and listen to the match between Ingemar and Floyd.

She leaned down and kissed me again.

Our tongues met like two young whales in the sea. I picked up faint signals of something I felt I ought to recognize and understand, but I didn't. And at the same time it was marvellous not to have to understand for once. She kissed me for a long time and I kissed her back even though her clock had stopped ticking. I was sure we could wind it up again. Everything would be all right.

I was so convinced that I didn't pay any attention to her funny ideas, but took them for the most natural ideas in the world. She said something in a hoarse whisper, then disappeared so quickly that I thought at first that I had misunderstood her. But then I thought in a way that it wasn't so strange after all. Even though she had not taken part in the general confirmation hysteria, she knew all right that we'd all been fitted out in the town of Nybro.

I had to wear a suit, of course. Now or never I'd be a grown-up. It seemed quite natural to christen the suit for a civil occasion, if we can call it that.

It was difficult to get permission to go and listen to the match at Manne's grandfather's place. My uncle had imagined that I was going to stay up with him, so he was a bit disappointed. But I insisted and managed to smuggle out both the suit and my new black shoes to the summer-house in the garden. And later that evening I walked over to Saga's house like a thief in the night, with my shoes under one arm and my suit in a cardboard box under the other. When the time came to kneel down in front of the altar the congregation wouldn't be able to tell anything from the soles of my shoes.

The night arrived.

The village was already deserted. The lights unfolded like pale rags in the summer night, but that didn't make any difference. From Saga's house I could see the row of houses at the bottom of the hill where I lived with Auntie Auntie. She was asleep. What did she care about Ingemar Johansson?

I tiptoed to the kitchen door and let myself into the house from the back as agreed. At first I expected Oscar to start barking, but then I remembered he wasn't with us any more. Maybe his bark echoed across the firmament accusing us of not listening to him, but that night I didn't hear a sound. It was just my own blood making a noise which was worse than a sledgehammer against my eardrums. I took off my clothes in the kitchen. It felt strange to put on the dark suit before I was confirmed and I wondered absentmindedly where Mrs Lindmark had got to that evening. She was so easily duped I would never have wanted to be looked after by her. And actually it was just as odd Saga's parents leaving her on her own for so long. That sort of thing is damaging. You must not leave a dog on his own for more than three hours. It ought to be less with children even. I had to hurry up and make her grown-up.

I chose not to wear a tie. It felt strange as it was, a bit like being an impostor in my own suit. I walked into the hall and looked at myself in the mirror. The person I saw there wasn't too confident and I started to wonder whether I had taken on too much. But the wonderful night had arrived. And I knew what I had to do. To quote Gustavus Adolphus just before he rode off on his 'ah, but too swift' horse Streiff, on the battlefield of Luetzen: 'Once the spurs are touching the sides of the horse, forward, forward and do not pause.'

Nice! I made it up as I stood there in front of the mirror. It was things like that which made me impossible at school. Instead of dates I declaimed verses.

After having checked my outfit I marched into the living room up to the drinks cupboard, where a few drops of liqueur had been rescued after the thirsty grammar school boys had had a go at it. I got two glasses out and called:

'Darling! What would you like before dinner?'

'The same as you,' answered Saga from the top floor.

That is the advantage with a lot of TV-viewing. You know exactly what to say and how to behave. I poured out a few drops about as green as myself, and Saga came wandering down the stairs. She also looked like an impostor in her dress. But she was beautiful. We raised our glasses in silence and my arm did exactly what was required of it and no more. For the first time I managed to get the precious drops to my mouth without any nervous ticks. I let the few drops roll onto the tongue. Next time it would be Christ's blood and I suppose it was vinegar and water. We agreed to have a proper look at ourselves in the hall mirror. After all, this was the last time that we were virgins and we ought to say farewell to that state in some way. Then all we had to do was to pull down the blinds and get started. When I think about it, most Venetian blinds salesmen are wandering saints who do a lot of good to housewives.

We studied ourselves in the hall mirror for as long as was necessary to say farewell and we probably thought of the same thing. We wanted to memorize every detail in our eyes and the trembling corners of our mouths to see if there'd be any difference afterwards. Saga squeezed my hand and asked if I wanted something to eat, but my stomach felt quite full already and I suggested we go upstairs and listen to the radio. I wanted to have it over and done with as soon as possible.

The only radio in the house was in the parents' bedroom. From the maroon bakelite case Pekka Langer was babbling away uninterrupted. He really made his presence felt in the room. Someone ought to write and thank him. We were so scared that we were shaking when we crept down between the sheets. A cool and almost cellar-like gust of wind came from the bed and we both lay there stiff as corpses, miles away from each other. We shivered and moaned and would probably have remained in our fetters forever if Pekka Langer's happy chatter had not made us laugh about the absurdity of it all. From the balcony doors the night seemed unnaturally light. Far away on the other side of the Atlantic the sun was just setting. Suns and moons and all the planets were a collection of balls against a wall of time. We boxed and wrestled a bit first in the large bed and before we knew really how, we did the job as it is meant to be done. It was quick. And Saga's clockwork was creaking and squeaking and we both watered it with our tears. I didn't know why she was crying, but she felt like a furious taut steel spring underneath me, and I cried with the sudden knowledge. The victory was nothing but a defeat, after all. I was right when I said that you fall for someone as soon as you start screwing them. Before I could say Jack Robinson I had exchanged my mother for her. Now, if not before, the time had come to run around in mindless circles. It didn't feel at all as if I had grown up. I was just as scared as a baby, however much my body was growing. And however much it tried to be big and strong it was still a child's body. There was something stopping me from growing up. There was something inside me which made me not want to enjoy myself.

We cuddled up against each other and fell asleep long before the match of the century had even started. The radio droned on and covered our dreams like a quilt and now and again I surfaced and woke up in short bursts. Then I fell into a tired wanderer's sleep again. I had walked a long way for nothing and needed a rest before I could get out of Saga's grip.

I woke up too late. I should have noticed when Saga left the bed. Her scream made me sit up and I scrambled out of bed while lots of voices were babbling with excitement over the wireless. Ingemar Johansson had won on a knock-out!

I switched off the radio in the vain hope that that would make Saga's cries of despair die away, and slowly I put my trousers back on, but she went on screaming somewhere on the ground floor. I closed my eyes and covered my ears with both hands and didn't dare go downstairs. When I removed my hands in the end I could suddenly make out a voice which begged Saga to stand still. Then I ran downstairs at last and arrived in the middle of a macabre dance round the dining-table. Saga was screaming and throwing chairs around and she was stark naked. Stuff-the-hole Hardy came waddling behind with a worried expression on his face. I jumped up and climbed on his back, beating him with my fist. I too started to scream to get him away from Saga.

He suddenly stopped and threw me over his shoulder so I hit the wall behind me. He leaned over me and explained in a roundabout way that he just wanted to tell Saga to stop worrying. Ingemar Johansson had not suffered any damage in his defeat from her hands last spring. I started to laugh and cry at the same time. Finally Saga's confused story about our boxing match had penetrated through to Stuff-the-hole Hardy's thick brain. And now he had come to comfort her. But Saga stood there pressed hard up against the dresser, trembling. She had stopped screaming. Maybe she had sneaked downstairs to have a look at herself in the mirror and there was Stuff-the-hole Hardy's coarse face suddenly behind her. Somehow he'd frightened her and she'd started to scream. And obviously I wasn't the only one who'd heard her. The whole village was on their feet after the match. We stood there as if we were waiting for a search party to arrive and eager voices could be heard outside the house. I pushed Stuff-the-hole Hardy in the side and tried to tell him to clear out, but he just stayed there. The chase after Saga had made him so confused that he could only repeat his original statement. He mumbled again and again something about Ingemar Johansson winning on knock-out. I turned towards Saga. She too refused to move, even though I implored her to hurry upstairs before anyone arrived. I slapped her face to stop her staring. But nothing happened. She looked terrible. I might as well have tried to repair a clock mechanism with a sledgehammer.

And the first person to turn up of course was 'Jesus'. It couldn't have been worse. He really was richly rewarded. Christ! His voice was mellifluous. His jaws flopped about, his teeth were making a noise and his eyes darted expectant looks. At last something concrete! He was like a man possessed.

Evil shall be wiped out with evil. I growled, prepared myself and took a leap at his throat.

I never got confirmed. But they gave me a Bible with an inscription from the Psalms: 'Behold, I was shapen in wickedness; and in sin hath my mother conceived me.'

I understood the hint, although it was subtle. You don't screw any old how in Småland. Nor do you bite people's throats. And you don't growl either when people try to tell you off.

In the beginning I did it mainly because I had nothing intelligent to say. Then it became a habit. It was simpler that way. One day my poor father turned up. He came to take me home. Saga's mother came home too. When you get lumps in your sauce you have to use a sieve, as they say. I realized that was what the grown-ups were discussing, so I kept a low profile and spent most of my time in bed. But sometimes I woke up and found my uncle and my father standing over me. They looked so worried that I almost jumped out of bed and started to wag my tail as a distraction. I was quite aware that I didn't have a tail and that my tricks didn't matter one way or the other. I bided my time. My father slept in Auntie Auntie's bed to keep an eye on me. That was decent of him. I realized that I needed a strong person to look after me. But in a way, Auntie Auntie would probably have been better. She and I could have exchanged a few confidences.

In the middle of this mess Saga disappeared. Stupidly enough she went to a private confirmation camp where they obviously specialized in turning young girls into worthy virgins. My auntie was incredibly impressed and relieved when she told me how much Saga's parents had done for her. I was happy for her sake. Now there was just one lump left in the sauce.

One day Manne came to see me. He told me about the confirmation and showed me his watch. He said it was a gas. He said that about everything. Manne's grandfather had driven his lorry to church and on the way home he'd let Manne drive. 'It was a gas.' He was scared of me. I just kept growling. Then he said I should stop being so ridiculous, but I didn't take any notice.

I wasn't even curious to find out that Louise was hanging on the gate to get a glimpse of me. I burrowed down. I just couldn't help it. I had hit upon an idea how not to upset my uncle and auntie. Although they were the kindest people I knew I still didn't want to stay with them. I was afraid of them. They wanted me to forget. They didn't realize that I was struggling hard to remember – something I couldn't remember, but which filled the future with pain and sorrow all the time.

My father paced up and down through the village and didn't know what to do with me. The Sunday after that marvellous night the managing director was going to open his refurbished football ground at last. It was such a big event that my father thought I ought to go along too. I suspected that he wanted to convince people that I was back to normal again. I bided my time and let people think what they liked. Soon enough something would happen.

It was a brilliant day for fishing. But for the opening of the football ground it was disastrous. The rain kept pouring down and people gathered under umbrellas. The director had to stand there all alone by the microphone and create his own echo. His voice seemed to cover the football ground with several laps a second. He was really pleased. His speech earlier on that winter in the glass factory was now forgotten, because it had been amalgamated with two other glass factories and was going to be stronger than ever from now on. It sounded like a marriage, although a little martial, the way he talked about it. Every glass factory should be one unit and one division. The director actually said that the future depended on whom you went to bed with. Yes! 'As you make your bed, so you must lie on it.' That's what he said. I remember it well because that's when I started to get angry. Without any real reason I started to think of Venetian blinds. Then I thought of the Manufacturer and then I thought of Saga and I allowed myself a few doubts about the future too. I was young but I already had cold feet. People like Weedon Scott are a dying species. You can't trust anyone.

I actually got so angry that I decided to run up and bite him in the leg. My poor father hadn't got used to me yet. He was so surprised that he didn't realize he could have stopped me. I growled and thought of Mr Holdst. At last I'd make up for my passive role in the glass works that time and act as his true guide-dog. I jumped up and bit the director in his Achilles tendon. His scream echoed across the sports ground while we tumbled about in the soaking wet grass.

I didn't mean any harm. He deserved a better finale to his opening ceremony. I probably mixed up too many things at once. I must say in my defence that it was I who let go in the end. I told my father that too.

I felt very sorry for him. He bundled me up in the car, which he had borrowed from the Manufacturer, and he wanted to get out of Småland as soon as possible. I was rocking gently in the back seat while we drove up the dirt track towards the crossroads. Suddenly I felt that someone was hot on our heels and I sat up to look out of the back window of the car. It was Manne. He was pedalling away as fast as he could on his racing bike. It had stopped raining. His mouth was half open and his eyes were desperately red. And he cried more than I could have managed even. It was like an old silent movie. The car rolled on. All I could see was him. My father drove slowly. Manne chased after us and his face was distorted with grief. I couldn't hear what he was shouting, but he kept moving his lips all the time. He was the only person in Småland with green hair and he cried for my sake! He was another original.

We disappeared behind the corner where Karl Evert had his toy factory. I wondered who he'd marry one day in order to secure the toy manufacturing business. Then we got to the big road. The car stopped so abruptly that I turned round to see what was happening. It was only the Artist. He had hired a tractor with a trailer to get his 'Mother with baby' from Kalmar. The council there didn't want his sculpture after all. They didn't dare exhibit it. But there she was swinging away on the open-sided trailer and there was the child which was modelled on me. Well partly, anyway. The idea the Artist wanted to convey was that the child was pulled out of the mother's womb and held up towards the sky in one great big sweeping movement. When the town councillors saw that they took fright and said no. And the Artist told the newspapers that he'd put his sculpture on a concrete base in the forest. He probably did too. Those images of Berit and me are probably resting somewhere in the depths of the forest. The Artist waved cheerfully and smiled at me with his moon-like face and I felt a sting of envy. I should have been an artist. Then you could do what you like. Nobody took any notice of you then.

After that, I stared at my father's neck for exactly as long as it took us to get home to Happy Heights and the Great Wall of China. In a way, that neck belonged to an unfamiliar person: he didn't really belong in my life. He was simply someone who came home with fruit. That wasn't his fault. He probably tried to do his best to make things nice for us. I wished that he'd been around from the beginning and become half a mother to me at least. But he wouldn't have. He wouldn't have been able to. He wouldn't have understood what I meant even if I'd told him.

It was a shame that he was nothing but a neck, but there wasn't much we could do about that. He was all I had and still more of a stranger than anyone else. Once, we had dragged home as many friends as we could find so they could all wrestle with him and see for themselves how enormously strong he was. We had to take a run with our heads first and aim for his stomach. We bounced back straightaway. That's how hard he was. Whatever you did, you always bounced back from him. It is sad but true.

But I was still happy rocking to and fro in the back of the car. I had got my own way without upsetting my uncle or my aunt too much. It wasn't such a bad idea biting the director's leg. I left my uncle and aunt with mixed feelings of embarrassment and relief, and they probably didn't realize that I wanted to get away from their love. They were so kind in every respect and I really loved my uncle. The problem was that they wanted me to forget. They didn't know that there was a big hole in the middle of me. They didn't know that I was struggling hard to remember something. I didn't even know what I wanted to remember. But it must have been something. Sooner or later it would come to light.

My father is the type of person who doesn't say very much. He uses his elbows instead. And yet he's always worried about his children. He used to promise us a good beating if we drowned for instance. He probably meant it too. It was his way of worrying.

When he was a lot smaller than I am now he fell under a cart with iron-sheathed wooden wheels. He ended up a mess of broken bones, barely held together by a pouch of skin. When he was discharged from hospital after a tremendous ordeal he was pushed around by his brothers and sister like a piece of luggage. That's how he lived for a very long time, until one day he made up his mind to become really strong. He really did. He has always fought his way from a weak position. And just because he succeeded, he thinks that everyone else can succeed too – if they really want to, that is. That's why he loved it when we used him as a punch-bag. He thought that was good practice for us. To be fair, he used us as punch-bags too sometimes, but unfortunately we weren't quite so enamoured of the idea.

Anyway, we filled the flat at the Great Wall of China on Happy Heights with human voices again. 'Human' is a debatable choice of word, perhaps. He wasn't a great one for verbal intercourse and I kept growling most of the time. We sat there in the kitchen and stared at the striped table-cloth while I was dying to ask him when he'd be off again, and he wondered what was wrong with me. But he hated to ask questions like that and I couldn't explain myself. Instead I woke up in the middle of the night and walked into the hall to check if he was still there. It was a completely idiotic thing to do, like looking under the bed for ghosts, but I did it anyway. I stood there in the hall while the soles of my feet got colder and colder and the ice shot up through my legs. I was impressed, overawed by his snoring. In that bedroom of all places! Couldn't he feel the cold spreading from the bed beside him? Didn't he feel how the flat had turned into a grave-chamber? Didn't he remember his own nights?

I wanted to shake him, to tell him that I had seen them once making love with my own eyes just when I was on my way to the toilet. They did it. They made love, and now he was sleeping there in the same bed.

My father was really someone you wanted to copy. He lay there whole and indestructible like a marble statue in all his glory.

But during the day a migratory bird inside him was itching to get out. I saw it. What could I do to keep it in our cage?

Of all the things I could have done, I probably chose the worst.

He was wondering what was wrong with me of course and as long as he was worried he would stay. But I, silly lemon, thought I'd be a little co-operative and start talking again. So suddenly one day I stopped growling and even suggested I might get myself an honest job. That might be just what the doctor ordered. He was really grateful and couldn't understand why he hadn't thought of that himself. We both completely forgot that I hadn't finished school yet. I was due to carry on in my old class in the autumn. But never mind. I reckoned with being a juvenile delinquent anyway, especially as I couldn't spell, and after all, he'd finished school and started work when he was younger than me, even.

So we wandered down to the Job Centre where I was offered a job at once as an errand boy at a pharmacy called 'The Swan'. That would suit me. They might even be able to give me some pills for my restlessness.

They offered me a fortune in wages. I got forty-five crowns a week before tax – which was five crowns. I spared a thought for Mr Holdst and his pension fund and counted myself as fully eligible for his all-embracing pension scheme. It felt good. And the job was easy. Half the day I spent reading detective novels which one of the washers-up brought along. Her son was doing his military service so he lent her his books. Her name was Mrs Svensson and she was like a dried raisin dashing around in that large shiny steel scullery, talking incessantly about her strange wonderful life. She was happy if I just sat down beside her reading and nodding now and again to show that I was listening and that I had understood. It was a crying shame really – a good person like her. I am sure we would have adopted each other if the Fox hadn't called across the yard all the time to get me involved in some work or other. The Fox was the deputy boss at the pharmacy. With the best will in the world I can't claim that we had a loving relationship. It irritated her no end that I didn't have enough work to do. It was she who always said that Mrs Svensson's kindness was a crying shame.

When the Fox's cries echoed across the yard it meant that it was time to run through the town to save some old person who was dying. First the doctors came and then me. I have read millions of stories about heroic doctors who save dying patients, but I think it is time we admit that it was people like me who came with the healing ointment. I mean, what did the doctors do, except sign a piece of paper? Was it their signature or my fast bicycle trips through the town that saved lives, really? I shall not delve any further into the matter. He who dies himself one day will know the answer.

The pharmacy was always full of young girls who counted pills and sold Elastoplast. They were happy and they used to flirt with me, because they had no one else to flirt with. But I had learned my lesson with Berit and it wasn't very hard to resist them. I made do with a few cursory glances through the door to their changing room. Most of the time I just read Manhattan thrillers. That was nice. I had no one to compete with any more. In time I would probably read more books than my mother. When I wasn't reading or doing something else I walked around the stockroom in the basement trying to make up a new inventory of the contents. With a little help from a handbook I soon learned which substances were poisonous and which would explode and which would have a corrosive effect if you poured them out. The rest was uninteresting, I thought.

Most of all I was practising to become an indestructible marble statue like father. I was going to become just as big and strong as he and bloody dangerous to boot. He was impressed by my dedication and gave me a muscle-training programme. He didn't worry about me not getting confirmed. I had guts, and that's what counted. After all, there weren't that many kids who'd dare bite a managing director's leg. I think that's the way he looked at it. We never talked about it. Once he told me that Saga had come home and everything in the garden was lovely again down there.

I preferred not to listen to that sort of talk. I noticed that I had a talent for wiping out events and impressions that I didn't like to remember. That was something I'd been able to do for a long time, but now I was developing it even further. To me reality had become something you could switch on and off at will. I had a tap inside my head. I was the quietest, kindest errand boy who'd ever mounted a bike.

And so the days went by. My father made nice food even if it wasn't a patch on Auntie Auntie's. We adjusted ourselves so we didn't have to talk to each other too much. I asked no questions and got no answers either.

I was dying to know what had happened to my brother and sister, but I began to think that we were getting our lives together. My father wasn't too difficult to live with after all. He wasn't too depressed nor too happy and I didn't care how he spent his days. I was just pleased to have him around.

We avoided going to the living room. He thought it was strange that I didn't run out to play in the evenings after supper, but I pointed out to him that I was working now. It would be very immature to play with your old school chums and he was satisfied with that explanation. I couldn't very well tell him that I didn't want to go out because I was afraid of leaving him on his own. It was more like a home when I was there too. And I'd rather keep out of Little Frog's path. It was difficult to look your innocence squarely between the eyes. In a way I had always thought that she and I would end up doing it properly, but instead I had left the sanctuary and screwed someone else. I felt a bit rotten about it. I wanted to forget both her and Saga as soon as possible, cut off all the threads and spend the rest of my life as I pleased. No reins and whips, I wanted to mark out my own path in order to turn into something unique the day I could call myself an adult.

I was enthusiastic in a controlled way – like when a tortoise realizes that it can move forward without sticking its neck out.

But then the day arrived when I forgot myself completely and was incredibly happy. My father had brought new fish for the aquarium. He stood there in the hall cleaning it out when I came home. Then we both helped to pop all the usual things in. It was a wonderful evening. We sat in front of the aquarium, staring at the fish-life, and I even started to prattle in my usual old way to make us laugh.

But suddenly he became serious and put his arm round me and I remembered how the Wolf-Dog instinctively knew that Weedon Scott was leaving Alaska long before the decision had been taken. I ought to have followed my old trail and known better. I swallowed and swallowed and tried desperately not to listen to what he was saying. But I couldn't help hearing anyway. He said it was time I looked after the goldfish on my own. Their future safety lay in my hands now. It was all a bit like a staircase where one step led from his work down to me and another step from me down to the goldfish. It was as simple as that. He had to work to send me some money. And I must try and understand.

I understood.

Poor fish. They hadn't even asked to be born, even less end up at Happy Heights in the Great Wall of China.

My father left. As usual, the Swedish nation needed their bananas more than I needed my father.

He had arranged for me to go and have supper with his parents every day. I hadn't had much to do with my father's parents before, even though they lived in the same town. The reason was simple. They had twelve children and every one of them had a great number of children. I was just one of many grandchildren. They were happy if we kept out of the way. I suppose you could say that it was a question of stamina.

My father's parents were like strangers to me and they spoke quite differently from my other grandparents too. They always seemed to be quarrelling, even when they were just asking each other to pass the salt. They chased each other round like cats and dogs in the small one-room flat where they lived. Grandmother was the dog. She barked all the time. Grandfather got out of her way and tried to find some peace and quiet. When things went too far he just spat.

All my eleven aunties and uncles on my father's side of the family were like those statues I talked about. But they all insisted that grandmother and grandfather loved each other and that that's why they carried on like that. I had very strong doubts about that. I saw how grandfather really enjoyed injecting the insulin into grandmother's fleshy old thigh. He dug around for a good while with the needle while grandmother rocked nervously in her chair. Her pink shapeless bloomers lay there like a collapsed parachute around her feet, my grandfather was on his knees and the kitchen was electric with their charged words. I had a definite feeling of being in the way. Except when grandfather came out into the hall and gave me a crown. He was chewing his cigar and he whispered that grandmother was ill. It had gone to her nerves.

I didn't know anything about things like that. I slunk off as soon as I could to my princely three-room flat.

The first few weeks there I stuck to a strict schedule as if I was acting as my own home nurse. I really tried putting all my Home Economics knowledge into practice and the flat sparkled like some advertisement for washing powder. But then I suddenly got fed up with it all. I simply couldn't open the door to the fridge or the larder any more. Every day when I got home from my job at the pharmacy I rushed out into the kitchen as if activated by some automatic memory, to see what was in the larder, and I always realized too late that there was nothing there. I was the only one who could fill it up. With my hand on the key I stood there fantasizing: if my mother was an angel she'd know sooner or later that I needed her. She'd fly down to stock up the larder and sometimes she'd bake her lovely bread for me.

I opened the door slowly to have a peep. The dusty jars looked more and more lonely every day. Why couldn't I stop? Why did I always have to run to the larder? The larder was just as empty as my head. For hours I sat there in front of the kitchen window. I got into the habit of peering out between the curtains and the window frame because I didn't want to be seen. I could sit there all evening while the autumnal darkness was falling outside and sometimes my old mates would walk past. If my grandmother had seen me then she'd probably have said that I wasn't eating enough fruit. There were no vitamins left in my body. I didn't even react when someone told me that the government had decided that lions and tigers and other wild animals could not be shown in the circus any more. It should have made me happy. But no. The world around me didn't matter at all.

The only person who suspected something was the deputy pharmacist whom I called the Fox. She was after me every day, but her suspicions were never confirmed. Unfortunately, I must admit that her suspicions were justified. I don't know how it all began, but I decided to start stock-piling explosives, poisons and corrosives. Every day I sneaked down to the basement to pinch some of the yellow, white and green powders. I emptied one jar onto some long white strips which burnt with a sizzling stinking yellowish light. Things looked really bad for me. The exemplary boy was planning his career. My idiosyncracies were expressed in practical terms. After supper with my grandparents I used to go round to the Great Wall of China to see which of my friends' windows were lit up. Suddenly one evening without quite realizing how, I got the idea to throw something at one of those lit-up windows. I got a coin out of my pocket and threw it as hard as I could. Then I just got into the habit of smashing one window a week. The upset and surprised voices coming out of the dark made me feel strong. It was a nice feeling being something untamed and undefinable, something which everybody was afraid of.

Soon I had stuffed the fridge with chemicals. My brother would have turned green with envy if he'd seen it all. His shoe polish experiments were nothing compared to the concoctions I could mix if I wanted to.

Time passed without me taking any real part in it. I ticked away like a home-made time-bomb in a parcel. It was just a matter of time before it would go off. I didn't get round to writing to my father. He didn't get round to writing to me either. My grand-parents kept quarrelling. I'd become the invisible man in the district. I was the window-smasher who came in the night and terrorized the cosy family fishbowls. As soon as I spotted some-one who might suspect me of being the dreaded window-smasher I avoided him like the plague.

And then there was the damn door to the larder.

Soon long mouldy worms would crawl out and strangle me in my sleep. I would have to open it and clean it inside, but I didn't dare. I was in such a bad way that I even started to think of ringing up Sven Hansson in the council and ask him to send me a home nurse for a few hours every night. But then I decided to do something radical instead. Sooner or later I'd have to face the world around me. I couldn't just hang around with the people in the pharmacy. The time had come to enter the social life of my own age group. I decided to invite Little Frog and some other friends to a party. I, if anyone, could have a party without interference from parents.

I wrote and wrote and glued to my heart's content and invited the whole crowd for one Saturday night at six o'clock. Our gramophone was standing in the living room with the three promotion records. We never bought any more. One record was about a mounted policeman who sang to his sweetheart across the valley. The other one was Louis Armstrong and the third sounded like stewed fruit falling to the ground. Satchmo's record would have to do. I rolled up the carpets and I locked the bedroom door where the double bed was so nobody could go in there and indulge in sinful pleasures. I didn't trust in my friends' sense of direction.

All I had left to do was organize the menu.

For a talented apprentice pharmacist like myself, the sky was the limit. We couldn't offer cordial and cake so I smuggled out some 96% spirit, bought some liqueur extract to go with it and mixed some beautiful green and yellow drinks. After that, I just sat down and waited for my guests.

At seven o'clock I realized that they were not going to come. Half an hour later, when I was feeding my liqueur mixture to the goldfish, a note was pushed through the letterbox and I could hear quick steps disappearing down the stairs.

'BEWARE OF THE POLICE!'

That's what it said. I should have realized that all the parents in the Great Wall of China were upset. Not only was I sitting there totally depraved on my own, I was going to be a terrible influence on their children too.

I recognized Little Frog's handwriting. Her rounded letters were like a slap in my face, as I wandered out into the kitchen to pour the liqueur down the sink. I was obviously shunned like a leper by the others. The following morning I'd go to the police and give myself up. I'd tell them that it was I who had smashed the fifteen window-panes. I felt dizzy when I realized how many there were. I should probably end up in a reformatory. I just hoped it would be better than the children's home.

At that moment there was someone at the door.

And like I've always claimed: soon enough Fate will have its way. Chance coincidences drop like coins in pinball machines and suddenly everything goes: ding-dong!

But I didn't think like that then. I just thought Little Frog had changed her mind. I rushed into the hall and opened the door wide – and there was my brother, cold and shaking in a strange way and with eyes that seemed to stare into the distance. He looked as if he'd travelled through Alaska without any dry

213

clothes. I was very surprised to see him. I had almost forgotten that he existed. It was odd to find a brother just like that outside the door. Last time I'd tried to talk to him he'd thrown me out. Should I close the door on him now, I wondered.

He pushed past me before I'd made up my mind. Then he rushed to the bedroom door and pulled the handle when he realized that it was locked. We don't have the same sense of humour, my brother and I. He only got angry when I told him that I had locked the door because I didn't want anyone to go in there. I knew he'd start hitting me if I didn't give him the key, so I threw it in the aquarium. That was a silly thing to do, I know, but sometimes it is good to show that you've got a will of your own, even if it comes to nothing. Funnily enough, he just sighed and started to search for it in the aquarium. Several of the fishes had risen to the poisonous green surface. They looked like little hydrogen balloons, abnormally swollen, and had obviously not enjoyed their drink very much.

My brother dug out the key from among the corals and opened the door to the bedroom. I ventured up behind him. He went over to mother's bed and rummaged around under the mattress. It looked so odd it was really scary. But when he pulled out his old air gun I could not help admiring him. That was really cunning to hide the gun right there.

My brother examined the gun and told me that he and I must help each other now. I nodded and my mouth felt dry. Even from a distance of several metres, huge waves of hatred radiated from his body. I wondered what was the cause of it. I didn't have to wait long for an answer. He directed me to the kitchen and was clearly impressed by the leftovers there, so he too had a taste and then he got to the point pretty quickly.

We were going to take revenge.

I agreed ecstatically at once. It was obvious that he and I had to avenge ourselves. I liked the idea of revenge and I had actually prepared myself for it for quite a long time. If you count the smashed windows, I already had an impressive list of achievements and could be regarded as an extremely professional avenger. I poured out a little more liqueur to get him to talk faster. His lips were trembling and so was his hand and I had strong doubts about his ability to be a good avenger without my cool assistance. I wanted to have a go straightaway, before the evil intent had vanished into thin air. My burning

214

hatred was already quivering like an arrow about to be shot.

The reason for my brother's fury was that he'd discovered that Sickan was dead. They'd cheated us. I had known about Sickan's fate all along, but I hadn't dared admit it. She was dead even when they gave us all that talk about farms and kennels in the country.

My brother had discovered Sickan's fate by chance. And the reason why he suddenly turned up in town was easy to explain. My mother's parents didn't have much trust in our father. They wanted the urn with mother's ashes in it so they could bury it in a cemetery close to where they lived. In the end it was agreed that my brother should go and fetch the urn which hadn't been interred yet. Meanwhile, the Manufacturer had taken care of it and put it in his cellar. I could just imagine my brother going down to their cellar and looking at the shelf above the lagged water pipes, and by accident his eyes would have caught sight of the clothes hooks. And that's where Sickan's lead was hanging. It had probably been there all along. I ought to have noticed it.

Maybe I had seen it even, but preferred not to understand the implication.

How could I have lied like that to myself?

My blood was pulsating in my veins while my brother was telling me his story. But I couldn't get all that burning hatred out. Instead I was turning into a great big steaming puddle of water which was slowly being covered with ice. The ice floes were groping about trying to touch each other. The heat evaporated from the dark water and, slowly at first, but then with ever-gathering speed, the ice floes joined up and all that was left was a smooth cover of ice. Silence and cold. People and dogs calling in the distance. The heat was concealed. Only the icy cold remained. The machinery sparkled cold and hard.

I nodded eagerly when he presented his simple plan. At first he was going to avenge Sickan's death, then he and I would run away together. It was my job to maintain the positions. He gave me the air gun. He claimed that he was much better at handling knives. He took one out of the kitchen drawer and got ready to go.

I looked at him. My poor brother. Not even grandmother and grandfather could help him. Slowly but steadily the truth had dawned on him. I wondered what our sister would have said about our plans, but I didn't dare ask at that point. The hour of revenge had come, that's all.

We pushed the aquarium up to the front door so that I could barricade myself behind it as soon as he'd gone. I showed off my pyrotechnical stockpile and suggested that we might deviate a bit from the original plan if something should go wrong. If he failed and came running back with lots of people at his heels it would be a piece of cake igniting the lot. Afterwards I could always let myself down at the back of the building. He nodded and disappeared. Then I pushed the aquarium back against the door. Poor fish. My father wouldn't be very happy to see that so many of them were dead. But never mind. He could always comfort himself with a banana.

I was alone, waiting. I was leaning against the cool marble by the window and I was holding the air gun against my cheek so I could aim at one of the many streetlamps which lined the street down to the canal. The empty flat was beginning to claw at me as if ready to devour me. The steel was burning my cheek and as I peered into the sight the streetlight exploded into a star with a thousand points. As soon as I blinked the light changed shape; it moved like a jellyfish in soft waves, exploded again and was dispersed into the night like needle-sharp points.

The raw cold air swept through the small crack in the window. A few cars drove past and their headlights swept up towards the window, dazzling me. I quickly withdrew with the gun, stumbled back into the flat and listened carefully for distant sounds while I sunk into nameless terror. There was something I couldn't quite recall, an image that superimposed itself on everything else.

It was a picture of my mother from a strange angle: a sunny summer's day and I am lying under the white garden table in my grandparents' garden. My mother's dress touches her legs lightly. Her feet rock in high-heeled sandals and she holds out a hand towards me. In her hand she's got a strawberry. Her body above her ribs looks quite different. My heart beats fast and I refuse to accept the strawberry from her hand. Agitated voices penetrate to my hiding-place. My mother whispers to me not to be silly, but I know that she is going to leave us and that it's she who is silly, not me. She wants my forgiveness. I refuse to give it to her.

216

In the distance a car stops. Someone calls out. Grandmother and grandfather are quarrelling. Her legs disappear and then she is gone. I know that she is gone and I hate her more than anything else in this world and I decide to kill her.

The memory was so vivid that I almost thought it was real. All the jigsaw pieces fell into place without any effort. Everything happened so quickly. Finally I saw the connection with the Manufacturer. My mum had eloped with him, of course. I remembered things that I had listened to behind half-closed doors. I could visualize things that I had always known, but not understood fully before. I had stacked the secrets away because I didn't want to know. She ran away that summer with the Manufacturer. It was he who came and fetched her by car. She ran away from us and she ran away from her own mother. But the summer rain caught up with her somewhere by a lake far from home. I had seen a photo of it myself in the Manufacturer's photo album. The thin wet dress hugged her body and yet her face was laughing!

But the next day her cough must have been very noisy and the Manufacturer must have got scared. Even in those days she was doomed. He drove her home and was so full of remorse that he didn't know how to make amends. My father probably suspected something, but he never quite realized what had happened.

I, who had been hiding under that table when she was about to make her big escape from us, was now standing there in an ice-cold kitchen ten years after the event, trying to make some sense of that picture. My mum wasn't much better than anyone else when it came to the crunch. She had screwed and we had come along by mistake. And then she had screwed again to become free. It seems as if that's the only way people have of signalling to each other.

It wasn't the stupid Manufacturer that we were going to avenge ourselves on, though. He was just a dirty henchman. My mother was the one who'd pointed at Sickan and sent her to her death – in the same way that she'd pointed at me and shown through her actions that she didn't want anything more to do with me. I had wished her dead but at the same time I had longed for her love. She had only regarded me as a great lump, she had never wanted us in the first place. I had made myself invisible. I had dissolved into a floating sea surrounding her. And as the days went by it became obvious that my secret desire was going to be fulfilled. She was actually going to die. She was going to disappear and she was never going to love me. I had done everything to conceal that terrible truth from myself. I was such a clever liar that I had begun to believe in my own lies. One of the lies was that my mother was an angel. I was the one who had carried the burden of guilt. And that's how it would have gone on forever if she hadn't made the mistake of sending the dog to its death. It was so unnecessary and so cruel. I hated her and couldn't feel sorry for her any more. She had disintegrated in front of my eyes and turned into someone I wanted to kick and spit on. But she was dead. And she didn't even have a gravestone I could kick. There was nothing I could do. Not even the thought of running away with my brother could raise my spirits. There was a strange compass in my head like a legacy from my child-hood. Long before I could put up any resistance, even my mother had implanted the nervous compass needle in my head. Wherever I went I had to carry that great hatred inside me. Maybe one day I'd even decide over the fate of dogs myself?

I made up my mind not to be human.

I tossed the gun over my shoulder and started to aim at the streetlamps. The globes tinkled and cracked into white snow-flakes that fell down over the parked cars. I fired and loaded with cold resolution and wasn't the least bit surprised when the cop car drove up and parked outside the entrance to our flats. Either my brother had failed or some worried parent had decided to call the police. I growled and decided to put up a struggle at least. I closed the kitchen window with a bang and tried desperately to put up my planned smoke screens. My hands were trembling too much and I threw the matches down and made for the door to stop people from coming in. The aquarium was blocking the door, but unfortunately I have an incredible knack for doing everything the wrong way round even though my intentions are always good. Our front door opened outwards of course so the police had no trouble at all getting in. We stood on either side of the aquarium staring at each other through the water and I asked them if they'd come to give me some throat pastilles like the police in Smaland had done. They didn't appreciate the joke. With no further ado they started to move the aquarium aside and I tried to hang on to it. Suddenly the aquarium got disconnected from its stand and the water squirted into the hall with all the dead fish. It was pure massacre.

At the actual arrest they told me indignantly that I had bitten one of the constables' hands. But it is a known fact that policemen always exaggerate the dangers they are in so they have an excuse to use their batons with a little extra force.

I am just joking. They didn't even have any batons with them. In fact, they were just as surprised as I was. All they wanted was to ask me a few questions about all the smashed windows in the district. They happened to witness my furious attack at the streetlights purely by chance. That's what the inspector told me down at the station later and he didn't know anything about my brother's revenge plan in the night.

The inspector was poking about in his ear with a large paper knife and he stared at me with vacant eyes which lit up a little when the constables mentioned that I was in the habit of biting people. I nodded eagerly and was just about to growl, but to my great surprise I started to cry instead. I cried and told them about my father who was in the South Seas, I cried and said that my father would come back next week to fetch me, as soon as he'd finished loading his bananas down there. And I cried and said that if they wanted to wreck my whole future for the sake of a few smashed windows which I would pay for anyway, then it would weigh heavily on their consciences for the rest of their lives. My father had promised that I could go with him, but if I had a criminal record he wouldn't want me for anything. And surely they knew that there was no better cure for a young offender like myself than a life at sea? The inspector was so flabbergasted by my speech that he rang up the Manufacturer to check the facts. I counted on his keeping his mouth shut for his own sake. In that way, I could save my brother from ruin too. But that was not necessary. He was just sitting in the cellar playing with the model railway.

I think I can understand why.

The inspector never realized that I was living on my own in that flat. He promised that he wouldn't stop me from going to the South Seas, provided I asked everyone's forgiveness. The main thing was that I'd pay for all the broken windows and street-lamps. I promised I'd do that. I looked at him and realized that he'd probably picked out a large part from his brain earlier on when he was poking about in his ear with the paper knife. Either that or he was the sort of person who really believed in something in this life. I suppose he couldn't grasp that there were children around who were so completely lacking in parental control or care as I was, especially not in a country where there are even laws to protect wild animals.

One day I might tell somebody the truth. I know exactly how I'll begin:

The snowflakes had a hypnotic effect on me. I was getting more and more drowsy, but I needed to keep my eyes open. What if I missed my station and got off at the wrong one, rushed out into the white arctic tundra, totally dazed, only to be met by wolves who were ready to tear me to pieces. Now, that would be unforgivable . . .